18.12

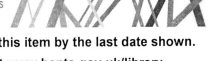

WITHDRAWN

FIGURES OF FEAR

Recent Titles by Graham Masterton available from Severn House

The Sissy Sawyer Series

TOUCHY AND FEELY
THE PAINTED MAN
THE RED HOTEL

The Jim Rook Series

DEMON'S DOOR
GARDEN OF EVIL

Anthologies

FESTIVAL OF FEAR
FIGURES OF FEAR

Novels

BASILISK
BLIND PANIC
CHAOS THEORY
COMMUNITY
DESCENDANT
DROUGHT
EDGEWISE
FIRE SPIRIT
FOREST GHOST
GHOST MUSIC
MANITOU BLOOD
THE NINTH NIGHTMARE
PETRIFIED
UNSPEAKABLE

FIGURES OF FEAR

Graham Masterton

This first world edition published 2014
in Great Britain and 2015 in the USA by
SEVERN HOUSE PUBLISHERS LTD of
19 Cedar Road, Sutton, Surrey, England, SM2 5DA.
Trade paperback edition first published
in Great Britain and the USA 2015 by
SEVERN HOUSE PUBLISHERS LTD.

British Library Cataloguing in Publication Data

Masterton, Graham author.
  Figures of Fear.
  1. Horror tales, English.
  I. Title
  823.9'2-dc23

ISBN-13: 978-0-7278-8446-6 (cased)
ISBN-13: 978-1-84751-552-0 (trade paper)
ISBN-13: 978-1-78010-599-4 (e-book)

All Severn House titles are printed on acid-free paper.

Severn House Publishers support the Forest Stewardship Council™ [FSC™],
the leading international forest certification organisation. All our titles that
are printed on FSC certified paper carry the FSC logo.

Typeset by Palimpsest Book Production Ltd.,
Falkirk, Stirlingshire, Scotland.
Printed and bound in Great Britain by
TJ International, Padstow, Cornwall.

AUTHOR'S NOTE

From the beginning of history, men and women have been haunted by figures of fear. They appear in many different shapes and disguises, from statues to animals to spiders to waif-like children. They frighten us to the point where we hang protective symbols and herbs around our doorways to keep them out, and say prayers to prevent them from harming us.

The reality is, however, that we have created these figures ourselves, in order to give a physical form to all of those things that we are afraid of: our dread of the inexplicable, and the terrible uncertainty we feel about never knowing what will happen to us next.

These figures represent everything from poverty and disease and madness and death to those horrors for which we have no names.

Many of them have become legendary. Satan is a prime example, with his horns and his hooves. Then there's the Indian goddess Kali, covered in blood, naked except for her belt of severed heads. Or Damballa, the slithery voodoo serpent god; and bristly Coyote, the Native American trickster. Or the Irish banshees, with their screeching voices and their ragged dresses, who gather outside your house as somebody comes close to breathing their last.

There are literally thousands of them, in every culture and religion, representing every possible terror that you can imagine, and some that you should be thankful that you can't.

But there are other figures of fear, closer to home. They are less well known but equally terrifying – if not more so – because they are so unfamiliar and yet so near to us.

That strange little girl with the deathly-white face who you see in your local churchyard, perhaps, but who vanishes when you turn away for a moment.

That limbless rubber doll that you find in a box in the attic, her pink skin turned amber with age, her eyes staring at you as if she knows what pain your future has in store for you, but refuses to tell.

That faceless statue in an alcove, in some small grey city in

Eastern Europe, with dead bouquets heaped around its feet where people have been praying – but for what? For the statue to protect them from ill fortune? Or not to come alive at night and tap at their windows, warning them that their time is up?

In this collection, you will discover many new figures of fear – some of which appear to be innocuous when they are first encountered; others which instantly bring shock and horror.

However, they all have one thing in common. They have all haunted my imagination for years, and still do; and if you choose to go further and read this book, they will haunt you, too. They will never leave you alone, ever again.

You might see one of them reflected in a shop window, right behind you; or gravely looking down at you from some high window in an unfamiliar city. Maybe one of them will be standing on the opposite side of a canal, with no reflection in the water, staring at you as if you have been picked out for the most calamitous fate of all.

You have a choice. If you believe that these figures can really bring you bad luck, then close this book now. There are happier books, sunnier books, books that will reassure you that you have nothing to be scared of. But if you decide that they are nothing more than stories intended to frighten you, then please read on.

Only you can figure out how fearful you are.

Graham Masterton, 2014

CONTENTS

EX-VOTO

'**S**eñor Foster! This way, señor!'
Henry stepped out of the shadow into the sunlight and into the middle of the marketplace. All around him, stalls were selling melons and tomatillos and decorated leather belts and scarves and holy statuettes and sticky-looking cakes and dishwashing brushes and bottles of Radiante floor cleaner.

Mariachi music was playing loudly from competing loudspeakers precariously wired on top of the stalls, and the noise of shouting and laughing and dogs barking and parrots squawking was so deafening that Henry felt as if he had found himself in the middle of a riot.

He caught up with Esmeralda, who unexpectedly took hold of his hand, as if he were a child rather than a forty-five-year-old man with thinning brown hair and a flappy white linen suit.

'You said that you wanted souvenirs, señor,' she reminded him.

'Well, yes. But something artistic, you know. Something truly Mexican, of course. But reasonably tasteful. I can't give the head of my sociology department a plastic cactus.'

'We will find something for you, señor,' said Esmeralda, and continued to tug him through the crowds. Henry had no choice but to follow her, as much as he didn't like being jostled. A gap-toothed man leered right in his face, holding up a necklace strung with large red chilli peppers.

'Show your girlfriend that you are hot stuff, señor!'

'She's my guide, thanks,' said Henry. 'Not my girlfriend.'

He didn't know why he had felt obliged to say that. After all, Esmeralda was stunningly pretty, with shiny brown curls and feline eyes and a mouth that seemed to be permanently pouting. The only trouble was that she was young enough to be his daughter.

'I know what we buy for you!' she said, as she pulled him through the acrid smoke that was wafting across from a *carne asada* stall. 'I know exactly for sure what you would like!'

She led him down a shady alley by the side of the marketplace, where old men with faces like wrinkled gourds were sitting on doorsteps together, smoking. At the end of the alley there was a makeshift stall constructed of packing cases and blankets and sacking.

A roughly painted metal sign outside the stall said *Retablos*. Inside, a woman was sitting on a kitchen chair with an easel in front of her, painting a small sheet of metal with enamel paints from twenty or thirty different little brightly coloured pots.

'*Buenos días*,' said Esmeralda. '*Mi amigo quiere comprar un retablo*.'

The woman turned toward them. She must have been about forty years old, with high, distinctive cheekbones and hooded eyes that were as shiny and colourless as ball bearings. She wore a black scarf twisted around her head and a black dress with grey serpentine patterns on it.

'Ah,' she said, and her voice was deep and throaty, as if she had been chain-smoking Delicados cigarettes since she was old enough to breathe. 'I have been waiting for you, señor.'

'Excuse me?' said Henry.

Without another word, the woman stood up and went to the back of her stall. She produced a small package wrapped in newspaper and handed it to him.

'What's this?' Henry asked her.

'Your *retablo*, señor. *Ex-voto*.'

Bewildered, Henry unwrapped the newspaper. Inside was a thin sheet of metal with a shiny picture painted on it, like a scene from a comic strip. It showed a city street, with a crowd of people standing on the sidewalk. A man in a white suit was lying in the middle of the street, with one arm pinned underneath the chassis of an over-turned truck. He was cutting his own arm off with a large saw, and there was blood all over his sleeve.

Up above him, floating in the sky, there was a saintly figure dressed in blue and gold, and attended by golden cherubs.

'I don't understand,' said Henry.

'It is simple,' the woman told him, pointing to the man in the white suit with a long, silver-polished fingernail. 'People come to me when they have survived a terrible accident, or a life-threatening sickness, or maybe they have been robbed and nearly killed. I paint for them an *ex-voto*, a thank you to the saint who saved their lives, which they will put up on the wall of their church.

'In this case I have painted yours *before* your accident. Sometimes I can do that. It depends on who you are, and which saint will preserve you. In this case it is *La Virgen de los Remedios*, Our Lady of the Remedies. She told me many weeks ago that you were coming, and what would happen to you, and how your life could be saved.'

Henry said, 'What? You think I'm going to be run down by a truck?'

'All fates are unavoidable, señor.'

'I'm going to be run over by a truck and I'll cut my own arm off to get free? That's insane.'

The woman shrugged. 'I do not decide the future, señor. I will sell you this *retablo* for twenty dollars. You will be able to thank Our Lady even before she has saved you.'

'This is sick,' said Henry. 'This is totally sick.'

He twisted his hand from Esmeralda's grasp and started to stalk back toward the marketplace.

Esmeralda called, 'Señor Foster! Señor Foster! Wait!' But Henry refused to turn around and angrily shouldered his way through the crowds.

He crossed the marketplace and walked back along the shadowy arcade that led to his hotel. His whole life people had treated him like he was some kind of a dupe and even now he was here in Mexico on business he was still being taken for a mark. He felt hot and sweaty and embarrassed and outraged.

If he hadn't been so angry, maybe he would have looked to his right before he stepped out into the blinding white sunlight at the end of the arcade and across the street in front of the Soledad Hotel. An old Dodge truck loaded with oil drums hit him at no more than fifteen miles an hour, but it knocked him through a wooden barricade that had been erected around a twelve-foot-deep excavation in the street, where the sewers were being replaced.

He fell right to the bottom, amongst the sewer pipes, and then the truck skidded on the dusty surface of the street and dropped into the hole on top of him, with a shattering, ramshackle crash.

He opened his eyes. It was gloomy and surprisingly chilly at the bottom of the excavation, and there was a strong smell of sewage and gasoline. He tried to sit up but found that he couldn't move an inch. His right shoulder was crushed under the right nearside wheel of the truck, and the truck itself was jammed at an angle.

He looked up. He could see anxious faces peering down at him from the sunlit street.

'Señor Foster!' a girl called out, and he recognized it as Esmeralda. 'Are you hurt, señor?'

'I can't – I can't get out,' Henry called back, his voice blurry with shock. 'My arm . . . it's stuck under the wheel.'

'Señor Foster, you have to get out. The truck is pouring gas.'

'I can't. It's my arm.'

Henry could hear Esmeralda talking to some of the men up on the street. Then there was a long pause. The stench of gasoline was growing stronger and stronger, and it was making his eyes water. It suddenly occurred to him that he was going to be roasted alive, down at the bottom of this stinking pit. That was how his life was going to end, and he had never even found anybody to love.

It was then that he heard a clanking noise. He lifted his head again, and realized what it was. A large carpenter's saw was being lowered down to him on the end of a length of cord.

It came to rest next to his left hand. He stared at it in horror.

Esmeralda called down to him. 'It is terrible, señor, I know! But what choice do you have?'

Henry picked up the saw and positioned it against his upper arm. The cross-cut teeth were so sharp that they snagged in the fabric of his linen coat. He closed his eyes tight, clenched his teeth, and pushed the saw as hard as he could. It cut through his coat and his shirt, and ripped into his skin. He had never felt anything so agonizing in his life, and he screamed, or he thought that he screamed. He was deafened with pain.

He dragged the saw back, and then pushed it across his shoulder a second time, cutting through muscle. So much blood welled up that his whole sleeve was flooded bright red, but he realized that he would have to push even harder, or cutting his arm off would take hours.

He pushed a third time, so forcefully that the teeth cut into his bone. But the saw also skidded against the iron sewer-pipe, and set off a spark. There was an instant *whoompph* of exploding gasoline fumes, and Henry's face was seared by a blast of 300-degree heat. His hair flared and shrivelled and his eyes were fried.

Henry blazed like an effigy. His linen suit turned brown and shrank and fell apart. His skin was scorched scarlet, and then charred black. But unlike an effigy he sawed harder and faster, with the jerky motions of one of those little figures on a weathervane. Within a few minutes he was a mass of flames, but he kept on sawing and screaming until he had cut right through his upper arm. He dropped backward, blackened and smoking, but free.

The painter of *retablos* had joined Esmeralda in the street above. She laid her silver-polished nails on Esmeralda's shoulder.

'*Le Virgen de los Remedios*, she warned him,' she said, in her throaty voice. 'He had no faith in her, no trust. But the Virgin of the Remedies . . . she has a remedy for everything, even that.'

WHAT THE DARK DOES

'**M**ummy – please don't close the door.'

His mother smiled at him, her face half lit by the landing light, the other half in shadow, so that she looked as if she were wearing a Venetian carnival mask.

'All right. But I can't leave the light on all night. Honestly, David, there's nothing to be scared of. You remember what Granpa used to say – dark is only the same stuff that's behind your eyelids, only more of it.'

David shivered. He remembered his granpa lying in his open coffin at the undertakers, his face grey and half-collapsed. He had thought then that Granpa would never see anything else, ever again, except the darkness behind his eyelids, and that *was* scary.

Darkness is only benign if you know that you can open your eyes whenever you want to, and it will have fled away.

He snuggled down under his patchwork quilt and closed *his* eyes. Almost immediately he opened them again. The door was still open and the landing light was still shining. On the back of his chair he could see his black school blazer, ready for tomorrow, and his neatly folded shorts.

In the corner of his room, lying sprawled on the floor, he could see Sticky Man, which was a puppet that his granpa had made for him. Sticky Man was nearly two feet tall, made of double-jointed sticks painted grey. His spine and his head were a long wooden spoon, with staring eyes and a gappy grin painted on to it. Granpa used to tell him that during the war, when he and his fellow soldiers were pinned down for days on end under enemy fire at Monte Cassino, they had made Sticky Men to entertain themselves, as many as ten or twelve of them. Granpa said that the Sticky Men all came to life at night and did little dances for them. Sometimes, when the enemy shelling was particularly heavy, they used to send Sticky Men to carry messages to other units, because it was too dangerous to do it themselves.

David didn't like Sticky Man at all, and twice he had tried to throw him away. But his father had always rescued him – once from the dustbin and once from a shallow leaf-covered grave at the end of the garden – because his father thought that Granpa's story about Sticky Men was so amusing, and part of family history. 'Granpa used to tell me that story when I was your age, but he never made *me* a Sticky Man. So you should count yourself privileged.'

David had never actually seen Sticky Man come to life, but he was sure that he had heard him dancing in the darkness on the wooden floorboards at the edge of his bedside mat: *clickety, clackety, clickety, clackety*. When he had heard that sound, he had buried himself even deeper under the covers, until he was almost suffocating.

What really frightened David, though, was the brown dressing gown hanging on the back of his bedroom door. Even during the day, it looked like a monk's habit, but when his father switched off the landing light at night, and David's bedroom was filled up with darkness, the dressing gown changed, and began to fill out, as if somebody were rising up from the floor to slide inside it.

He was sure that when the house was very quiet, and there was no traffic in the street outside, he could hear the dressing gown *breathing*, in and out, with just the faintest hint of harshness in its lungs. It was infinitely patient. It wasn't going to drop down from its hook immediately and go for him. It was going to wait until he was so paralysed with terror that he was incapable of defending himself, or of crying out for help.

He had tried to hide the dressing gown by stuffing it into his wardrobe, but that had been even more frightening. He could still hear it breathing but he had no longer been able to see it, so that he had never known when it might ease open the wardrobe door and then rush across the bedroom and clamber up on to his bed.

Next he had tried hanging the dressing gown behind the curtains, but that had been worse still, because he was sure that he could hear the curtain rings scraping back along the brass curtain pole. Once and once only he had tried cramming it under the bed. When he had done that, however, he had been able to lie there for less than ten minutes, because he had been straining to hear the dressing gown dragging itself out from underneath him, so that it could come rearing up beside him and drag his blankets off.

His school blazer was almost as frightening. When it was dark, it sat hunched on his chair, headless but malevolent, like the stories that early Spanish explorers had brought back from South America of natives with no heads but their faces on their chests. David had seen pictures of them in his school books, and even though he knew they were only stories, like Sticky Men were only stories, he also knew that things were very different in the dark.

In the dark, stories come to life, just like puppets, and dressing gowns.

He didn't hear the clock in the hallway downstairs chime eleven. He was asleep by then. His father came into his room and straightened his bedcover and affectionately scruffed up his hair. 'Sleep well, trouble.' He left his door open a little, but he switched off the landing light, so that his room was plunged into darkness.

Another hour went by. The clock chimed twelve, very slowly, as if it needed winding. David slept and dreamed that he was walking through a wood, and that something white was following him, keeping pace with him, but darting behind the trees whenever he turned around to see what it was.

He stopped, and waited for the white thing to come out into the open, but it remained hidden, even though he knew it was still there. He breathed deeply, stirred, and said, out loud, 'Who are you?'

Another hour passed, and then, without warning, his dressing gown dropped off the back of his bedroom door.

He didn't hear it. He had stopped dreaming that he was walking through the wood, and now he was deeply unconscious. His door was already ajar, but now it opened a little more, and a hunched brown shape dragged its way out of his bedroom.

A few moments later, there was a soft click, as the door to his parents' bedroom was opened.

Five minutes passed. Ten. David was rising slowly out of his very deep sleep, as if he were gradually floating to the surface of a lake. He was almost awake when something suddenly jumped on top of him, something that clattered. He screamed and sprang upright, both arms flailing. The clattery thing fell to the floor. Moaning with fear, he fumbled around in the darkness until he found his bedside lamp, and switched it on.

Lying on the rug next to his bed was Sticky Man, staring up at him with those round, unblinking eyes.

Trembling, David pushed back the covers and crawled down to the end of the bed, so that he wouldn't have to step on to the rug next to Sticky Man. What if it sprang at him again, and clung to his ankle? As he reached the end of the bed, and was about to climb off it, he saw that his dressing gown had gone. The hook on the back of his bedroom door had nothing hanging on it except for his red-and-white football scarf.

His moaning became a soft, subdued mewling in the back of his throat. He was so frightened that he squirted a little warm pee into his pyjama trousers. He looked over the end of the bed but his dressing gown wasn't lying in a heap on the floor, as he would have expected.

Perhaps Mummy had at last understood that it scared him, hanging up on the back of the door like that, and she had taken it down when he was asleep. Perhaps she had taken it away to wash it. He had spilled a spoonful of tomato soup on it yesterday evening, when he was sitting on the sofa watching television – not that he had told her.

He didn't know what to do. He knelt on the end of the bed, biting at his thumbnail, not mewling now but breathing very quickly, as if he had been running. He turned around and looked down at Sticky Man, but Sticky Man hadn't moved – he was still lying on his back on the rug, his arms and legs all splayed out, glaring balefully at nothing at all.

Whatever David did, he would have to change his wet pyjama trousers, and that would mean going to the airing cupboard on the landing. Mummy always liked to keep his clean pyjamas warm.

Very cautiously, he climbed off the bed and went across to his bedroom door. He looked around it. The landing was in darkness, although the faintest of green lights was coming up the stairs from the hallway, from the illuminated timer on the burglar alarm, and that was enough for David to see that his parents' bedroom door was open, too.

He frowned. His parents *never* left their door open, not at night. He hesitated for a few long moments, but then he hurried as quietly as he could along the landing until he reached his parents' bedroom, and peered inside. It was completely dark in there, although he could just make out the luminous spots on the dial of his father's bedside alarm clock.

He listened. Very far away, he could hear a train squealing as it made its way to the nearest station, to be ready for the morning's commuters. But when that sound had faded away, he could hear nothing at all. He couldn't even hear his parents breathing, even though his father usually snored.

'Mummy?' he called, as quietly as he could.

No answer. He waited in the doorway, with his wet pants beginning to feel chilly.

'*Mummy?*' A little louder this time.

Still no answer.

He crept into his parents' bedroom, feeling his way round the end of the bed to his mother's side. He reached out and felt her bare arm lying on top of the quilted bedcover. He took hold of her hand and shook it and said, hoarsely, 'Mummy, wake up! I've had an accident!'

But still she didn't answer. David groped for the dangly cord that switched on her bedside reading light, and tugged it.

'*Mummy! Daddy!*'

Both of them were lying on their backs, staring up at the ceiling with eyes so bloodshot that it looked as if somebody had taken out their eyeballs and replaced them with crimson grapes. Not only that, both of them had black moustaches of congealing blood on their upper lips, and their mouths were dragged grotesquely downward. Two dead clowns.

David stumbled backward. He heard somebody let out a piercing, high-pitched scream, which frightened him even more. He didn't realize that it was him.

He scrabbled his way back around the end of the bed, and as he did so he caught his foot and almost tripped over. His brown dressing gown was lying tangled on the floor, with its cord coiled on top of it.

He didn't scream again, but he marched stiffly downstairs like a clockwork soldier, his arms and legs rigid with shock. He picked up the phone and dialled 999.

'Emergency, which service please?'

'Ambulance,' he said, his lower lip juddering. 'No, no, I don't need an ambulance. I don't know what I need. They're dead.'

The red-haired woman detective brought him the mug of milky tea that he had asked for, with two sugars. She sat down at the table next to him and gave him a smile. She was young and quite pretty, with a scattering of freckles across the bridge of her nose.

'You didn't hear anything, then?' she asked him.

'No,' David whispered.

'We're finding it very difficult to work out what happened,' she said. 'There was no sign that anybody broke into your house. The burglar alarm was on. And yet somebody attacked your daddy and mummy and whoever it was, they were very strong.'

'It wasn't me,' said David. He was wearing the purple hooded top that his uncle and aunt had given him for his last birthday, and he looked very pale.

'Well, we know for certain that it wasn't you,' said the detective. 'We just need to know if you saw anything, or heard anything. Anything at all.'

David looked down into his tea. He felt like bursting into tears but he swallowed and swallowed and tried very hard not to. He was too young to know that there was no shame in crying.

'I didn't hear anything,' he said. 'I don't know who did it. I just want them to be alive again.'

The detective reached across the table and squeezed his hand. She couldn't think of anything to say to him, except, 'I know you do, David. I know.'

Rufus said, 'Did they ever find out how your parents died?'

David shook his head. 'The coroner returned a verdict of unlawful killing by person or persons unknown. That's all he could do.'

'You must *wonder*, though, mate. You know – who could have done it, and why. And *how*, for Christ's sake!'

David took a swig from his bottle of Corona. The Woolpack was crowded, even for a Friday evening, and they were lucky to have found somewhere to sit, in the corner. An enormously fat man sitting next to them was laughing so loudly that they could hardly hear themselves speak.

Rufus and David had been friends ever since David had started work at Amberlight, selling IT equipment. He had been there seven months now, and last month he had been voted top salesman in his team. Rufus was easy-going, funny, with a shaven head to pre-empt the onset of pattern baldness and a sharp line in grey three-piece suits.

David heard himself saying, 'Actually . . . I *do* know who did it.'

'Really?' said Rufus. 'You really *do* know? Like – have you known all along, right from when it happened? Or did you find out later? Hang on, mate – why didn't you tell the police? Why don't you tell them now? It's never too late!'

David thought: *Shit, I wish I hadn't said anything now. Why did I say anything? I've kept this to myself for seventeen years, why did I have to come out with it now? It's going to sound just as insane now as it would have done then.*

'I didn't tell the police because they would never have believed me. Just like you won't believe me, either.'

'Well, you could try me. I'm famous for my gullibility. Do you want another beer?'

'Yes, thanks.'

Rufus went to the bar and came back with two more bottles. 'Right, then,' he said, smacking his hands together. 'Who's the guilty party?'

'I told you you wouldn't believe me. My dressing gown.'

Rufus had his bottle of beer poised in front of his mouth, his lips in an O shape ready to drink, but now he slowly put the bottle down.

'Did I hear that right? Your dressing gown?'

Trying to sound as matter-of-fact as possible, David said, 'My dressing gown. I had a brown dressing gown that used to hang on the back of my bedroom door and it looked like a monk. I always used to think that when it was dark it came alive. Well, one night it did, and it went into my parents' bedroom and it strangled them. In fact it garrotted them, according to the police report. It strangled them so hard it almost took off their heads.'

'Your dressing gown,' Rufus repeated.

'That's right. Sounds bonkers, doesn't it? But there is absolutely no other explanation. Unlawful killing by night attire. And there was something else, too. I had a puppet that my grandfather made for me, like it was all made out of grey sticks, with a wooden spoon for a head. Sticky Man, I used to call it. When my dressing gown went to murder my parents, Sticky Man jumped on me and I think he was trying to warn me what was going to happen.'

Rufus bent his head forward until his forehead was pressed against the table. He stayed like that for almost ten seconds. Then he sat up straight again and said, 'Your puppet warned you that your dressing gown was going to kill your mum and dad.'

'There – I told you that you wouldn't believe me. Thanks for the beer, anyway.'

'You know who you need to talk to, don't you?' said Rufus.

'A shrink, I suppose you're going to say.'

'Unh-hunh. You need to talk to Alice in accounts.'

'Alice? That freaky-looking woman with the white hair and all of those bracelets?'

'That's the one. Actually she's a very interesting lady. I had a long chat with her once at one of the firm's bonding weekends. It was down somewhere near Hailsham, I think. Anyway, Alice is a great believer in crustaceous automation, I think she called it.'

'What? Crustaceous? That's like crabs and lobsters, isn't it?'

'Well, I don't know, but it was something like that. What it meant was, things coming to life when it gets dark. She really, really believes in it. Like your dressing gown, I suppose. One of the things she told me about was this armchair that came to life when anybody fell asleep in it, and it squeezed them so hard that it crushed their ribcage. It took forever before somebody worked out what was killing all these people.

'What she said was, it's the dark that does it. The actual darkness. It changes things.'

David looked at Rufus narrowly. 'You're not taking the piss, are you?'

'Why would I?'

'Well, I know you. Always playing tricks on people. I don't want to go up to this Alice and tell her about my dressing gown if she's going to think that I'm some kind of loony.'

'No, mate,' said Rufus. 'Cross my heart. I promise you. I'm not saying that *she's* not loony, but I don't think you're any loonier than she is, so I doubt if she'll notice.'

They met in their lunch break, at their local Pizza Hut, which was almost empty except for two plump teenage mothers and their screaming children. David ordered a pepperoni pizza and a beer while Alice stayed with a green salad and a cup of black tea.

When he started talking to her, David realized that Alice was much less freaky than he had imagined. She had a short, severe, silvery-white bob, and he had assumed that she was middle-aged, but now he saw that her hair was bleached and highlighted and she couldn't have been older than thirty-one or thirty-two. She had a sharp, feline face, with green eyes to match, and she wore a tight black T-shirt and at least half a dozen elaborate silver bangles on each wrist.

'So, what did Rufus say when you told him?' she asked, lifting up her cup of tea with both hands and blowing on it.

'He was all right about it, actually, when you consider that he could have laughed his head off. Most of the rest of the team would have done.'

'Rufus has his own story,' said Alice. David raised an eyebrow, expecting her to tell him what it was, but she was obviously not going to be drawn any further.

'You know the word "shoddy"?' she said.

'Of course.'

'Most people think it means something that's been badly made. You know, something inferior. But it can also mean a woollen yarn made out of used clothes. They rip up old coats and sweaters to shreds and then they re-spin them, with just a bit of new wool included. Most new clothes are made out of that.'

David said, 'I didn't know that, no.'

'In Victorian times, these guys used to go around the streets ringing a bell and collecting used clothes. They called them "shoddy-men". These days it's mainly Lithuanians who pinch all of those bags of clothes that people leave out for charities. They ship them all back to Lithuania, turn them into new clothes and then sell them back to us.'

'I'm not too sure what you're getting at.'

Alice sipped her tea, and then she said, 'Sometimes, those second-hand clothes have belonged to some very violent people. Murderers, even. And clothes take on their owners' personalities. You know what it's like when you try on another man's jacket. It makes you feel as if you're *him*.'

'So what are you trying to tell me? My dressing gown might have had wool in it that once belonged in some murderer's clothes?'

Alice nodded. 'Exactly.'

'But it's not like *I* put it on, and *I* killed my parents. The dressing gown came alive. The dressing gown did it on its own!'

David suddenly realized that he was talking too loudly, and that the two teenage mothers were staring at him.

He lowered his voice and said, 'How did it come alive on its own? I mean, how is that possible?'

Alice said, 'The scientific name for it is "crepuscular animation". It means inanimate objects that come alive when it begins to get dark. Most people don't understand that darkness isn't just the absence of light. Darkness is an element in itself, and darkness goes looking for more darkness, to feed itself.

'That night, when your light was switched off, the darkness in your room found whatever darkness that was hidden in your dressing gown, and filled it up with more of its own dark energy, and brought it to life.'

'I'm sorry, Alice. I'm finding this really hard to follow.'

Alice laid her cool, long-fingered hand on top of his. Her green eyes were unblinking. 'What else could have happened, David? You said yourself that nobody broke into the house, and that you didn't do it. You *couldn't* have done it, you simply weren't strong enough. And your puppet man came alive, too, didn't he? How do you think that happened?'

David shrugged. 'I haven't a clue. And why should my dressing gown have come to life *then*, on that particular night? It was hanging there for *months* before that. My mother bought it for me in October, so that I could wear it on fireworks night.'

'Well, I don't know the answer to that. But it could have been some anniversary. Perhaps it was a year to the day that somebody was murdered, by whoever wore the wool that was woven into your dressing gown. There's no way of telling for certain.'

David sat for a long time saying nothing. Alice continued to fork up her salad and sip her tea but he didn't touch his pizza.

'How do you know all this?' he asked her. 'All about this – what did you call it – screspusular stuff?'

'Crepuscular animation. "Crepuscular" only means "twilight". My great-grandmother told me. Something happened to one of her sons, during the war. There was a lot of darkness, during the black-outs. So much darkness everywhere. She said there used to be a statue in their local park, a weeping woman, on a First World War memorial. Apparently her son and one of his friends took a shortcut through the park at night, and the statue came to life and came after them. Her son's head was crushed against the metal railings and his neck was broken.

'Of course nobody believed the other little boy, but my great-grandmother did, because she knew him and she knew that he always told the truth. She made a study of inanimate objects coming to life when it begins to get dark, and she wrote it all down in an exercise book and that exercise book got passed down to me. Nobody else in the family wanted it. They thought it was all cuckoo.'

To emphasize the point, she twirled her index finger around at the side of her head.

'I don't know what to think,' David told her.

'Just beware of the darkness,' said Alice. 'Treat it with respect. That's all I can say. And if you see a dressing gown that looks as if might come alive, then believe me, it probably will.'

He returned home late that night. The bulb had gone in the hallway and he had to grope his way to the living room.

The living room was dimly lit from the nearby main road. He lived on the ground floor of what had once been a large family house, but which was now divided into eight different flats. His was one of the smallest, but he was very fastidious, and he always kept it tidy. Up until the end of last year, he had shared a large flat with two colleagues from work, and that had been horrendous, with dirty plates stacked in the kitchen sink and the coffee table crowded with overflowing ashtrays and empty Stella cans. Worst of all had been the clothes that were heaped on the floor, or draped over the backs of chairs, or hanging from hooks on the back of every door.

He switched on the two side lamps, and the television, too, although he pressed the mute button. On the left-hand wall stood a bookcase, with all of his books arranged in alphabetical order, according to author. In front of them stood two silver shields, for playing squash, and several framed photographs of his father and mother, smiling. And then, of course, there was Sticky Man, perched on the edge of the shelf, staring at him with those circular, slightly mad eyes.

When Sticky Man had jumped on David on the night that his parents had been murdered, he had terrified him, but David had come to believe that he had been trying to warn him, and that was why he had kept him all these years. Hadn't Sticky Men always been helpers, and facilitators – entertaining the troops in Italy during the war, and carrying messages under shellfire? When David was little, Sticky Man may have frightened him by coming alive during the night, but he had only been dancing, after all.

'Hey, Sticks,' he said, but Sticky Man continued to stare at him and said nothing.

Although he had eaten only one slice of his pizza at lunchtime, David didn't feel particularly hungry, so he opened a can of Heinz vegetable soup, heated it up in the microwave and ate it in front of the television, watching *Newsnight.*

Afterwards, he showered and brushed his teeth and climbed into bed. He tried to read *The Girl With The Dragon Tattoo* for a while, but he couldn't stop thinking about Alice, and what she had said about inanimate objects coming to life when darkness fell. He still couldn't remember exactly what it was called. Crispucular automation?

Just beware of the darkness. Treat it with respect. That's all I can say. And if you see a dressing gown that looks as if it might come alive, then believe me, it probably will.

After his parents' murder, David had been brought up by his Aunt Joanie and his Uncle Ted. They had bought him a new dressing gown, a tartan one, but on the day that he had left home he had thrown it in the dustbin and he had never bought himself another one since. He never hung any clothes from the hook on his bedroom door, not even a scarf. Even before he had talked to Alice, he had always kept his clothes shut up in closets and wardrobes, out of sight. No jackets were hunched over the back of his chair. No shirts hung drip-drying in the bathroom, like ghosts.

He switched off the light and closed his eyes. He felt very tired for some reason. Alice had disturbed him quite a lot, even though he found it very hard to believe everything that she had told him. The statue of the weeping woman he found quite unsettling. And he wondered what Rufus's story was? Rufus was so pragmatic, and so straightforward. What on earth had appeared out of the dark to frighten Rufus?

He slept, deeply, for over an hour, but then he abruptly woke. He was sure that he had heard a clicking noise. His bedroom was unusually dark, and when he lifted his head from the pillow he realized that the digital clock beside his bed was no longer glowing. There were no street lights shining outside, either. There must have been a power cut, which might explain the clicking noise that had woken him up: the sound of the central-heating pipes contracting as they cooled down.

As he laid his head back down on the pillow, he heard more clicking. More like clattering this time. He strained his ears and listened. There was a lengthy silence, and then a quick, sharp rattling sound. He thought he heard a door opening.

He sat up. Something was outside his bedroom, in the hallway. Something that made a soft, dragging noise. It sounded as if it were coming closer and closer, and then it bumped into his bedroom door. Not loudly, but enough to give him the impression that it was big and bulky.

His heart was hammering against his ribcage. 'Who's there?' he called out. 'Is anybody out there?'

There was no answer. Nearly half a minute went by. Then suddenly there was another clatter, and he heard his door handle being pulled down. His door swung open with the faintest whisper, almost like a sigh of satisfaction.

He waited, listening, his fingers gripping the bedcovers. What had somebody once said about bedcovers? Why do we pull them up to protect ourselves when we're scared? Do you think a murderer with a ten-inch knife is going to be deterred by a quilt?

'Who's there?' he called out, hoarsely.

No answer.

'For God's sake, who's there?'

It was then that the power came back on again, and his digital bedside clock started flashing green, and the central heating began to tick into life again, and he saw what it was that was standing in his bedroom doorway.

It was his navy-blue duffel coat, with its hood up. It looked like a dead Antarctic explorer, somebody whose body had been found in the snow a hundred years after they had died.

Beside it, tilting this way and that, as if it couldn't get its balance right, was Sticky Man. Sticky Man must have opened the door to the closet, in the hallway, so that the duffel coat could shuffle out, and Sticky Man had opened his bedroom door, too. There was nobody else in the flat, so who else could it have been?

It was then that he realized that on the night his parents had been killed Sticky Man hadn't been trying to warn him. Sticky Man had probably been trying to wake him up, so that he too would go into his parents' bedroom, to be garrotted along with them.

'*You traitor, Sticks*,' he whispered, but of course Sticky Man wasn't a traitor, because Sticky Man was a creature of the dark, just as much as his dressing gown, and his duffel coat. It wasn't *them*, in themselves. They were only inanimate objects.

David's duffel coat rushed across his bedroom floor toward him. He lunged sideways across to the other side of the bed, trying to reach his phone.

'Emergency, which service please?'

'—*dark*—!'

Then a struggling sound, and a thin, reedy gasp, followed by a long continuous tone.

It was what the dark does.

SAINT BRÓNACH'S SHRIFT

'God has forgiven you, Michael,' said Father Bernard. 'Now you have to find it in your heart to forgive yourself.'

'And do you honestly think that I haven't tried?' Michael retorted. 'I've even tried mortification of the flesh. Stubbing out cigarettes on the back of my hand. Hitting my head against the wall again and again until I couldn't see for the blood running down my face. I had to tell Kate I hit myself on a cupboard door.'

Father Bernard shook his head. 'That's not the way, Michael. Castigating yourself now isn't going to change what you did all those years ago.'

Michael was standing by the window, looking out over the steeply sloping garden. It had started raining again, and he could hear the raindrops crackling through the hydrangeas. At the bottom of the garden ran the River Lee, the colour of badly tarnished silverware, and beyond the river rose the misty hills that led to the airport, and beyond, to Riverstick and Belgooly and Garrettstown. And of course to Kinsale Sands, where day and night the grey Atlantic washed, and washed, but could never wash away Michael's guilt.

Father Bernard said, 'Nobody blamed you, Michael. Your parents didn't blame you. The Gardaí said there was no cause to think that it was anything else but an accident so. Even your Kate didn't blame you.'

Michael turned away from the window. He had celebrated his thirty-fifth birthday only last Thursday, but he looked much older. His light brown hair stuck up like a cockatoo's crest but it was beginning to thin and recede at the temples, and there were deep creases in his cheeks as if somebody had cut him with a craft-knife. When he sat down the daylight was reflected in his rimless spectacles, making him look blind.

Father Bernard leaned forward and laid a liver-spotted hand on his knee. 'Would you care to pray?' he suggested.

Michael said, 'What's the use? The only person who can answer my prayers is me.'

'You're still having the same dream?'

Michael nodded.

'Are you not still taking the pills the doctor gave you?'

'Twice the dose, Father. Washed down with two glasses of Paddy's.'

Father Bernard sat back. He steepled his hands and stared at Michael for a long time without saying anything. He was obviously thinking hard. Behind him, the pendulum in the long-case clock wearily swung, but the passing seconds couldn't help Michael, either.

'Try once more tonight, Michael,' said Father Bernard. 'Try it without the pills and the whiskey. If you have the nightmare again, come back to me in the morning, early. Before ten if you can. I have to be visiting Mrs O'Leary in Ballyhooly. Poor old girl may not last another week.'

They both stood up. Father Bernard's knees clicked like two shots from a cap-pistol. His eyes were a very pale agate, as if they had been leached of their natural colour by all the years of pain that he had witnessed, and the endless rain.

He laid his hands on Michael's shoulders. 'O my God,' he intoned, 'we love You above all things, with our whole hearts, because You are good and worthy of our love. We love our neighbours as ourselves for the love of You. We forgive all who injured us and we ask pardon of all whom we have injured.'

Michael said, 'Amen.' When he looked up, his eyes were glistening with tears, and he had to wipe his nose with the back of his hand.

Little Kieran had been fractious all day and Kate was exhausted by the time Michael put the key in the lock and stepped into the hallway.

He hung up his coat. He could hear Kieran upstairs, honking in his crib like a baby seal. Kate came out of the kitchen in her apron, all red and flustered, her russet hair awry. She smelled of frying onions and ground lamb so he guessed it must be shepherd's pie tonight. He kissed her and then he said, 'Sounds like he's teething again, poor little beggar.'

'It's those two big back ones,' Kate told him. 'I gave him Calpol to take his temperature down but he's still so miserable. He nods off but then the pain wakes him up again.'

I know the feeling, thought Michael. *It's the pain that can follow*

*you everywhere, no matter how many glasses of whiskey you drink,
no matter how many Sominex tablets you swallow. It comes after
you through the fog of your exhaustion like the crocodile coming
after Captain Hook and its ticking is the ticking of your bedside
clock.*

He went into the living room and unscrewed the half-empty bottle
of Jacob's Creek shiraz that was standing on the sideboard. He could
see himself in the mirror as he poured out two glasses. He didn't
think that he looked like himself at all, more like some rat-faced
private detective who had been hired to see what he was up to. His
eyes were so dead and watchful, in spite of all the turmoil that he
was feeling inside.

He took the wine through to the kitchen. Kate was standing over
the range, stirring the lamb in a large saucepan. The kitchen floor
was only half-finished and every time she wanted to go to the
cupboard she had to step over a missing floorboard.

'You should have booked a babysitter,' he told her. 'We could
have gone to Isaac's for dinner tonight, and given you a break.'

Kate said, 'You're joking, aren't you? I wouldn't wish Kieran on
anybody right now. Besides, we can't afford it. And you look like
you could do with an early night.'

He intercepted her as she stepped over the missing floorboard
and picked her up in his arms. 'Hey!' she said, with a wooden
spatula in one hand and a jar of dried thyme in the other.

'You're the one who suggested an early night.' He smiled, and
kissed her on her perspiring forehead.

'Not *that* kind of an early night. I'm totally flahed out.'

'We'll see.' He kissed her again and let her go. She went back
to stirring the lamb and he pulled out a kitchen chair and sat down
to watch her. He never tired of it, she was so magical, even when
she was hot and messy like this. Her red hair, her high forehead,
her wide-apart blue eyes, so blue that they were almost indigo. Her
little straight nose with the spattering of freckles across it.

Most of all he loved her slight overbite, the way her top teeth
rested on the moist pink cushion of her lower lip.

She was small and trim with narrow hips and she could dance like
a flame-haired fairy, her eyes full of mischief, spinning around and
around and always seeming to be teasing him, because she shouldn't
be his, not really. Not that she should have been Sean's, either.

They ate on their laps in the living room, watching television. Upstairs, Kieran was sleeping at last, snuffling as he slept, his cheeks as red as tomatoes.

'Did you sell that gorgeous house in Lover's Walk yet?' asked Kate, flapping her hand in front of her face because her mouthful of shepherd's pie was so hot.

Michael shook his head. 'They wanted me to drop the price by another two thousand. I told them to stuff it. Not in so many words, though. Polite, like.'

'How's your old mamo?'

'Oh, she's grand, except for her knee.'

'You should see her more often.'

Michael didn't answer. Calling in to see his grandmother in Glanmire had been his pretence for visiting Father Bernard at St Dominic's Retreat House. He had confessed only to Father Bernard what he had done, nineteen years and two months ago. At the time, he had told the Gardaí what had happened, blurting it out between his tears, but he hadn't told them that he had done it deliberately, nor what had provoked him to do it, and he had never admitted it to Kate.

He had never told Kate what he had seen through Sean's bedroom door, either. Sometimes he wondered what would happen if he did. But it didn't take much imagination to realize that it would bring down every ceiling in the house, and their marriage would be over, and little Kieran, like Michael, would be fatherless.

He placed two Sominex tablets on his nightstand, next to his alarm clock, just in case he really needed them, but Father Bernard had given him the courage to try to sleep without them. *God has forgiven you*, he told himself. *Now you have to find it in your heart to forgive yourself.*

By the time he had climbed out of the bath and towelled himself, Kate had climbed into bed, switched off her bedside lamp and turned her back to him. The freckles on her bare shoulders looked like a faded map of the stars. He eased himself into bed, leaned over and breathed in deeply, just so that he could smell her. Chanel Eau Premiere, light and flowery.

He knew that he wouldn't be able to go to sleep immediately, so he propped his pillows up behind him and watched a nature

programme about fishermen somewhere off the coast of east Africa,
keeping the volume muted so that he wouldn't disturb Kate. After
a while one of the fishermen came walking along the glossy wet
sand, holding up a feathery-looking fish. It seemed to take him
hours to approach the camera, but when he finally came close enough
he gave a gappy smile and waved the fish from side to side in front
of the lens, and shouted at the top of his voice, '*You see this,
Michael? This is a devil firefish, Michael! It stings! Very dangerous
to humans! A fish like this can take a terrible revenge on you!*'

Michael jerked and opened his eyes. The nature programme must
have finished almost twenty minutes ago. It was eleven p.m. now
and the RTE weatherman was predicting another day of soft weather
tomorrow. Michael got up and switched the television off. The
bedroom was engulfed in darkness, and all he could hear was the rain
sprinkling against the window and the deep throbbing of oil tankers
moored on the opposite side of the Lee.

The dream began as it always began. He was walking along the
upstairs corridor of The Far Horizon Hotel, where the O'Connor
family stayed every summer for two weeks. Outside the day was
blurry and hot, but inside the hotel it was always cool and smelled
of damp.

All along the white-painted corridor hung wooden-framed photographs of the few survivors from the *Lusitania*, which had been
sunk by a German submarine in 1915 only eight miles off the Old
Head of Kinsale. Michael had often stopped to study these survivors,
wrapped in blankets and surrounded by local fishermen, their faces
strangely expressionless, as if they accepted that one day they would
be dead, too, nothing more than pictures of themselves on a hotel
wall.

Michael was returning to the room he shared with Sean because
he had forgotten his towel and his swimming trunks. He knew what
he was going to see when he reached the door, because he had
dreamed this dream so many times before, but somehow he always
felt the same shock when he saw it, like scores of cockroaches
scuttling down his back.

He heard Kate sigh a second before he saw them, a high sweet
note of happiness, almost as if she were singing. The door was only
an inch or two ajar, but he could see them reflected in the mirror

in the huge mahogany press – Sean lying on his back, his skin as white as the sheet he was lying on, and Kate sitting upright on top of him, her elbows raised, both hands buried in her tangled red hair. '*Sissikins*,' said Sean, and he made her pet name sound so lubricious.

Michael stood breathless in the corridor, watching with horror and fascination as Kate slowly rose up and down, as if she were wading in the sea.

Neither she nor Sean could see him, and he stayed completely still, barely breathing, not knowing what he should do. Eventually he took one careful step back, and then another, and then he turned and hurried softly downstairs. He crossed the hotel reception area and pushed his way out of the front door and stood on the porch in the wind and the sunshine with the sea almost blinding him.

It was then he realized that he was not only shocked but grievously hurt. Ever since the O'Connors had brought him home when he was six years old, he and Kate had always been close, playing make-believe games together while Sean was out kicking footballs with his school friends, telling each other stories, sharing secrets. He had never articulated the thought before, but he had assumed that he and Kate would stay together for the rest of their lives, and it had never occurred to him that she might feel such affection for anybody else, especially her own natural brother.

The dream continued. He sat on the steps as the afternoon passed, and the shadows of the clouds fled across Kinsale Sands, rising and falling as they crossed over the dunes like the steeplechasers at Leopardstown. After twenty minutes or so, Sean appeared, his shirt hanging out of his crumpled khaki shorts, his carroty hair tousled and his cheeks flushed. He sat on the step next to Michael and gave him a playful push on the shoulder. 'What's the matter with you, boy? I thought you were going swimming, like. You left your badinas upstairs.'

'I changed my mind,' said Michael, standing up.

He started to walk away from the hotel, toward the beach. In the dream he always walked very quickly and jerkily, like a speeded-up film, and Sean followed him, about twenty yards behind.

He walked over half a mile, until he reached the dunes. He wanted to be alone but Sean kept following him. He sat down and covered his face with his hands. Sean circled around him, kicking at the sand. The sea looked like smashed-up mirrors, and the inside of Michael's head felt the same.

'We should dig ourselves a hideout like,' Sean suggested.

Michael looked up at him, one eye closed against the sunshine.

'We could pinch some bottles of beer from the bar, see, and sit in the hideout and drink it and nobody could see us.'

Michael thought: *That's exactly the kind of stupid idea that Sean was always coming up with, ridiculous impractical plans for shop-lifting from Dunnes with plastic bags safety-pinned inside their coats or making a periscope to spy on the women's changing room at Mayfield swimming pool.*

He said nothing, but Sean picked up a flat piece of driftwood and started to dig into the side of the dune.

'You could help,' he panted, after he had been shovelling sand for over half an hour.

Michael looked up at him again. He hated him so much he could have jumped up and grabbed him by the throat and strangled him.

'Oh well, please yourself,' said Sean, and carried on digging.

The sun was sinking and the wind began to rise, whistling thinly through the grass. Sean had dug a tunnel into the dune almost two metres deep, so that only his rubber dollies were showing. He came crawling back out of it and brushed himself down, shaking his head like a dog to get the sand out of his hair.

'I'm a genius,' he announced. 'I'm the greatest digger of hideouts that ever was. All I have to do now is make it just a bit more wider. Then we can go and pinch ourselves a few bottles of Satz and have us a party.'

He got down on his hands and knees and crawled back into the tunnel. He had only been digging for a few minutes, though, before Michael heard a very soft thump, and a muffled shout. He looked around and saw that the sand had collapsed, and that Sean was buried. He couldn't even see his rubber dollies.

He stood up, his heart banging.

'Sean!' he called out. 'Sean! Can you hear me? Sean, are you all right?'

A brief flurry of sand was kicked up where Sean's feet must have been, but then there was nothing but absolute stillness. Michael knelt down and frantically started scooping at the sand with his cupped hands, but the more sand he scooped, the more slid down from higher up the dune, faster and faster, like a nightmarish parody of an hourglass, and he soon realized that he was making things worse.

He stopped, and stood up. 'Hold on, Sean! I'll go for some help! Just hold on!'

He started to run along the beach toward the hotel. His long shadow ran in front of him, with a tiny head. At first he ran as fast as he could, but then he slowed down to a trot, and then a walk, and after a while he stopped.

There was nobody in sight for over half a mile, only a woman in a billowy red dress walking her dog by the water's edge. Three seagulls circled overhead, crying like lost children. Michael looked back at the dunes. He hesitated for a moment and then he took a deep breath and held it for as long as he could, timing himself with his wristwatch. A little more than a minute. Even if Sean could hold his breath for twice as long, he must have suffocated by now.

Michael started running again. As he approached the hotel, he could see his father climbing the front steps, smoking his pipe. He waved his arms and screamed out, '*Da! Da! Come quick! It's Seanie! Seanie's been buried in the sand!*'

He opened his eyes. He thought at first that he might have been shouting out loud in his sleep, but if he had, he hadn't disturbed Kate, who was still breathing softly and evenly and hadn't stirred.

He lay on his back for nearly an hour, staring at the ceiling and listening to the rain chuckling in the gutters outside. He knew where he would have to go tomorrow. Prayers hadn't helped. Years of counselling hadn't helped. He couldn't imagine what Father Bernard had in mind, but he doubted if that would help, either.

He said, 'Holy Father . . .' But then he stopped himself, and stayed silent with his lips pressed tightly together until he heard the clock in the hallway strike two.

The following day was one of those dark Cork days when the rain holds off but the sky remains relentlessly grey from morning till night.

Father Bernard was sitting in his study drinking a cup of coffee when Michael knocked at the door. He unhooked his spectacles and said, 'Michael! I was hoping against hope that I wouldn't be seeing you this morning.'

Michael sat down in the leather-upholstered chair on the opposite side of Father Bernard's desk. The chair was so low that he felt like the schoolboy Stephen Dedalus explaining to the rector that he had broken his glasses on the cinder path. 'I was hoping so, too, Father. But I had the dream again. And just as vivid as always.'

Father Bernard sat back with his hand pressed over his mouth as if he didn't trust himself to say any more. But after a short while he stood up and went across to his bookcase, lifting out of his soutane a bunch of keys on a long chain. He unlocked the front of the bookcase and took out a grey porcelain jar with a lid that was fastened with twisted wire. He brought it back across the room and set it down on his desk between them.

Michael could see that the jar was decorated with a pattern of green leaves and small purplish flowers. Father Bernard said, 'Inside this jar is a powder that was made up for me by a very dear friend, at a time in my life when I had my own ghosts to lay. It's a compound of bishopswort, more commonly known as betony, and marigold petals, as well as numerous other ingredients including the dried and ground-up hearts of several moles.'

Michael didn't know how to respond to that – whether he ought to make a joke of it, or look serious, and nod. He settled for a brief twitch at the sides of his mouth, and an interested frown.

Father Bernard prised the lid open, and tilted the jar so that Michael could see the soft purplish-grey powder inside. 'They call this Saint Brónach's Shrift, because it was first compounded by Saint Brónach the Virgin of Glen-Seichis in the sixth century. She was an abbess, with great mystic powers, and according to legend she was very beautiful.

'A fiery young Irish chieftain named Fergus had wounded a rival named Artan and left him for dead. However, he was overcome with remorse for what he had done and became a pilgrim of penance until he was a very old man. He was so wracked with guilt that he finally came to the abbey to seek the help of Saint Brónach, and she gave him an infusion of this powder to drink.

'That night Fergus had a dream in which he returned to the skirmish in which he had wounded Artan, and Artan, as he lay bleeding on the ground, forgave him.'

Michael peered into the jar again. 'And what you're proposing is that *I* should drink some of this stuff?'

Father Bernard said, 'It's a very powerful mixture, Michael. It might have some side-effects, mystical as well as physical. The physician to the Emperor Caesar Augustus used a similar preparation of betony to protect the emperor from epidemics and to guard him against witchcraft, but one of its greatest benefits was to give him peace of mind.

'Peace of mind could be yours, Michael, if you're prepared to try it.'

'And you say that you've tried it, yourself?'

Father Bernard nodded.

Michael hesitated. But then he thought about those endless dreams, hammering through his head almost every night like a flicker-book. The wind blowing through the grass. The soft thumping sound as the sand collapsed and Sean was buried. The woman in the red billowy dress, and the sea continuing wearily to whisper to itself because the sea was like his ageing grandmother and had forgotten who he was.

'Well, I'll try it, like,' Michael agreed. 'What do I have to do?'

Father Bernard with shaking hands poured some of the powder into a white envelope. 'Three teaspoonfuls should be enough, stirred up well with hot water. Drink it about an hour before you go to bed.'

'You said something about side-effects,' said Michael, as he opened the door to leave.

Father Bernard laid a hand on his shoulder. 'Everything we do in life has side-effects, Michael. God be with you.'

Kate was too tired to cook so they ordered a margherita pizza from Valentino's and when it arrived they sat in front of the television and shared it out of the box.

'You're awful quiet,' said Kate.

Michael wiped his mouth on a paper napkin and swallowed a mouthful of warm red wine and then he leaned over and kissed her on the cheek.

'You don't think I'm a bad person, do you?' he asked her.

'Of course not! Whatever made you ask me that?'

'I've never meant to hurt anybody, Kate, not ever. And if I have, they've been sins of omission, if you know what I mean. Not deliberate.'

'You're strange,' said Kate, looking at him with those wide-apart blue eyes of hers that were almost indigo. 'When you first came to live with us, Sean told me that you were a goblin child that none of the other goblins wanted. I suppose in a way it was kinder than crowing that your da and your ma had been killed in a car crash.'

'Maybe Sean was right,' Michael told her. 'Maybe I *am* a goblin. I don't remember my parents at all. What they looked like, of course, from the photos. But I can't hear their voices, not at all. I can't remember what they *felt* like.'

Kate went upstairs for a bath first and Michael went into the kitchen and made her a mug of chocolate. He took out the envelope that Father Bernard had given him and tipped the powder into a tumbler. He sniffed it but it didn't smell of anything at all. He poured hot water over it and stirred it until it dissolved.

He held the tumbler up to the light. Saint Brónach's Shrift was a pale agate colour, the same colour as Father Bernard's eyes. Perhaps it would give him the same insight, too. He drank it, and it tasted very slightly bitter, but nothing more.

After his bath, he and Kate sat up in bed and watched television for a while. He glanced at her sideways from time to time and wondered if she had really been in love with Sean and how young she had been when they first went to bed together – questions that he could never ask her.

At the end of *CSI: Miami*, Kate twisted herself into her sheets and her blankets as she always did and went to sleep. Michael sat up a little longer but he was beginning to feel oddly light-headed, as if he had taken too many flu tablets.

He switched over channels, and found that he was watching the same nature program about east African fishermen that he had watched last night, or *thought* he had watched. Here was the same wet shoreline, and the same fisherman walking slowly towards the screen, holding up that spiny devil firefish. Michael switched the television off while the fisherman was still a hundred yards away.

He lay in the darkness for over half an hour, not moving. There was no wind tonight and no rain, only the throbbing of the oil tankers. The river amplified the deep drumbeat of their engines and sometimes he felt as if the whole house was throbbing, as if every-thing was going to be loosened, nuts and bolts and dovetail joints and screws, and finally shaken apart.

He closed his eyes. When he opened them again it was daylight and the sun was shining through the windows and he was walking along the corridor at The Far Horizon Hotel, past the framed photographs of the *Lusitania* survivors.

He heard Kate let out that sweet high cry of pleasure. He heard Sean say, '*Sissikins*'. He looked in horror through the open doorway and saw their reflection in the press, Kate with her fingers buried in her curly red hair.

He ran downstairs and out through the door and into the wind and the sunshine. He felt as if he had been in the same head-on crash that had killed his father and mother on the N25 at Churchquarter. He was too shocked even to cry. He was still sitting there when Sean came out with his shirt untucked, his cheeks flushed, his upper lip beaded with clear perspiration.

'What's the matter with you, boy? I thought you were going swimming.'

He didn't answer. Instead, he stood up and started to walk quickly towards the beach. He prayed that, this time, Sean wouldn't follow him, but without even turning his head he knew that Sean was only ten yards behind him.

He reached the dunes and sat down. Sean circled around him, kicking the sand.

'We should dig ourselves a hideout, like.'

'No,' said Michael.

'Don't be so soft. We could pinch some bottles of beer from the bar and we could sit in our hideout and drink them and nobody would know.'

'No,' Michael repeated.

Sean picked up a piece of driftwood and started to dig. 'You're not going to help me, then?'

'No.'

'All right then, please yourself so.'

Sean went on digging and the wind began to rise, keening through the grass like the banshees that were supposed to wail whenever an O'Connor was close to death. When Sean had excavated a tunnel into the side of the dune that was more than four feet deep, Michael stood up and said, 'Stop, Seanie! Don't! Don't dig any more! It's too dangerous!'

Sean waggled his head and crossed his eyes and stuck out his tongue. 'You're a header, Mikey. It's a hole in the sand, that's all.'

'Just stop it. I'll go tell Da what you're doing, else.'

'Go on, then! What do you think *he's* going to say? We're on a seaside holiday and I'm digging in the sand. What else are you supposed to do on a seaside holiday?'

Michael stepped up to him and tried to grab the piece of driftwood away from him but Sean hit him on the elbow with it, hard, right on the funny bone.

'If you don't want to help, then you can bog off. I mean it. And if you try to do that again I'll drop you.'

Michael stayed where he was, rubbing his elbow. He had got into fights with Sean dozens of times, and Sean had always beaten him, because he was a year older and at least a stone heavier. He should have turned around and walked away and left Sean to the fate that was waiting for him, but he knew that he couldn't.

Sean dug and grunted and dug and grunted. Michael sat down on the side of the dune while the sun began to sink and the cloud shadows fled across the beach. Eventually Sean came crawling out of the tunnel, sandy backside first. He scrabbled sand out of his hair and said, 'I'm a genius! The greatest hideout digger ever known! All I have to do now is make it a bit more wider. Talk about *The Great Escape!*'

'No, Seanie!' Michael shouted, standing up again, but his voice was snatched out of his mouth by the wind, and Sean was already elbowing his way back into the tunnel.

In three long leaps, like an astronaut walking on the moon, Michael bounded across the side of the dune and seized Sean's ankles, twisting his fingers into the laces of his rubber dollies so that he couldn't get himself free. Sean bellowed, 'Let go of me, you gowl! What the do you think you're feckin' doing? Let go of me!'

Sean struggled and twisted and kicked at him, but Michael held on to him and tried to drag him backward. He wasn't strong enough or heavy enough to pull him more than a few inches, but in the end, Sean grew so furious that he struggled his way out of the tunnel himself, and stood up, and punched Michael on the left cheek.

Michael staggered backward and fell over, rolling down the side of the dune and landing on his back, winded. Up above him he saw ragged white clouds, and seagulls.

Sean shouted, 'You're a feckin' eejit, do you know that? You're the biggest feckin' eejit I ever knew! I wish to God that my da and my ma had never took you in, you gimp!'

He stalked back toward his tunnel, but as he did so it collapsed, with the same soft thump that Michael had heard so many times in his dreams.

Sean stood in front of the dune with his arms spread wide. 'Now look what you've done! Now look what you've feckin' done! I spent all feckin' afternoon digging that hideout and that's it!'

He kicked at the sandy depression where the tunnel had been, and then he came back down the dune and stood over Michael and kicked him in the hip. 'Gimp,' he repeated, and then he started walking back along the beach towards the hotel.

Michael sat up, dabbing at his cheek with his fingertips. His eye was beginning to close up already. But he turned and watched Sean shrinking smaller and smaller and thought: *I saved him. I hate him but I did the Christian thing and I saved him, even if I made him so angry. I don't need God's forgiveness any more. I don't need Sean's forgiveness either.*

He hadn't felt such inner peace in years. He closed his eyes and the wind gradually died down and the sea whispered softer and softer. Soon there was absolute silence, except for the surreptitious ticking of a clock.

Somebody laid a hand on his shoulder and said, 'Michael? Michael? You must have fallen asleep. Come on, Michael, we have to get to Togher before seven.'

He opened his eyes. He was sitting in a brown leather chair in a gloomy oak-panelled room, lined with bookcases. Through the windows he could see that the clouds were deep grey and that it was raining.

He looked up. Father Bernard was standing over him, smiling.

'I must be working you too hard,' said Father Bernard. 'Maybe I should let you have a day off. Maybe we should *both* take a day off, and do some fishing. The salmon are running in the Blackwater.'

Bewildered, Michael turned his head. Beside him, on a side table, there was a half-empty cup of milky tea and a copy of *Bethada Náem Nérenn*, the lives of the Irish saints, open at the life of Máedoc of Fern, with a thirty-cent-off coupon from Valentino's the pizza parlour as a bookmark.

'I'm sorry, Father. I must have dropped off.'

'Never mind. But we should be making haste now. We don't want to be late for the needy of Saint Arran's, do we?'

'No, Father.'

Michael stood up and brushed biscuit crumbs from the front of his soutane. He couldn't think why he felt so disoriented. He couldn't remember coming into the library or where he had been before. He couldn't even remember getting up this morning.

'How's the eye?' asked Father Bernard.

'The eye?' Michael reached up and touched his left eye. It was swollen and tender, and it felt greasy, as it if had been smeared with butter to relieve the bruising. 'I don't know. Better, I think.'

Father Bernard laid a hand on his shoulder and steered him across the room. On the panelled walls around the door frame hung several hand-coloured engravings of fish. A salmon, a gurnard, a John Dory and an ugly-looking tropical fish with staring eyes and feathery spines. *Pterois miles*, the devil firefish. Michael was sure that he had seen this before. Not just here, in the library, but somewhere else, although he couldn't think where. A house, somewhere in the city. A bedroom, where somebody else was sleeping beside him.

But then Father Bernard steered him out into the corridor and out through the front doors and into the rainy street outside, where his old blue Honda was parked.

He climbed into the passenger seat and the doors slammed and he forgot where he had seen the devil firefish before, for ever.

At the same time, which was five eighteen in the morning in New York, Kate was woken up by Kieran starting to grizzle again. She eased herself out of bed and out of the bedroom and walked across the living room to Kieran's crib. She lifted him out and he was hot and damp and smelled of pee.

'There,' she said, jiggling him up and down. 'Is it those nasty teeth again?'

She carried him across to the window and looked down at East 13th Street. It had been raining during the night and there were stacks of sodden cardboard on the sidewalk. There was no traffic, although she could hear a fire truck honking somewhere in the distance, and the warbling of sirens.

'There, there,' she sang, rocking Kieran from side to side. And then she sang, '*Chip, chip, my little horse. Chip, chip again, sir. How many miles to Dublin town? Fourscore and ten, sir. Will I get there by candlelight? Yes, and back again, sir.*'

She felt a hand on her shoulder, and then a kiss on the back of her neck, and then another kiss. She turned and said, 'We tried not to wake you, didn't we, baby?'

'That's all right, Sissikins. I couldn't sleep anyway. Every time I closed my eyes I had dreams about Michael. I can't think why, like. I haven't thought about Michael for years.'

Kate reached up with one hand and touched his cheek. 'Poor Michael,' she said. She kissed the top of Kieran's gingery hair and for a long moment Kieran was silent, as if she had given him a blessing.

THE BATTERED WIFE

Halfway through the afternoon it began to rain, almost laughably hard, and they retreated under the canvas awning of the bric-a-brac stall.

'You should leave him,' said Heather, over the syncopated drumming of the rain. 'You should pack everything up, take the kids and walk out. You could always come to Tunbridge Wells and stay with us until you find somewhere else to go.'

'How can I?' said Lily. 'And why *should* I? Poppy's only just started at Elm Trees – she'd be so upset if we had to move – and Jamie keeps wetting the bed as it is. Apart from that, damn it, Heather, half of that house belongs to me, and I've spent three years decorating it exactly the way I want it.'

'But you can't go on the way you are, Lily. One day he's going to kill you.'

Lily didn't know what to say. She knew that Heather was right. It was a gloomy wet afternoon in late September but she was wearing dark glasses to conceal her two bruised eyes. Two nights ago Stephen had come home in one of his moods. He had been drinking, although he wasn't incoherently drunk, like he sometimes was. She had cooked him a chicken-and-tomato casserole, one of his favourites, but for some arcane reason he had interpreted this as mockery.

'What? You think I'm some kind of a peasant, all I ever want to eat is chicken-and-tomato casserole?'

He had dropped the Le Creuset casserole on the kitchen floor, cracking the tiles and splashing her ankles with scalding red sauce, and then he had punched her, once, on the bridge of the nose.

'Me – I would have called the police,' said Heather.

'Oh, yes. And then Stephen would tell them that he's suffering from stress at work and how sorry he is and how he'll never ever lay another finger on me.'

'At least see a counsellor, Lily. Please.'

Lightning crackled behind the horse chestnuts that bordered the village green, followed by an indigestive grumble of thunder. Children scurried in the rain between the tents, screaming.

Heather said, 'Why does it *always* rain whenever we hold a fête? You would have thought that God was all in favour of us raising money for a donkey sanctuary. His son went everywhere by donkey.'

But Lily wasn't really listening. She was frowning at a woman who was sheltering under the cake stall opposite. The woman was wearing a grey knitted hat and a grey three-quarter-length raincoat, and she had a pale, drained face, with tightly pursed lips. She had a small grey Bedlington terrier with her, which repeatedly shook itself.

What Lily found unsettling was the way that the woman was staring at her, unblinking. She turned her head away for a few seconds, but when she looked back the woman was still staring at her.

'Do you see that woman?' she asked Heather.

'What woman?'

'*That* woman – the one in the grey raincoat, with the dog – next to the cake stall.'

'What about her?'

'She's staring at me. She's been staring at me for the past few minutes.'

Heather pulled a face. 'Perhaps she knows you.'

'Well, I certainly don't know her. And look. She's *still* staring at me.'

There was another rumble of thunder, but it was much further away now and the rain was easing off. After a few minutes, Lily and Heather stepped out from under the awning, and soon the aisles between the tents were crowded again. Lily tried to see if the woman in the grey hat and the grey raincoat was still standing at the cake stall, but she had vanished.

Before she picked up Poppy from Elm Trees, Lily parked on a double yellow line in the High Street to buy pork chops and runner beans and a fresh loaf of bread. She went into the off-licence, too, and bought two bottles of Merlot on special offer.

Stephen usually drank Merlot, and she thought that if she showed him that she didn't disapprove of his drinking, so long as he did it in moderation, he might not feel that she was judging him so much. 'You're always *judging* me. Just because you're a solicitor's daughter. Who the *hell* do you think you are?'

She was waiting at the counter in the off-licence when she turned towards the window to make sure that there were no traffic wardens around. Standing outside the window, peering in at her, was the woman in the grey hat and the grey raincoat, with her Bedlington terrier beside her.

Lily was about to go outside and ask her what she wanted when the assistant took her bottles of Merlot from her and said, 'Afternoon, madam. Like to put your card in?'

By the time she had paid and stepped out of the off-licence, the woman had gone. She looked up and down the High Street, but there was no sign of her.

She put Poppy and Jamie to bed early that evening and read them a story, *Chris Cross in Snappyland*, about a boy who kept losing his temper until he was taken away by monsters who could all shout much louder than he could.

'Mummy,' said Poppy, as Lily tucked her in. 'We're not going to go away, are we?'

'Of course not, sweetie.'

'But Daddy is always shouting and makes you cry. I don't like it when he shouts and makes you cry.'

'Daddy has a lot of worry at work. Sometimes it makes him cross like Chris Cross in Snappyland. He doesn't really mean it.'

'I heard you tell Daddy that you were going to take us away.'

'Well, that's because *I* get cross, too. But I don't mean it, either.'

'That lady said you mustn't take us away.'

'Lady? What lady?'

'She was standing outside the playground today and she called me. She said, *Poppy*. Then she said "your mummy mustn't leave your daddy".'

Lily stared at her. 'What did this lady look like?'

'She had a grey woolly hat and a grey raincoat and she had a dog that looked like a dirty lamb.'

'And that was all she said? She didn't tell you what her name was, or how she knew what your name was?'

Poppy shook her head. 'The bell went and I had to go inside.'

Stephen still hadn't come home by ten fifteen. Lily stood in the living room with a glass of Merlot in her hand, almost motionless, looking at herself in the mirror over the mantelpiece as if she were someone that she didn't recognize. A thirty-five-year-old woman with blonde, short-cropped hair, and two black eyes that were now turning rainbow-coloured, as if she were wearing a pierrette's mask. She didn't know whether to start supper or not. It was so late now that she herself had lost her appetite, and she didn't know what state Stephen would be in when he eventually arrived home.

She was still standing in front of the mirror when the doorbell chimed. She went into the hallway to answer it. Through the green and yellow stained-glass window in the front door she could a dark distorted shape.

'Who is it?' she called out.

There was a moment's pause, but then a woman's voice said, *'Don't open the door. There's no need to. But don't take the children away.'*

'What?' she demanded. 'Who are you?'

She unfastened the latch and threw the door open wide. In the porch stood the woman in the grey hat and the grey raincoat, her face as grey as newspaper. As soon as she saw Lily, she screamed out, *'Don't take the children away! Not tonight! Something terrible will happen if you do!'*

Terrified, Lily slammed the door shut. After she had done so, she stood in the hallway quaking. From upstairs, she heard Poppy calling out, 'Mummy! Mummy! Jamie's wet the bed!'

She approached the front door again. The light in the porch was shining through the stained-glass window, but she couldn't see the shape of the woman any more. She slid the security chain into place, and then she opened the door a little way.

The woman had disappeared. All she could see were street lights flickering through the trees, and all she could hear was the muffled sound of traffic.

She switched off the lights in the living room and she was just about to go upstairs to run a bath when the front door burst open with a deafening crash.

'Lily! Lily? Where the eff are you?'

She went through to the hallway. Stephen was leaning against the open door, his hair sticking up like a schoolboy's, his tie crooked. She could smell alcohol and regurgitated curry.

'Stephen,' she said.

'Oh, you recognize me! You know who I am! That makes a change!'

He took three stumbling steps forward, lost his balance, and almost collided with her.

'Get away from me,' she told him.

'Get *away* from you? That's not what you said on our wedding night, you bitch!'

'Stephen, you're drunk and you stink. Go upstairs and take a shower and go to bed.'

Stephen stood in the hallway, swaying. He had a faraway look in his eyes, and he was smiling.

'Stephen,' she repeated, and it was then that he slapped her so hard that she bounced against the wall, knocking her head and jarring her shoulder.

She fell to the floor, but Stephen gripped the front of her dress, tearing it wide open. He dragged her on to her feet and slapped her again and again.

'*You know what you are?*' he kept yelling at her. '*You know what you are?*'

Both Poppy and Jamie were crying as she bundled them into her Meriva. She heaved the big blue travelling bag into the back and slammed the door.

As she climbed into the driver's seat, Stephen reappeared in the porch.

'Lily!' he shrieked at her. 'You're not taking my kids, Lily! You're not going anywhere, you bitch!'

He staggered down the front steps towards them. Lily turned the key in the ignition and revved the engine. Poppy was screaming now and Jamie was crying in a high, panicky whistle.

Stephen banged his fist on the Meriva's rear window, and Lily put her foot down so that it hurtled out of the driveway in a spray of pea-shingle.

There was a deep, clumsy thump, and Lily saw a body tumbling in the air in front of her. It turned over and over before it hit the road, but immediately, another car ran over it and its arms flew up and its hands clapped together, *smack*, as if it were applauding.

Shaking with shock, Lily climbed out of the driver's seat and stepped out into the road. The woman in the grey woolly hat and the grey raincoat was lying on her back, staring up at her blind-eyed.

Lily turned around. A small crowd had already gathered and the driver of the second car was phoning for an ambulance. Standing next to her front gate, however, was the same woman, in her grey hat and her grey raincoat, with her Bedlington terrier on its lead.

Lily walked across to her. The woman's image appeared to ripple, as if she were seeing her through running water.

'*You're dead*,' Lily whispered. '*That's you, lying in the road. You're dead.*'

'I did try to warn you, Lily,' the woman told her. 'You should have walked out over a year ago, when he first started to hit you. But you were too frightened of being on your own. And – secretly – you *enjoy* being his victim, don't you? It makes you feel wanted. You should have stayed. Because *now* look what you've done.'

Lily said, 'I'm so sorry.' But the woman turned around and walked away, leaving her dog standing on the pavement. As she turned the corner, and disappeared from sight, Lily called out, '*I'm so, so sorry!*'

THE NIGHT HIDER

D awn was dreaming of Christmas and snow and jingle bells. She was sitting in a black-painted sleigh, sliding across a frozen lake under a charcoal-grey sky. The steel runners hissed on the ice, the jingle bells jingled. Strangely, the sleigh seemed to be self-propelled, and as it came closer and closer to the edge of the lake, she began to worry about how she was going to stop it.

Help! she called out, or thought she called out. But there was nobody in sight, only snowdrifts, and fir trees, and the louring grey sky, and the sleigh continued to glide across the ice with its runners hissing and its jingle bells merrily jingling.

Somebody help me! She was panicking now, but seconds before the sleigh could reach the edge of the lake, she woke up, and opened her eyes. She wasn't in a sleigh at all, she was lying in bed, in her own flat in Chiswick.

The jingling, however, carried on. She frowned, and listened. *Jing-a-ling-jing-ching.* She couldn't work out where it was coming from, but she could hear it quite distinctly. How could she still be hearing the sleigh bells from her dream, when she was awake?

She lifted her head from the pillow and reached across to the bedside table for her mobile phone. As she did so, she heard a soft creaking sound, like a door being opened. The jingling grew louder for a moment, *jing-chingle-jing-ching*, but then it became softer, and more sporadic, as if the sleigh had come to a halt. Then it stopped altogether, and there was silence. She pressed her phone and saw that it was 2.37 a.m.

Another creak, but more like a floorboard this time. She sat up in bed, her heart thumping painfully hard. Her curtains were velvet, and tightly closed together, and so her bedroom was totally dark. Yet another creak, and now she was so frightened that she didn't even have the breath to ask if there was anybody there.

There was a long, long silence. She remained sitting upright, one hand gripping the bedcover, listening. She could hear her own blood rushing through her ears, so loudly that she wasn't sure if she could hear somebody breathing, too. Was there somebody else in the room? How could there be, when her bedroom door was locked and her window was bolted? And yet she was sure that she could feel somebody's presence. She sniffed, and she thought that she could smell something *burnt*.

Very slowly and carefully, she leaned sideways until her fingertips found the button on the base of her bedside lamp. She stayed in the dark for a few seconds longer, still listening, and then she pressed it. Her bedroom was instantly lit up: her white wickerwork chair, with her smiling pink teddy bear sitting on it; her dressing table, crowded with creams and lipsticks and nail polish; her own watercolour painting, on the wall, of the blood-red autumn trees in Firestone Copse.

And standing by the door, with his hand reaching out for the handle, there was a man.

Dawn was too shocked even to gasp. The man was dressed entirely in black, with black hair and a black face, not African black but soot-black, although his eyes and his eyebrows and his mouth were ghostly white, as if he were a photographic negative. He was wearing a flat cap, although it looked frayed, or burnt into tatters, and his jacket was tattered, too.

He appeared to be grinning at her, or scowling. With his negative face, it was difficult for Dawn to tell which. He didn't move. His hand remained two inches away from the door handle.

'*Get out*,' Dawn heard herself saying, although she said it so quietly that she couldn't be sure if the man had heard her. He stayed where he was, motionless, staring at her with his black teeth bared. Then, with a harsh snortling sound, almost like a pig, he took a step toward her bed.

'*Get out!*' she screamed, but at that moment the bulb in her bedside lamp popped out, and she was left in overwhelming darkness. '*Get out! Go away! Don't touch me!*'

She scrambled out of bed, although the bedcover twisted itself tightly around her left leg as if it were trying to stop her. She half-hopped, half-hobbled to the window and dragged back the curtains, so that her bedroom was lit up by the sodium lamp in the street outside. Panting with fear, she turned the key in the window lock and tried to pull up the window. It wouldn't budge. The frame had been recently repainted and the window was stuck solid.

Dawn grasped both handles and tried again to heave the window up, although she knew she wasn't strong enough. She was weeping with helplessness, tugging and tugging and gritting her teeth with effort.

She was ready to give up when she heard a door slam behind her – and then again, she heard jingle bells. She turned slowly around. The black-faced man had vanished. After a few seconds, the bells stopped, too.

'Hallo?' she said, although she knew how empty and ridiculous that sounded. 'Hallo?'

She went across to the bedroom door and turned the handle. It was still locked, and the key was still in it. So the man couldn't have gone out that way. She sniffed. She could still faintly smell something burnt, like paper, or wool, or horsehair.

She tilted her head sideways and looked quickly under the bed, even though it was a divan bed with less than a two-inch gap underneath it, and he would have to be as flat as a sheet of paper to have hidden himself there.

There was only one other place where the man could have concealed himself. He must have had been hiding in there all the time, and the thought made Dawn feel shivery and sick. She had come home at ten o'clock that evening, after working late at the restaurant, and she had taken a long shower and then sat naked in front of her dressing-table, with her hair in a towel-turban, filing and polishing her fingernails. Supposing he had been watching her?

She circled around the bed and approached the wardrobe. It was huge, and shiny, covered in light brown walnut veneer with darker streaks in it. It had a single door with an arched top that could almost have suited a chapel, with decorative Gothic beading around it. Dawn had always thought that the walnut veneer appeared to have the face of a werewolf.

The wardrobe had been given to Dawn last month by her Aunt Selina who owned an antiques business in Oxfordshire. All Dawn had really wanted was a simple Ikea flat-pack wardrobe, but Aunt Selina had insisted. 'Let's say that it's a premature inheritance, for when I die. It's worth a fortune, I promise you. It belonged to somebody quite famous, that's what I was told. Cyril Connolly, or Charlie Chaplin. Somebody beginning with "C" anyway. I forget.'

But now Dawn was standing in front of it with her hand pressed over her mouth, wondering if she had the nerve to open it. What if the burnt-smelling man was standing inside it, amongst all of her dresses and her jumpers? He couldn't be anywhere else, could he? Yet when she had come home last night, she had hung up the long black skirt that she had to wear for work, and he hadn't been inside her wardrobe then.

She was utterly confused. Perhaps the most sensible thing to do was to lock the wardrobe, and then call the police. But what if she had simply imagined him? What if she hadn't woken up when the sleigh had been sliding nearer and nearer to the edge of the lake, but only *dreamed* that she had woken up, and only *dreamed* that the man had been standing by the door? What if she hadn't really woken up until the moment she had opened the curtains?

What if she called the police and told them that there was a strange black-faced man hiding in her wardrobe, but there was nobody there?

She went up to the wardrobe and turned the key in it, and rattled the handle to make sure that it was locked. Then she leaned close to it and said, 'Is there anybody in there? Because if there's somebody in there I'm going to give you one chance to come out of there, and then I'm going to call the police.'

She waited, but there was no response. Perhaps it was stupid of her to expect him to answer, if he was in there, and did she really want him to come out? What if he attacked her? But what else was she going to do? Even though the wardrobe was locked, she wouldn't be able to go back to sleep, knowing that a man could be hiding inside it. And if he wanted to, he could probably kick the door open.

She picked up her mobile phone and dialled Jerry's number. It rang and rang for almost a minute. When he answered he sounded sleepy and clogged-up.

'Dawn? What the hell time is it?'

'Jerry,' she blurted, 'there's a man in my bedroom!'

'What? What do you mean?'

'I woke up and there was this man in my bedroom. He was all black like he'd been burnt and then the light bulb went and now I think he's hiding in my wardrobe. I've locked the door but I don't know what to do!'

'Dawn – say that again, slowly.'

Dawn repeated herself, trying to explain more clearly what had happened, although she couldn't stop herself from repeatedly sniffing and wiping the tears away from her eyes with the back of her hand. When she had finished, Jerry said, 'Leave the bedroom, sweetheart, like *now*. Lock the door. You *can* lock the bedroom door, can't you? Go into the living room and lock that door, too. Wait for me. I'll be there in ten minutes, OK? But if you hear this bloke trying to break out, call the police – like, immediately.'

The front doorbell chimed. Dawn unlocked the living-room door and went into the hallway, and through the frosted-glass window in the front door she could see Jerry. She unlocked the door and flung her arms around him.

'Hey!' he said. 'Hey. Everything's going to be OK. It's probably just some nutter who wandered in by mistake. He didn't try to hurt you, did he, so that's something.'

Jerry was tall and stockily built, with short brown hair that was no more messed up tonight than it usually was. He was handsome in a slightly overweight, rugby-player way, with very blue eyes. Dawn was blonde and very skinny and, up until Jerry, all of her boyfriends had been almost as skinny as she was, and older, too. Jerry, though, gave her a feeling of being physically protected. He wasn't artistic, like she was, but he had the boundless confidence of a young man who was sure that he could take care of himself in almost any situation, and she found that strongly attractive.

'OK,' he said. 'Let's see what this character thinks he's doing, shall we?'

Dawn gave him the key and he unlocked her bedroom door. The wardrobe door was still closed and undamaged, so the man obviously hadn't made any attempt to break out of it. Jerry walked up to the wardrobe and banged on it with his fist.

'Hey! You in there! I'm opening the door now and I don't want any trouble! You got it! You're not dealing with a girl now, mate, I warn you!'

He twisted the key in the wardrobe door and flung it open, stepping back two paces after he had done so, both hands raised defensively in front of him. On one side of the wardrobe rail there were six or seven empty wire coat hangers, which jangled for a moment and then stopped jingling.

All of Dawn's coats and dresses and skirts were hanging in the wardrobe, and all of her shoes and boots were neatly arranged underneath them. On one side, there were six shelves on which she kept her sweaters and her underwear and her socks.

But there was no man standing or sitting in the wardrobe, and the only smell was the light flowery fragrance of Allure, Dawn's favourite perfume, on her clothes.

Dawn looked up at Jerry and shook her head. 'He's gone. I don't understand it. Where did he go? He *must* have hidden in the wardrobe. There's absolutely nowhere else.'

Jerry reached into the wardrobe and rapped his knuckles on the back of it. 'Solid. No false back to it. And in any case, it's right up against the wall.'

'Oh, Jerry,' said Dawn, and she suddenly burst into tears. 'I must be going mad! I swear I saw him! I swear it! His face was all black and horrible like he'd been burnt or something and he grunted at me and he was coming to get me but the light bulb popped and it all went dark again and I was so *scared*, Jerry! I thought he was going to kill me!'

Jerry held her close and shushed her. 'You had a nightmare, that's all. Plenty of people have nightmares when they think they've woken up but they haven't really.'

'I'm going mad! I *know* I'm going mad!'

'You're not going mad, silly. You've just been overworking, that's all. Too many split shifts at that crappy restaurant. You haven't been very well, either, have you?'

'No,' she said, miserably.

'Listen, come back to my place and spend the rest of the night with me. I'll call up the restaurant tomorrow for you and tell them that you have to go to the dentist or something. I'll take a day off and we can go for a walk around Kew Gardens or down by the river or something. It's about time you had a break.'

Dawn nodded, and said, 'All right. I'd like that. Thanks, darling.'

She dressed and brushed her hair and collected a few clothes together in case she wanted to change later, including her favourite pink jumper. When she was ready, she closed the wardrobe door. Jerry was waiting for her in the hallway and he smiled when he saw her locking it, too.

'There's no horrible black-faced man inside there, sweetheart, I promise you.'

Dawn said nothing. She still found it hard to believe that the man had been nothing more than a nightmare. She locked the bedroom door, too, and set the burglar alarm before they left.

Jerry put his arm around her and gave her a comforting squeeze. 'I think that's the first time I've ever seen somebody setting an alarm to stop an intruder from breaking *out*.'

The following evening Jerry drove her home and came in to check the wardrobe and reassure her that there was nobody in there, or anywhere else in her flat. He even lifted up the cushions on the sofa bed in her living room, in case there was a black-faced man hiding inside it.

'There's nobody here, sweetheart. You can see for yourself.' He walked through to the kitchen and opened up the oven door and said, 'See? Empty. You're completely on your own.'

'You don't have to make fun of me.'

'I'm not. I'm just trying to convince you that you're perfectly safe. I wouldn't leave you alone here if I thought that there was a prowler around. But – listen – if you do hear anything, or get frightened about anything – just give me a call. I'll come over straight away.'

'Thanks, Jerry,' she said, and put her arms around him and gave him a kiss. 'It's just me being stupid, you know that.'

'That's why I love you, stupid.'

That night she dreamed that she was sitting on a veranda overlooking a weedy, unkempt garden. The grass was almost knee-high and all the laurel bushes surrounding the lawn were overgrown. Above her the sky was heavy and grey, and the garden smelled as if it had just stopped raining.

At the far end of the veranda a wind chime was jingling. *Jing-a-ling-jing-ching.* She found the sound of it irritating rather than soothing, and she wondered why it was jingling at all, since there wasn't any wind.

Then she thought: *The wind chimes sound just like the sleigh bells in my other dream. But how can I remember another dream, when I'm dreaming this one?*

She opened her eyes. Her bedroom wasn't completely dark, because she had deliberately left the curtains three inches apart. She could see her teddy bear's eyes glistening in the gloom, and on the wall behind his chair, a shadow was flickering, a shadow that looked like a witch nodding her head. Dawn knew that it was only the shadow from the plane tree which stood in the garden at the front of her block of flats, but all the same she couldn't keep her eyes off it, in case it moved, and the witch suddenly came tapping at her window.

Jingle-jingle-ching went the wind chimes. Only they weren't wind chimes out of her dream, nor sleigh bells from the black-painted sleigh. They were coat hangers, jingling inside her wardrobe.

Oh God, oh God, please don't let it be him. Please don't let it be the black-faced man inside my wardrobe. Please God, don't let him get out.

Dawn stretched across the bed for her mobile phone, but as she did so the whole wardrobe creaked, and she could hear something heavy shifting inside it.

Oh God, please don't let it be him.

She groped around for her phone – *where was it?* But the wardrobe creaked again, much louder this time, almost a groan, and the groan was followed by a shuffling sound. She was so startled that when she found her phone she accidentally tipped it over the edge of her nightstand. She heard it drop on to the carpet but when she looked over the edge of the bed she couldn't see where it had gone.

The door's locked. He can't get out. Please don't let him get out.

She threw back the covers and climbed out of bed and went down on her hands and knees. Her phone wasn't anywhere in sight so she guessed that it must have bounced underneath the bed. She reached into the narrow gap between the bed and the carpet, pushing her arm in as far as she could, and after sweeping her hand from side to side three or four times, she touched it with her fingertips.

She tried to flick her phone back toward her, but it was a fraction of an inch too far away, and she succeeded only in pushing it even farther out of reach. The bed was much too heavy for her to lift, so all she could do was force her arm in deeper, even though the rough hessian lining scraped against her skin.

She was still straining to reach her phone when she heard the key slowly turning in the wardrobe door. *Click, click, click* – pause – *kerchick.*

She turned her head around and looked back up at the wardrobe. It was impossible. You couldn't unlock the door from the inside. Yet as she lay there, on her side, with her left arm pinned underneath the bed, she saw that the wardrobe door was slowly opening.

'*Go away!*' she screamed. '*Don't come out of there! Leave me alone! Don't come out of there! Don't! Don't come out of there!*'

She dragged her arm out from underneath the bed, grazing her forearm all the way from her elbow to her wrist. Then she threw herself on to the bed, rolled over it, and went for the bedroom door. She tried to turn the key but it jammed, like it often did, because it was old and worn and always needed coaxing. What had she been thinking about when she locked it? She should have realized that she might need to escape.

She glanced frantically over her shoulder, and as she did so the black-faced man stepped out of the wardrobe and turned toward her. He not only *looked* burnt, he was actually wreathed in acrid-smelling smoke, which lazily curled its way across her bedroom. His white eyes were staring at her and his black teeth were bared in a snarl. He started to make his way around the end of the bed, with both hands raised in front of him like blackened claws.

Dawn jiggled the key in the lock and at last managed to turn it. As soon as she pulled open the door, though, the black-faced man came up behind her and slammed it shut again.

'*Bitch!*' he said. His voice was so harsh he sounded as if he had grit between his teeth. He stank so strongly of charred wool that Dawn could hardly breathe. 'Why'd you tell 'em it was me, you bitch? You see what they done to me? You see what they done?'

Dawn was unable to speak. She sank down on to her knees, her hands crossed over her breasts like a religious supplicant, and all she could do was whimper.

The black-faced man stood over her. She was too frightened to lift her head and look up at him, and all she could see was his black, ragged trousers and his burnt lace-up boots, with smoke leaking out of them.

He seized her upper arms. His fingers were blistered and rough, and he gripped her so tightly that she felt that he was trying to twist her arms out of their sockets. With a deep grunting noise he hoisted her up off the floor and flung her backward across the bed. Immediately he climbed on top of her, straddling her hips. He glared down at her, with his black flaking nose only an inch away from hers.

'Please,' she said. 'I don't even know who you are.'

'Oh, you really *are* a bitch, aren't you?' he growled at her, and she felt his spit prickling on her face. 'You don't even know who I am? You knew who was I right enough when they came asking questions about your babby. You knew who was I then, all right.'

Dawn dug her heels into the mattress and tried to kick herself out from under him, but he clenched his thighs together even tighter and then he slapped her across the face, twice. Her eyes burst out with tears and her cheeks felt as if he had set them on fire.

'*Bitch!*' he said, each time he slapped her. '*Bitch!*'

With his left hand he kept her shoulder pinned against the bed, while he reached down with his right hand and started to tug at his belt buckle.

'Might as well do it, if I'm to be blamed for it!' he spat at her. 'Might as well relish what I was punished for! What do you say, bitch? What do you say to that?'

He wrestled his trousers halfway down to his knees. The hair on his thighs was thick and crisp and scratchy. She felt his hardened penis press against her leg, and that felt rough and dry, too, as if he were jabbing at her with a wooden rolling pin. He grabbed the hem of her cotton nightshirt and tore it upward and sideways, so that the buttons were pulled off.

Dawn struggled furiously, but the black-faced man was far too strong for her. She screamed, again and again, or at least she thought she did. All she could see was his white eyes, staring down at her, and all she could smell was his burnt body hair and his charred woollen clothes, and all she could feel was his weight bearing down on her, crushing all the breath out of her, crushing her ribcage.

He forced her thighs apart, and pushed one knee in between them. As he did so, however, somebody rapped against the window, very sharply. The black-faced man hesitated, and looked around, although he still kept Dawn pressed down on the bed.

The rapping was repeated, and then Dawn heard a muffled voice outside the window say, 'Dawn? Dawn? It's Jerry! Are you awake?'

'Jerry!' she called out, but the black-faced man immediately covered her mouth with his horny, claw-like hand. '*Mmmffff! Jerry! Jerry!*'

Jerry rapped again. 'Dawn? It's me, Jerry! Are you awake?'

The black-faced man hesitated for a few seconds, and then he heaved himself off her, and stood up, pulling up his trousers and buckling his belt.

'I'll get my revenge on you one day, you bitch!' he told her. 'You just wait and see!'

With that, he stalked back round to the wardrobe, opened the door and climbed inside. He closed the door behind him and Dawn heard the key turn.

Shaking, she slid off the bed. She knelt beside it for a moment, breathing deeply, and then she managed to stand up.

'Dawn? Are you there, Dawn?'

Unsteadily, barely able to keep her balance, she went to the window. Jerry was standing outside, precariously perched on the edge of a wooden planter so that he could reach up and rap on her window.

'What is it?' he shouted, through the glass. 'What's happened?'

Dawn pointed toward the bedroom door to indicate that she would let him in. He jumped awkwardly down from the planter and she went to the front door and opened it for him. She put her arms around him and clung on to him and sobbed so hard that it hurt.

Gently, he walked her through to the living room and sat her down on the couch.

'What's happened? Look at you, your nightie's all torn! And look at your face! You look like somebody's been hitting you!'

'He came out again. That black-faced man. There's no way he could have unlocked that wardrobe door – not from the inside. But he *did*, and he came out again. And I dropped my phone and I tried to get away but the key got stuck. He pushed me on to the bed and he was going to rape me.'

Jerry stood up. 'Right,' he said, 'I'm going to settle this, once and for all.'

'Jerry, no! He's really, really strong. He'll hurt you.'

'We'll see about that. Where did he go? Back into your wardrobe? I bet it has a false back, or some secret compartment, and he's been hiding in it.'

'Please, Jerry, no! Let's just go back to your place and come back tomorrow. Then we can see if he really is hiding in the wardrobe and if he is we can call the police.'

But Jerry said, 'Sorry, Dawn. I'm not letting anybody get away with hurting you and trying to rape you. I don't care how bloody strong he is! I don't care if he's King bloody Kong!'

With that, he went through to the bedroom, marched up to the wardrobe and hammered on it, hard. 'Right! You in there! I'm warning you! You've got a count of three to come out and show yourself! If you don't I'm coming in after you, and I'm going to find you, mate, even if I have to chop this wardrobe up into firewood!'

Dawn stood in the bedroom doorway watching him as he turned the key in the wardrobe door and opened it. The wire coat hangers softly jingled for a while, and then stopped jingling.

'Right, then! You've got one – two – *three!*'

He waited, but no black-faced man stepped out of the wardrobe. Almost half a minute went by, but all they could hear was the traffic outside in the street. Dawn said, 'Perhaps *this* was a dream, too. Oh, God. Perhaps I need to see a psychiatrist.'

'You can't slap your own face, Dawn, especially in a dream. Look at you. In the morning you'll have two black eyes.'

He reached into the wardrobe and parted Dawn's dresses and coats. He banged on the back of it, much harder than he had the night before. Then he took out all of Dawn's shoes and boots and thumped with his fist on the floor.

'If you're hiding under there, you'd better show yourself, quick!'

He thumped on the floor again, and then turned to Dawn and said, 'Bring me a knife, would you? Any old knife.'

Dawn went to the kitchen and came back with a carving knife with a broken tip which she always used for cutting up vegetables. She handed it to Jerry and said, 'He's not actually in *there*, is he, under the floor? There's not enough room, surely.'

Jerry dug the broken knife blade into the side of the wardrobe's plinth. Carefully, he pried a board upward, but underneath there was only a dark, empty space, containing nothing at all, not even spiderwebs. He peered inside and then shook his head. 'Not in here,' his voice sounding hollow. 'Wouldn't really be room enough, anyway. You'd have to be a bloody midget to hide in here.'

'You see?' said Dawn. She felt as if her brain were bursting apart into a thousand glittering fragments, like a mirror being smashed in slow motion, and she had to sit down on the side of the bed. 'I *was* dreaming it. Or else I *am* going mad. I think I'm going mad.'

Jerry sat down next to her and put his arm around her. 'No, sweetheart, you didn't dream it, and no, you're not going mad. To be honest, I wasn't too sure if I believed you yesterday about this black-faced man, but I was lying in bed tonight and I couldn't sleep because I was thinking to myself, Dawn's not the hysterical type, not at all. In fact you're the most level-headed girl I ever went out with. Why do you think I came round here at two o'clock in the morning? I just wanted to be sure.'

Dawn gave him a kiss, and snuggled in closer to him. 'But if I'm not *dreaming* him, and I'm not going mad, then what is he? He felt real, and he really hurt me, but how can he be real if he can disappear like that? Perhaps he's a ghost or an evil spirit or something. He kept saying that I was a bitch. He said he'd got the blame for something I'd done, but I couldn't really understand what he meant. Something to do with a baby.'

Jerry said, 'I'm sure that it's something to do with the wardrobe. How long have you been living here now?'

'It'll be a year at the end of September.'

'And when was the wardrobe delivered?'

'A month ago. Less than a month.'

'And you didn't see this black-faced man before then?'

Dawn shook her head.

'I'll tell you what we're going to do,' said Jerry. 'Tomorrow we're both going to throw a sickie and we're going to drive up to Oxford and see your Aunt What's-Her-Name.'

'Selina. But what for?'

'Let's find out where she got this wardrobe. Maybe it used to belong to a coven of witches. Or a stage magician. I'll bet that's it. I'll bet you it belonged to The Great Lumbago or somebody like that, only he got trapped inside it.'

'So why is he all burnt like that? I could feel the hair on his legs was burnt. It was all crunchy and horrible.'

'Maybe he was waiting for somebody to let him out of the wardrobe and he lit up a cigarette to pass the time, and he accidentally dropped it.'

Dawn sat up and gave Jerry a slap on the shoulder. 'Be serious, will you, Jerry? I've never been so frightened in my life. If you hadn't knocked at the window he would have raped me.'

Jerry said, 'I know, sweetheart. I'm sorry. I'm trying to make a joke of it because I'm just as frightened for you as you are. I don't believe in ghosts and spirits and stuff like that, I really don't. But I believe you're telling the truth and I can't find any black-faced man hiding in that wardrobe, so what else can he be, except a ghost or a spirit? Or maybe some kind of horrible creature that we've never even heard of?'

As they arrived outside Aunt Selina's antiques shop, it started to rain almost laughably hard, drumming on the fabric roof of Jerry's BMW so loudly that they could hardly hear themselves. Times Gone By stood on a corner of Windmill Road, a long, depressing street of semi-detached Victorian villas in Headington, a suburb of Oxford. Jerry parked in Margaret Road and opened the passenger door so that Dawn could scamper into the antiques shop doorway with her jacket held over her head.

The doorbell jingled as they went inside. Times Gone By was a very small shop, but it was crowded with armchairs and occasional tables and whatnots and mirrors. On the side wall hung oil paintings of rural landscapes and decorative dinner plates and barometers, and at the very back of the shop they could just see long-case clocks and tall display cabinets and wardrobes, like the skyline of a wooden city. The whole shop was filled with a strong, musty smell of old upholstery and varnish.

Aunt Selina came out from her little office, still holding a cup of tea in her hand. '*Dawny!* I wasn't expecting you till *much* later! And this must be Barry!'

'Jerry,' Dawn corrected her. 'There was hardly any traffic, I don't know why. We didn't leave till half past ten.'

Aunt Selina was taller than Dawn's mother, but just as thin. She had iron-grey hair cropped in an angular bob, and a face like an elderly eagle, with high cheekbones and a pointed chin. Her eyes were as grey as two pebbles, and her eyebrows were plucked so fine and so high that they gave her an expression of permanent disbelief.

She was wearing a long purple dress with a sagging grey cardigan over it, and her pockets bulged with crumpled tissues and dirty orange dusters.

'You said you had a problem with that wardrobe I gave you,' said Aunt Selina. 'It doesn't have *woodworm*, does it? I promise you I checked it thoroughly before I let the storage people take it.'

'No, Auntie. Nothing like that. I don't know how to explain it, exactly.'

'Go on, Dawn,' Jerry coaxed her. 'We've come all this way; you might as well tell her.'

Aunt Selina gave her a bright, encouraging smile, even though her eyebrows still made her look amazed.

'Yes, come on, Dawny. Whatever it is, I swear I won't be cross.'

Dawn hesitated for a moment, and then she said, 'It's haunted. There's a ghost in it.'

'There's a *ghost* in it? *No!* Are you serious? What kind of a ghost?'

'A man. He's black all over, like he's been burnt. He's come out of the wardrobe twice now and last night he tried to rape me. If Jerry hadn't turned up and knocked on the window, I think he would have done.'

'My dear Dawny! How dreadful! But what makes you think he's a ghost, and not some horrible common-or-garden sex maniac?'

'He went back into the wardrobe after he attacked her,' Jerry put in. 'But I checked it thoroughly myself, top to bottom, and there was nobody inside it. I even pulled up the floor.'

'You're sure he went back in there? He didn't hide under the bed or behind the curtains or somewhere like that?'

'I'm absolutely sure. I just want to know where the wardrobe came from. You know, if it's got any kind of history behind it. I'm going to have to get rid of it, Auntie, I'm sorry about that.'

Aunt Selina frowned, as much as her eyebrows would allow her to. Then she said, 'Wait a minute. Ron Hackett did give me some notes about it, along with the invoice. That's who I got it from, Ron Hackett. Well, you said you needed a wardrobe and I remembered seeing it in the corner of his warehouse. *He* got it from old Mister Chesney, who used to own a storage business in Risinghurst, before he died.'

She went back into her cramped little office and rummaged around in her filing cabinet. Dawn and Jerry waited uncomfortably among her antiques, and Dawn began to wish that she had never come. She should have simply called a house-clearance firm and asked them to take the wardrobe away, whether they paid her anything for it or not. She just wanted to be rid of it.

At last, however, Aunt Selina came out again, and she was holding up an old notebook with a marbled green cover. A folded invoice was attached to it with three elastic bands, but Aunt Selina took these off, opened the notebook and began to read what was written in it, silently mouthing the words to herself as she did so.

'Well?' asked Dawn, impatiently. 'Is there anything about my wardrobe in it?'

'Oh, I'm sorry,' said Aunt Selina. 'Yes, there most certainly is. I mean, there's not a lot, but it's *all* about your wardrobe. This was written by Harold Chesney right back in October of 1930. I mean, just look how faded his writing is! Do you want me to read it to you?'

'Yes, that would be a good idea,' said Dawn, trying not to sound impatient.

'Very well . . . let me see . . . "October thirteenth, 1930 . . . Jack Lewis came into the warehouse and asked if I could take away a wardrobe for him as soon as possible. I told him that my driver Leonard was up in Leicester and wouldn't be back till the following morning. He said he didn't mind what it cost, he wanted the wardrobe out of the house before it got dark. I telephoned Bill Leppard at the Morris plant at Cowley and he said he had a lorry available and could shift Jack Lewis's wardrobe for him by half past three, although it would cost him £5. I thought that was a bit steep and said so but Jack Lewis didn't hesitate and agreed at once.

"'Bill Leppard brought the wardrobe around at ten to four. I must say it was quite a fine piece of furniture, burr walnut veneer, made around 1880. I asked Jack Lewis what he wanted for it but he said that I should just keep it in store for the time being and he would pay me whatever it cost. There were two ropes tied around it so that the doors couldn't be opened but Jack Lewis said he wanted those to stay fastened at all costs. I asked him why but he wouldn't tell me."'

Aunt Selina said, 'That's all he wrote. The rest of the pages are all blank. Oh, except for this Jack Lewis's address and telephone number.'

She paused, and then she said, 'My God! Do you know who he was, this Jack Lewis?'

Dawn shook her head. 'I have absolutely no idea.'

'It's his address, it's famous. The Kilns, Headington Quarry. That's the house where C.S. Lewis used to live. You know, the writer. Narnia, and all that. *The Lion, the Witch and—*'

'The wardrobe,' Dawn finished, and although she didn't really understand why, she felt flooded by a deep sense of dread, as if they had come across a secret that nobody had ever been supposed to find out.

They all went to a large noisy pub called the Britannia Inn for a drink and cheese sandwiches.

After they had found a table in a corner of the bar, Aunt Selina said, 'You must tell me more about this black-faced ghost of yours, Dawny. I'm fascinated!'

Dawn said, 'I'm sorry. I don't really want to talk about it. It was horrible.'

'But supposing yours was the actual wardrobe that inspired C.S. Lewis to write all of those stories!'

'That's what scares me even more. I mean – it makes it all the more believable, doesn't it? Why was he so desperate to have the wardrobe taken out of his house before it got dark? And why did he tie its door shut with ropes?'

'I think *he* saw your ghost, too,' said Aunt Selina. She laid her ring-encrusted hand on top of Dawn's and gave her an affectionate squeeze. 'I really don't blame you for wanting to get rid of the wardrobe. If you like, I'll ask Ron Hackett to take it back.'

'But then he'll sell it again, won't he, and I don't want the same thing to happen to some other poor girl.'

'In that case, you really need to find out more about it. Where it originally came from, and who this black-faced man is, and why he was burnt. Now you're up here in Oxford, why don't you go to The Kilns and see if you can find somebody who knows a bit more about it? It's a kind of study centre now for the life and work of C.S. Lewis. It's only in Risinghurst, so it's not very far.'

After they had taken Aunt Selina back to her antiques shop, they drove to the C.S. Lewis house in Risinghurst. The rain had eased off now, and the wet streets were blinding with reflected sunshine.

They turned into Lewis Close, a small estate of detached 1960s houses which had been built on the eight-acre garden that used to surround C.S. Lewis's house. Once grandly isolated, the rambling red-tiled country house now stood close to the road. Jerry parked and they walked up the pathway and knocked at the front door.

They waited. The roses on either side of the pathway were sparkling with raindrops and somewhere a pigeon was monotonously cooing for its mate. Although it wasn't particularly cold, Dawn found herself shivering.

'Maybe there's nobody in,' said Jerry, but at that moment the front door suddenly opened and they were confronted by a bald, bespectacled man in a bright yellow sweater and brown corduroy trousers.

'May I *help*?' he asked them in a pained voice, as if that was the last thing he wanted to do.

'I'm sorry,' said Dawn. 'I hope we're not disturbing you, but we were wondering if there was anybody here who knew something about C.S. Lewis when he first moved in here.'

The man took off his spectacles and blinked at her. 'I'm not at all sure what you mean by that. This is a Christian study centre now, where we discuss the Christian inspiration in C.S. Lewis's novels and essays.'

'But we've discovered that something might have happened to him – something that really scared him, but which changed his whole life.'

'Something that *scared* him? I still don't see what you're getting at.'

'Did he keep a diary, at that time? Maybe he wrote about it but nobody understood what he meant.'

'Of course, yes, he kept diaries – and, yes, some of what he wrote was a little obscure. But, with respect – unless you yourself are a C.S. Lewis scholar, madam – I doubt if you will be able to interpret what he wrote with any greater clarity than anybody else has been able to do so far. Now, unless there's anything else—'

'I have his wardrobe,' said Dawn.

'*What?*' said the man.

'I have his wardrobe. His original wardrobe. The one he got rid of.'

The man quickly looked right and left, as if he were frightened that somebody might be overhearing them. 'How do you know it's *his* wardrobe?'

'Because my aunt bought it from a storage company in Headington and *they* got it from the storage company in Risinghurst that C.S. Lewis originally asked to take it away.'

'You're sure about this?'

'Absolutely sure. Not only that, I know what's inside it.'

'Listen,' said the man, and he was clearly very agitated. 'You'd better come in.'

He led them into the long, narrow hallway, and then into a study. It was a gloomy, old-fashioned room, with a view of the garden. Its walls were lined with bookshelves and a faded blue Persian rug covered the floor. 'Here, sit down,' said the man, and she and Jerry sat side by side on a worn-out velvet sofa while he pulled up an armchair and sat close to them.

The study was airless and smelled of floor polish and the man's breath smelled of coffee, and Dawn would have done anything to have a window open.

'You know what's inside it?' the man repeated.

Dawn nodded. 'Do you want me to tell you?' she asked him. 'It seems to me that you already know.'

The man said, 'I'd better introduce myself. Geoffrey Walmsley – Professor Geoffrey Walmsley. I'm a scholar-in-residence here at the moment. C.S. Lewis has been my life's work. His life, his conversion to Christianity, his novels. I probably know more about C.S. Lewis than he did himself.'

'So you know about the wardrobe?'

'I know *all* about the wardrobe,' said Professor Walmsley. 'It was here in the house already when Jack Lewis and his brother and Mrs Janie Moore moved into the property in 1930. His family and friends always called him Jack, by the way. He recorded what happened next in his diary, but that *particular* diary contains specific instructions that it is not to be published and not to be made available to any critics or biographers.'

He paused, and then he said, 'When he moved in, Jack Lewis was puzzled to find that the wardrobe in the guest bedroom was facing the wall, with its back toward the room. Because of this, of course, its door couldn't be opened. He and his brother Warnie turned it around so that Jack could hang some of his clothes in it. The wardrobe was quite empty, he said, but he did detect a lingering smell of burning.

'That night, he heard a noise on the landing, and when he went to see what it was, he saw a strange man just about to open the door to Mrs Moore's bedroom.'

'The man's face was black, and his clothes looked as if he had been burnt,' Dawn put in.

Professor Walmsley looked at her sagely. 'You *have* seen him, then?'

'He came out of the wardrobe and attacked me. I've never been so frightened in my life.'

'Jack shouted out, and the man rushed back into the spare bedroom and Jack heard the wardrobe door slam shut. He took a poker from the fireplace and went to open the door, but when he did so he found that it was locked, which could only have been done from the outside. All the same, he opened the door, only to discover that the wardrobe appeared to be empty.'

'So what did he do?'

'At that time of night, there wasn't much that he could do. But he woke his brother and told him what had happened, and between them they shifted the wardrobe around again so that its door was up against the wall.

'The next day, he got up early and went to the village as it then was and made some enquiries. In the end, he was directed to a man called Briggs who had lived in the village all his life. Briggs told him that The Kilns had been built in 1922 on the site of an old Victorian brickworks, which is why it was called The Kilns.

'The story went that the owner of the brickworks, a man called Stephenson, had a very pretty young daughter called Sophie. Sophie fell in love with one of the young workers at the kiln, whose identity we don't know, but she became pregnant. When her father demanded to know who was responsible, she blamed an older man called Henry Bell – claimed that he had raped her. Obviously she wanted to protect her young lover from her father's retribution, and Henry Bell was apparently a bad-tempered man, and much disliked.

'Although there was never any proof of this, Stephenson was said to have paid two of his workers to throw Henry Bell into the brick kiln, when it was all fired up. Bell was hideously burned but managed to escape. A local woman later claimed that a man "all black and smouldering" had entered her house in the middle of the night. She had called her husband, who slept in a separate room, but when he came to her assistance the man had disappeared – even though the window was closed and there was no other means of escape.

'She had opened her wardrobe to see if he was hiding in it, and her wardrobe had been filled with smoke, but that was all. No black and smouldering man.'

'So where did C.S. Lewis think the man had gone?' asked Dawn. 'Or was he just totally baffled, like I am?'

'He wrote pages and pages about it. He conjectured that this particular wardrobe must somehow have acted as a way through to another plane of existence – a way that was open only to those in extreme distress, or in need of succour.

'He became convinced that there was another world there, beyond the wardrobe, but it could be found only under very special circumstances. He did strongly suspect, though, that Henry Bell had been allowed to find a retreat there because he had been the victim of a terrible injustice.

'The world beyond the wardrobe, he theorized, was a world where Christian justice and Christian mercy had at last prevailed, and all our trespasses forgiven, as we forgive those who trespass against us. However, he thought that Henry Bell was not yet ready to forgive the lie told by Sophie Stephenson, which is why he had reappeared in search of revenge.'

'And what do *you* think?' asked Dawn.

'Up until you came here, I had no way of knowing if this story was true or not. But there is one thing I do know. Briggs told Jack that the only way to prevent Henry Bell from coming back through the wardrobe was to destroy it – by burning, preferably, since that would finish the job that Stephenson's men had started.'

'So why didn't Jack just take it out in his garden and set fire to it?'

'Because he was such a committed Christian,' said Professor Walmsley. 'Henry Bell was an innocent man, after all, and Jack couldn't accept the responsibility for taking what was left of his life. "Whatever my failings, I can never act an executioner." That was what he wrote.'

Jerry took hold of Dawn's hand. Neither of them spoke but then they didn't need to. They both knew what they were going to have to do next.

Jerry's friend Mick had a Transit van which he used for his mobile car-cleaning business. He came around to Jerry's house the following day and picked them both up, and they all drove around to Dawn's flat. On the way they stopped at the Esso service station on Chiswick High Road and filled up a red plastic petrol container.

'What are you two up to, then?' asked Mick. He had a gingery buzz cut and a gap in his teeth he could whistle through, and he always splashed himself in too much Lynx aftershave, in the hope of attracting a girlfriend. 'Spot of arson, is it? Never quite know with you two.'

'We're having a bonfire,' said Dawn. 'Kind of an early fireworks night.'

When she opened the door of her flat and stepped inside, Dawn sniffed. She could smell jasmine, from her Yankee Candle, but she could also smell that sour burnt odour of the black-faced man. She went into the bedroom with Jerry close behind her, and there it was, the wardrobe, with its door still locked. But she knew now that this wasn't just any wardrobe. This was the wardrobe that had terrified C.S. Lewis, but also inspired him to invent a world where purity battled against evil, and the innocent were sacrificed for the greater good.

She pressed her hand flat against its polished walnut door, and said, '*Narnia*,' and thought of all those bedtime stories that her mother used to read to her when she was young, with the White Witch and Mr Tumnus the faun and Aslan the lion. It gave her the strangest of feelings, both frightening and sad.

With Mick's help, they dragged and heaved the wardrobe out of the bedroom, along the hallway, out of the front door and bumped it down the steps. They paused to rest for a moment or two and then they lifted it, grunting, into the back of Mick's van.

Mick knew just the place. A developer was demolishing a block of 1920s flats on the Sheen Road. The site was screened off from the road with a green-painted hoarding, almost ten-feet high, and there were fires burning there constantly, so one more shouldn't attract any attention.

While Dawn and Jerry kept watch, Mick unfastened one of the wire security fences at the end of the hoarding. Cars and buses roared past, cyclists cycled past, but nobody took any notice of them. They lifted the wardrobe out of the van and carried it through the gap. The sun was going down now, and the hoarding blocked it out almost completely, so that the demolition site was chilly and filled with shadows. The ground was strewn with rubble and broken bricks, and so they had to carry the wardrobe almost to the far end of the site before they found somewhere level enough to put it down.

'Right, then, you going to burn it?' said Mick. 'Should have brought some hot dogs and stuff. We could have had a barbie.'

'Sorry, Mick,' Jerry told him. 'I want you to go now, and leave us alone.'

'Oh, that's nice! I practically break my flipping back helping you carry that bleeding great wardrobe. I find you a great place to burn it, and now you won't let me even watch!'

'There's a good reason, Mick. Honestly. Besides, if somebody sees us and we get into trouble, you don't want to get involved, do you?'

'All right. But you owe me five pints for this, got it?'

'Mick – whatever you want, mate, it's yours.'

'All right. Five pints and a night with Rihanna.'

'Whatever. I promise you.'

Mick went stumbling off over the mountains of broken yellow bricks. When he had climbed back through the security fence, Jerry unscrewed the lid of the petrol container and said, 'OK, then, sweetheart. Here goes nothing.'

He circled around the wardrobe, splashing it with petrol. Then he took out a box of matches, lit one, and tossed it toward the wardrobe door. With a soft *whoomppphh*, the wardrobe was enveloped in rippling flames.

Dawn and Jerry stood side by side watching it burn. The walnut veneer crackled and curled, and soon the oak underneath was being scorched black. Sparks flew up into the evening air like fireflies.

'I wonder what's going to happen to him now?' asked Dawn.

'What do you mean?'

'Well – this wardrobe is like his only doorway to the real world, isn't it? Now he's going to be trapped forever in Narnia – although I don't suppose it's anything like the Narnia that's in the books.'

The wardrobe was blazing furiously now, and the flames were licking nine or ten feet into the air. Dawn could see that a woman was watching them from a third-floor window in the block of flats next to the demolition site.

After five more minutes, the flames began to subside a little. Suddenly, however, there was a loud cracking noise, and then another, and then another, and the whole fiery wardrobe was violently shaken with every crack.

Dawn stepped back a few paces. 'What's that?' she said. 'It's not . . .'

There was yet another crack, even louder, and the wardrobe door burst open and fell flat on to the rubble. Dawn couldn't stop herself from screaming. Out of the skeletal remains of the wardrobe, a fiery figure of a man appeared, blazing from head to foot. He was burning so fiercely that it was impossible to see his face, but she knew that it must be the black-faced man.

'*Aaaaaahhhhhhh!*' he roared at her, and it was a roar of rage and agony and utter desperation. He stepped out of the wardrobe and came toward her, both blazing arms raised, walking with his knees half-bent as if he were almost on the verge of collapse.

'*Bitch!*' he bellowed, and a gout of flame rolled out of his mouth. '*I'll have you, you bitch!*'

He began to stagger toward Dawn much faster. Jerry said, 'Run, Dawn! For God's sake! Run!'

Dawn hesitated, and then she started to run, jumping and scrambling over the broken bricks. When she was halfway across the demolition site, she turned, to make sure that Jerry was running too. The fiery man was still staggering after her, and he was much closer than she had realized. She saw Jerry kick out at him, trying to knock him over, but then Jerry lost his balance and fell backward, and the fiery man kept on coming toward her. His flames made a soft rushing sound as he approached, and she could feel their heat.

'*Aaaaaahhhhhhh!*' he roared again, but this time he sounded even more desperate.

She started to run again, but the broken bricks gave way beneath her feet in a tumbling cascade, and she had to scrabble for a handhold to stop herself from sliding backward.

The fiery man had almost reached her, and she twisted around and held up her arm to shield herself.

'*I'm not Sophie!*' she shrilled at him. '*I'm not Sophie Stephenson!*'

The fiery man stopped still.

'I'm not Sophie Stephenson,' she repeated, much more softly.

The fiery man lowered his fiery head, and began to turn away. As he did so, however, Jerry jumped on his back, even though he was blazing, and wrapped his arms around him.

'*Aaaaaaaahhhhh!*' roared the fiery man, and Jerry roared, too, except that Jerry's roar came from nothing but pain, as the flames shrivelled his skin and cauterized his nerve-endings.

The fiery man lurched, and spun around, but he didn't fall over. Jerry was still clinging tightly to his back, but now he had no choice because the two of them were irrevocably welded together by the heat. They went around and around, and each time they went around, Dawn saw that Jerry's face was burning scarlet, and then crimson, like a Satanic mask. His arm muscles were charring, so that his white bones began to gleam through the black.

Dawn sank to her knees, stricken with shock. There was nothing she could do but watch Jerry and the fiery man as they continued to teeter around in circles, like some terrible children's wind-up toy. After less than two minutes they were blazing so fiercely that she couldn't see which of them was which. Then, quite abruptly, they collapsed, and lay amongst the bricks, still burning.

Over on the far side of the demolition site, the back of the wardrobe fell to the ground with a clatter.

Dawn didn't hear the sirens, but she saw the blue flashing lights, and she heard the firefighters crunching across the demolition site toward her. A firefighter laid his hand on her shoulder and leaned down to look into her face.

'Are you all right, love? What happened here?'

'You're not Aslan, are you?' she asked him.

'No, love. Alan. Come on, let's get you out of here.'

He reached down and picked her up as easily as if she were a little girl and carried her back to reality.

UNDERBED

As soon as his mother had closed the bedroom door, Martin burrowed down under the blankets. For him, this was one of the best times of the day. In that long, warm hour between waking and sleep, his imagination would take him almost anywhere.

Sometimes he would lie on his back with the blankets drawn up to his nose and his pillow on top of his forehead so that only his eyes looked out. This was his spaceman game, and the pillow was his helmet. He travelled through sparkling light years, passing Jupiter so close that he could see the storms raging on its surface, then swung on to Neptune, chilly and green, and Pluto, beyond. On some nights he would travel so far that he was unable to return to Earth, and he would drift further and further into the outer reaches of space until he became nothing but a tiny speck winking in the darkness and he fell asleep.

At other times, he was captain of a U-boat trapped thousands of feet below the surface. He would have to squeeze along cramped and darkened passageways to open up stopcocks, with water flooding in on all sides, and elbow his way along a torpedo tube in order to escape. He would come up to the surface into the chilly air of the bedroom, gasping for breath. Then he would crawl right down to the very end of the bed, where the sheets and the blankets were tucked in really tight. He was a coal-miner, making his way through the narrowest of fissures, with millions of tons of Carboniferous rock on top of him. He never took a flashlight to bed with him. This would have revealed that the inside of his space helmet didn't have any dials or knobs or breathing tubes; and that the submarine wasn't greasy and metallic and crowded with complicated valves; and that the grim black coalface at which he so desperately hewed was nothing but a clean white sheet.

Earlier this evening he had been watching a programme on potholing on television and he was keen to try it. He was going to be the leader of an underground rescue team, trying to find a boy who had wedged himself in a crevice. It would mean crawling through one interconnected passage after another, then down through a water-filled sump, until he reached the tiny cavern where the boy was trapped.

His mother sat on the end of the bed and kept him talking. He was going back to school in two days' time and she kept telling him how much she was going to miss him. He was going to miss her, too – and Tiggy, their golden retriever, and everything here at Home Hill. More than anything, he was going to miss his adventures under the blankets. You couldn't go burrowing under the bedclothes when you were at school. Everybody would rag you too much.

He had always thought his mother was beautiful and tonight was no exception, although he wished that she would go away and let him start his potholing. What made her beauty all the more impressive was the fact that she would be thirty-three next April, which Martin considered to be prehistoric. His best friend's mother was only thirty-three and she looked like an old lady by comparison. Martin's mother had bobbed brunette hair and a wide, generous face without a single wrinkle, and dark-brown eyes that were always filled with love. It was always painful, going back to school. He didn't realize how much it hurt her, too; how many times she sat on his empty bed when he was away, her hand pressed against her mouth and her eyes filled with tears.

'Daddy will be back on Thursday,' she said. 'He wants to take us all out before you go back to school. Is there anywhere special you'd like to go?'

'Can we go to that Chinese place? The one where they give you those cracker things?'

'Pang's? Yes, I'm sure we can. Daddy was worried you were going to say McDonald's.'

She stood up and kissed him. For a moment they were very close, face to face. He didn't realize how much he looked like her – that they were both staring into a kind of mirror. He could see what he would have looked like, if he had been a woman; and she could see what she would have looked like, if she had been a boy. They were two different manifestations of the same person, and it gave them a secret intimacy that nobody else could understand.

'Good night,' she said. 'Sweet dreams.' And for a moment she laid a hand on top of his head as if she could sense that something momentous was going to happen to him. Something that could take him out of her reach for ever.

'Good night, Mummy,' he said, and kissed her cheek, which was softer than anything else he had ever touched. She closed the door.

He lay on his back for a while, waiting, staring at the ceiling. His room wasn't completely dark: a thin slice of light came in from the top of the door, illuminating the white paper lantern that hung above his bed so that it looked like a huge, pale planet (which it often was). He stayed where he was until he heard his mother close the living-room door, and then he wriggled down beneath the blankets.

He cupped his hand over his mouth like a microphone and said, 'Underground Rescue Squad Three, reporting for duty.'

'Hello, Underground Rescue Squad Three. Are we glad you're here! There's a boy trapped in Legg's Elbow, two hundred and twenty-five metres down, past Devil's Corner. He's seventeen years old, and he's badly injured.'

'OK, headquarters. We'll send somebody down there straight away.'

'It'll have to be your very best man – it's really dangerous down there. It's started to rain and all the caves are flooding. You've probably got an hour at the most.'

'Don't worry. We'll manage it. Roger and out.'

Martin put on his equipment. His thermal underwear, his boots, his backpack and his goggles. Anybody who was watching would have seen nothing more than a boy-shaped lump under the blankets, wriggling and jerking and bouncing up and down. But by the time he was finished he was fully dressed for crawling his way down to Devil's Corner.

His last radio message was, 'Headquarters? I'm going in.'

'Be careful, Underground Rescue Squad Three. The rain's getting heavier.'

Martin lifted his head and inhaled a lungful of chilly bedroom air. Then he plunged downwards into the first crevice that would take him down into the caves. The rock ceiling was dangerously low, and he had to crawl his way in like a commando, on his elbows. He tore the sleeve of his waterproof jacket on a protruding rock and he gashed his cheek, but he was so heroic that he simply wiped away the blood with the back of his hand and carried on crawling forward.

It wasn't long before he reached a tight, awkward corner, which was actually the end of the bed. He had to negotiate it by lying on his side, reaching into the nearest crevice for a handhold, and heaving himself forward inch by inch. He had only just squeezed himself around this corner when he came to another, and had to struggle his way around it in the same way.

The air in the caves was growing more and more stifling, and Martin was already uncomfortably hot. But he knew he had to go on. The boy in Legg's Elbow was counting on him, just like the rest of Underground Rescue Squad Three, and the whole world above ground, which was waiting anxiously for him to emerge.

He wriggled onwards, his fingers bleeding, until he reached the sump. This was a ten-metre section of tunnel which was completely flooded with black, chill water. Five potholers had drowned in it since the caves were first discovered, two of them experts. Not only was the sump flooded, it had a tight bend right in the middle of it, with rocky protrusions that could easily snag a potholer's belt or his backpack. Martin hesitated for a moment, but then he took a deep breath of stale air and plunged beneath the surface.

The water was stunningly cold, but Martin swam along the tunnel with powerful, even strokes until he reached the bend. Still holding his breath, he angled himself sideways and started to tug himself between the jagged, uncompromising rocks. He was almost through when one of the straps on his backpack was caught and he found himself entangled. He twisted around, trying to reach behind his back so that he could pull the strap free from the rock, but he succeeded only in winding it even more tightly. He tried twisting around the other way, but now the strap tightened itself into a knot.

He had been holding his breath for so long now that his lungs were hurting. Desperately, he reached into his pocket and took out his clasp knife. He managed to unfold the blade, bend his arm behind his back and slash at the tightened strap. He missed it with his first two strokes, but his third stroke managed to cut it halfway through. His eyes were bulging and he was bursting for air, but he didn't allow himself to give in. One more cut and the strap abruptly gave way.

Martin kicked both legs and swam forward as fast as he could. He reached the end of the sump and broke the surface, taking in huge, grateful breaths of frigid subterranean air.

He had beaten the sump, but there were more hazards ahead of him. The rainwater from the surface was already beginning to penetrate the lower reaches of the cave system. He could hear water rushing through crevices and clattering through galleries. In less than half an hour, every pothole would be flooded, and there would be no way of getting back out again.

Martin pressed on, sliding on his belly through a fissure that was rarely more than thirty centimetres high. He was bruised and exhausted, but he had almost reached Devil's Corner. From there, it was only a few metres to Legg's Elbow.

Rainwater trickled from the low limestone ceiling and coursed down the side of the fissure, but Martin didn't care. He was already soaked and he was crawling at last into Devil's Corner. He slid across to the narrow vertical crevice called Legg's Elbow and peered down it, trying to see the trapped boy.

'Hallo!' he called. 'Is anybody there? Hallo, can you hear me? I've come to get you out!'

Martin listened but there was no answer. There wasn't even an *imaginary* answer. He forced his head further down, so that he could see deeper into the crevice, but there was nobody there. Nobody crying; nobody calling out. No pale distressed face looking back up at him.

He had actually reached the bottom of the bed, and was looking over the edge of the mattress, into the tightly tucked dead-end of blankets and sheets.

He had a choice, but there was very little time. Either he could climb down Legg's Elbow to see if he could find where the boy was trapped, or else he could give up his rescue mission and turn back. In less than twenty minutes, the caves would be completely flooded, and anybody down here would be drowned.

He decided to risk to it. It would take him only seven or eight minutes to climb all the way down Legg's Elbow, and another five to crawl back as far as the sump. Once he was back through the sump, the caves rose quite steeply towards the surface, so that he would have a fair chance of escaping before they filled up with water.

He pushed his way over the edge of Legg's Elbow, and began to inch down the crevice. He could slip at any moment, and his arms and legs were shaking with effort. He could feel the limestone walls starting to move – a long slow seismic slide that made him feel as if the whole world were collapsing all around him. If Legg's Elbow fell in, he would be trapped, unable to climb back out, while more and more rainwater gushed into the underground caverns.

Panting with effort, he tried to cling on to the sides of the crevice. There was one moment when he thought he was going to be able to heave himself back. But then everything slid – sheets, blankets, limestone rocks, and he ended up right at the bottom of Legg's Elbow, buried alive.

For a moment, he panicked. He could hardly breathe. But then he started to pull at the fallen rockslide, tearing a way out of the crevice stone by stone. There had to be a way out. If there was a deeper, lower cavern, perhaps he could climb down to the foot of the hill and crawl out of a fox's earth or any other fissure he could locate. After all, if the rainwater could find an escape route through the limestone, he was sure that *he* could.

He managed to heave all of the rocks aside. Now all he had to do was burrow through the sludge. He took great handfuls of it and dragged it behind him, until at last he felt the flow of fresh air into the crevice – fresh air, and wind. He crawled out of Legg's Elbow on his hands and knees, and found himself lying on a flat, sandy beach. The day was pearly-grey, but the sun was high in the sky and the ocean peacefully glittered in the distance. He turned around and saw that, behind him, there was nothing but miles and miles of grey tussocky grass. Somehow he had emerged from these tussocks like somebody emerging from underneath a heavy blanket.

He stood up and brushed himself down. He was still wearing his waterproof jacket and his potholing boots. He was glad of them, because the breeze was thin and chilly. Up above him, white gulls circled and circled, not mewing or crying, their eyes as expressionless as sharks' eyes. In the sand at his feet, tiny iridescent shells were embedded.

For a moment, he was unable to decide what he ought to do next, and where he ought to go. Perhaps he should try to crawl back into the pothole, and retrace his route to the surface. But he was out in the open air here, and there didn't seem to be any point in it. Besides, the pothole was heavily covered in grass, and it was difficult to see exactly where it was. He thought he ought to walk inland a short way, to see if he could find a road or a house or any indication of where he might be.

But then, very far away, where the sea met the sky, he saw a small fishing boat drawing in to the shore, and a man climbing out of it. The fishing boat had a russet-coloured triangular sail, like a fishing boat in an old-fashioned watercolour painting. He started to walk towards it; and then, when he realized how far it was, he started to run. His waterproof jacket made a chuffing noise and his boots left deep impressions in the sand. The seagulls kept pace with him, circling and circling.

Running and walking, it took him almost twenty minutes to reach the fishing boat. A white-bearded man in olive-coloured oilskins was kneeling down beside it, stringing fat triangular fish on to a line. The fish were brilliant, and they shone with every colour of the rainbow. Some of them were still alive, thrashing their tails and blowing their gills.

Martin stopped a few yards away and watched and said nothing. Eventually the man stopped stringing fish and looked up at him. He was handsome, in an old-fashioned way – chiselled, like Charlton Heston. But his eyes were completely blank: the colour of sky on an overcast day. He reminded Martin of somebody familiar, but he couldn't think who he was.

Not far away, sitting cross-legged on a coil of rope, was a thin young boy in a hooded coat. He was playing a thin, plaintive tune on a flute. His wrists were so thin and the tune was so sad that Martin almost felt like crying.

'Well, you came at last,' said the man with eyes the colour of sky. 'We've been waiting for you.'

'Waiting for me? Why?'

'You're a tunneller, aren't you? You do your best work underground.'

'I was looking for a boy. He was supposed to be stuck in Legg's Elbow, but . . . I don't know. The whole cave system was flooded, and it seemed to collapse.'

'And you thought that you escaped?'

'I did escape.'

The man stood up, his waterproofs creaking. He smelled strongly of fresh-caught fish, all that slime on their scales. 'That was only a way of bringing you here. We need you to help us, an experienced tunneller like you. What do you think of these fish?'

'I never saw fish like that before.'

'They're not fish. Not in the strictest sense of the word. They're more like ideas.'

He picked one up, so that it twisted and shimmered, and Martin could see that it *was* an idea, rather than a fish. It was an idea about being angry with people you loved, and how you could explain that you loved them, and calm them down. Then the man held up another fish, and this was a different fish altogether, a different idea. This was a glittering idea about numbers: how the metre was measured by the speed of light. If light could be compressed, then distance could, too – and the implications of that were quite startling.

Martin couldn't really understand how the fish managed to be ideas as well as fish, but they were, and some of the ideas were so beautiful and strange that he stood staring at them and feeling as if his whole life was turning under his feet.

The sun began to descend towards the horizon. The small boy put away his flute and helped the fisherman to gather the last of his lines and his nets. The fisherman gave Martin a large woven basket to carry, full of blue glass fishing floats and complicated reels. 'We'll have to put our best foot forward, if we want to get home before dark.'

They walked for a while in silence. The breeze blew the sand in sizzling snakes, and behind them the sea softly applauded, like a faraway audience. After four or five minutes, though, Martin said, 'Why do you need a tunneller?'

The fisherman gave him a quick, sideways glance. 'You may not believe it, but there's another world, apart from this one. A place that exists right next to us, like the world that you can see when you look in a mirror . . . essentially the same, but different.'

'What does that have to do with tunnelling?'

'Everything, because there's only one way through to this world, and that's by crawling into your bed and through to the other side.'

Martin stopped in his tracks. 'What the hell are you talking about, *bed*? I tunnel into caves and potholes, not beds.'

'There's no difference,' said the fisherman. 'Caves, beds, they're just the same . . . a way through to somewhere else.'

Martin started walking again. 'You'd better explain yourself.' The sun had almost reached the horizon now, and their shadows were giants with stilt-like legs and distant, pin-size heads.

'There isn't much to explain. There's another world, beneath the blankets. Some people can find it, some can't. I suppose it depends on their imagination. My daughter Leonora always had the imagination. She used to hide under the blankets and pretend that she was a cave-dweller in prehistoric times; or a Red Indian woman, in a tent. But about a month ago she said that she had found this other world, right at the very bottom of the bed. She could see it, but she couldn't wriggle her way into it.'

'Did she describe it?'

The fisherman nodded. 'She said that it was dark, very dark, with tangled thorn-bushes and branchy trees. She said that she could see shadows moving around in it – shadows that could have been animals, like wolves; or hunched-up men wearing black fur cloaks.'

'It doesn't sound like the kind of world that anybody would *want* to visit.'

'We never had the chance to find out whether Leonora went because she wanted to. Two days ago my wife went into her bedroom to discover that her bed was empty. We thought at first that she might have run away. But we'd had no family arguments, and she really had no cause to. Then we stripped back her blankets and found that the lower parts of her sheets were torn, as if some kind of animal had been clawing at it.' He paused, and then he said, with some difficulty, 'We found blood, too. Not very much. Maybe she scratched herself on one of the thorns. Maybe one of the animals clawed her.'

By now they had reached the grassy dunes and started to climb up them. Not far away there were three small cottages, two painted white and one painted pink, with lights in the windows, and fishing nets hung up all around them for repair.

'Didn't you try going after her yourself?' asked Martin.

'Yes. But it was no use. I don't have enough imagination. All I could see was sheets and blankets. I fish for rational ideas – for astronomy and physics and human logic. I couldn't imagine Underbed so I couldn't visit it.'

'Underbed?'

The fisherman gave him a small, grim smile. 'That's what Leonora called it.'

They reached the cottage and laid down all of their baskets and tackle. The kitchen door opened and a woman came out, wiping her hands on a flowery apron. Her blonde hair was braided on top of her head and she was quite beautiful in an odd, expressionless way, as if she were a competent oil-painting rather than a real woman.

'You're back, then?' she said. 'And this is the tunneller?'

The fisherman laid his hand on Martin's shoulder. 'That's right. He came, just like he was supposed to. He can start to look for her tonight.'

Martin was about to protest, but the woman came up and took hold of both of his hands. 'I know you'll do everything you can,' she told him. 'And God bless you for coming here and trying.'

They had supper that evening around the kitchen table – a rich fish pie with a crispy potato crust, and glasses of cold cider. The fisherman and his wife said very little, but scarcely took their eyes away from Martin once. It was almost as if they were frightened that he was going to vanish into thin air.

On the mantelpiece, a plain wooden clock loudly ticked out the time, and on the wall next to it hung a watercolour of a house that for some reason Martin recognized. There was a woman standing in the garden, with her back to him. He felt that if she were able to turn around he would know at once who she was.

There were other artefacts in the room that he recognized: a big green earthenware jug and a pastille-burner in the shape of a little cottage. There was a china cat, too, which stared at him with a knowing smile. He had never been here before, so he couldn't imagine why all these things looked so familiar. Perhaps he was tired, and suffering from *déjà vu*.

After supper they sat around the range for a while and the fisherman explained how he went out trawling every day for idea-fish. In the deeper waters, around the sound, there were much bigger fish, entire theoretical concepts, swimming in shoals.

'This is the land of ideas,' he said, in a matter-of-fact way. 'Even the swallows and thrushes in the sky are little whimsical thoughts. You can catch a swallow and think of something you once forgot; or have a small, sweet notion that you never would have had before. You – you come from the land of action, where things are *done*, not just discussed.'

'And Underbed? What kind of a land is that?'

'I don't know. The land of fear, I suppose. The land of darkness, where everything always threatens to go wrong.'

'And that's where you want me to go looking for your daughter?'

The fisherman's wife got up from her chair, lifted a photograph from the mantelpiece and passed it across to Martin without a word. It showed a young blonde girl standing on the seashore in a thin summer dress. She was pale-eyed and captivatingly pretty. Her bare toes were buried in the sand. In the distance, a flock of birds was scattering, and Martin thought of 'small, sweet notions that you never would have had before'.

Martin studied the photograph for a moment and then gave it back. 'Very well, then,' he said. 'I'll have a try.' After all, it was his duty to rescue people. He hadn't been able to find the boy trapped in Legg's Elbow: perhaps he could redeem himself by finding Leonora.

Just after eleven o'clock they showed him across to her room. It was small and plain, except for a pine dressing table crowded with dolls and soft toys. The plain pine bed stood right in the middle of the longer wall, with an engraving of a park hanging over it. Martin frowned at the engraving more closely. He was sure that the park was familiar. Perhaps he had visited it when he was a child. But here, in the land of ideas?

The fisherman's wife closed the red gingham curtains and folded down the blankets on the bed.

'Do you still have the sheets from the time she disappeared?' Martin asked her.

She nodded, and opened a small pine linen chest at the foot of the bed. She lifted out a folded white sheet and spread it out on top of the bed. One end was ripped and snagged, as if it had been caught in machinery, or clawed by something at least as big as a tiger.

'She wouldn't have done this herself,' said the fisherman. 'She *couldn't* have done.'

'Still,' said Martin. 'If she didn't do it, what did?'

By midnight Martin was in bed, wearing a long white borrowed nightshirt, and the cottage was immersed in darkness. The breeze persistently rattled the sash window like somebody trying to get in, and beyond the dunes Martin could hear the sea. He always thought that there was nothing more lonely than the sea at night.

He didn't know whether he believed in Underbed or not. He didn't even know whether he believed in the land of ideas or not.

He felt as if he were caught in a dream – yet how could he be? The bed felt real and the pillows felt real and he could just make out his potholing clothes hanging over the back of the chair.

He lay on his back for almost fifteen minutes without moving. Then he decided that he'd better take a look down at the end of the bed. After all, if Underbed didn't exist, the worst that could happen to him was that he would end up half-stifled and hot. He lifted the blankets, twisted himself around, and plunged down beneath them.

Immediately, he found himself crawling in a low, peaty crevice that was thickly tangled with tree roots. His nostrils were filled with the rank odour of wet leaves and mould. He must have wriggled into a gap beneath the floor of a wood or forest. It was impenetrably dark, and the roots snared his hair and scratched his face. He was sure that he could feel black beetles crawling across his hands and down the back of his collar. He wasn't wearing nightclothes any longer. Instead, he was ruggedly dressed in a thick chequered shirt and heavy-duty jeans.

After forty or fifty metres, he had to crawl right beneath the bole of a huge tree. Part of it was badly rotted, and as he inched his way through the clinging taproots, he was unnervingly aware that the tree probably weighed several tons and, if he disturbed it, it could collapse into this subterranean crevice and crush him completely. He had to dig through heaps of peat and soil, and at one point his fingers clawed into something both crackly and slimy. It was the decomposed body of a badger that must have become trapped underground. He stopped for a moment, suffocated and sickened, but then he heard the huge tree creaking and showers of damp peat fell into his hair, and he knew that if he didn't get out of there quickly he was going to be buried alive.

He squirmed out from under the tree, pulling aside a thick curtain of hairy roots, and discovered that he was out in the open air. It was still night-time, and very cold, and his breath smoked in the way that he and his friends had pretended to smoke on winter mornings when they waited for the bus for school – which was, when? Yesterday? Or months ago? Or even years ago?

He stood in the forest and there was no moon, yet the forest was faintly lit by an eerie phosphorescence. He imagined that aliens might have landed behind the trees. A vast spaceship filled with narrow, complicated chambers where a space-mechanic might get lost for months, squeezing his pelvis through angular bulkheads and impossibly constricted service tunnels.

The forest was silent. No insects chirruped. No wind disturbed the trees. The only sound was that of Martin's footsteps, as he made his way cautiously through the brambles, not sure in which direction he should be heading. Yet he felt that he was going the right way. He felt drawn – *magnetized*, almost, like a quivering compass needle. He was plunging deeper and deeper into the land of Underbed: a land of airlessness and claustrophobia, a land in which most people couldn't even breathe. But to him, it was a land of closeness and complete security.

Up above him, the branches of the trees were so thickly entwined together that it was impossible to see the sky. It could have been daytime up above, but here in the forest it was always night.

He stumbled onwards for over half an hour. Every now and then he stopped and listened, but the forest remained silent. As he walked on he became aware of something pale, flickering behind the trees, right in the very corner of his eye. He stopped again, and turned around, but it disappeared, whatever it was.

'Is anybody there?' he called out, his voice muffled by the encroaching trees. There was no answer, but now Martin was certain that he could hear dry leaves being shuffled, and twigs being softly snapped. He was certain that he could hear somebody *breathing*.

He walked further, and he was conscious of the pale shape following him like a paper lantern on a stick, bobbing from tree to tree, just out of sight. But although it remained invisible, it became noisier and noisier, its breath coming in short, harsh gasps, its feet rustling faster and faster across the forest floor.

Suddenly, something clutched at his shirtsleeve – a hand, or a claw – and ripped the fabric. He twisted around and almost lost his balance. Standing close to him in the phosphorescent gloom was a girl of sixteen or seventeen, very slender and white-faced. Her hair was wild and straw-like, and backcombed into a huge bird's nest, decorated with thorns and holly and moss and shiny maroon berries. Her irises were charcoal-grey – night eyes, with wide black pupils. Eyes that could see in the dark. Her face was starved-looking but mesmerically pretty. It was her white, white skin that had made Martin believe he was being followed by a paper lantern.

Her costume was extraordinary and erotic. She wore a short

blouse made of hundreds of bunched-up ruffles of grubby, tattered lace. Every ruffle seemed to be decorated with a bead or a medal or a rabbit's foot, or a bird fashioned out of cooking-foil. But her blouse reached only as far as her navel, and it was all she wore. Her feet were filthy and her thighs were streaked with mud.

'What are you searching for?' she asked him, in a thin, lisping voice.

Martin was so confused and embarrassed by her half-nakedness that he turned away. 'I'm looking for someone, that's all.'

'Nobody looks for *anybody* here. This is Underbed.'

'Well, *I'm* looking for someone. A girl called Leonora.'

'A girl who came out from under the woods?'

'I suppose so, yes.'

'We saw her passing by. She was searching for whatever it is that makes her frightened. But she won't find it here.'

'I thought this was the land of fear.'

'Oh, it is. But there's a difference between fear, isn't there, and what actually makes you frightened?'

'I don't understand.'

'It's easy. Fear of the dark is only a fear. It isn't anything real. But what about things that really do hide in the dark? What about the coat on the back of your chair that isn't a coat at all? What about your dead friend standing in the corner, next to your wardrobe, waiting for you to wake?'

'So what is Leonora looking for?'

'It depends what's been frightening her, doesn't it? But the way she went, she was heading for Under-Underbed; and that's where the darkest things live.'

'Can you show me the way?'

The girl emphatically shook her head so that her beads rattled and her ribbons shook. 'You don't know what the darkest things are, do you?' She covered her face with her hands, her fingers slightly parted so that only her eyes looked out. 'The darkest things are the very darkest things; and once you go to visit them in Under-Underbed, they'll know which way you came, they'll be able to smell you, and they'll follow you back there.'

Martin said, 'I still have to find Leonora. I promised.'

The girl stared at him for a long, long time, saying nothing, as if she were sure that she would never see him again and wanted to remember what he looked like. Then she turned away and beckoned him to follow.

They walked through the forest for at least another twenty minutes. The branches grew sharper and denser, and Martin's cheeks and ears were badly scratched. All the same, with his arms raised to protect his eyes, he followed the girl's thin, pale back as she guided him deeper and deeper into the trees. As she walked, she sang a high-pitched song.

> *The day's in disguise*
> *It's wearing a face I don't recognize*
> *It has rings on its fingers and silken roads in its eyes . . .*

Eventually they reached a small clearing. On one side the ground had humped up, and was thickly covered with sodden green moss. Without hesitation the girl crouched down and lifted up one side of the moss, like a blanket, revealing a dark, root-wriggling interior.

'Down there?' asked Martin, in alarm.

The girl nodded. 'But remember what I said. Once you find them, they'll follow you back. That's what happens when you go looking for the darkest things.'

'All the same, I promised.'

'Yes. But just think *who* you promised, and why. And just think who Leonora might be, and who I am, and what it is you're doing here.'

'I don't know,' he admitted; and he didn't. But while the girl held the moss-blanket as high as she could manage, he climbed on to his side and worked his way underneath it, feet-first, as if he were climbing into bed. The roots embraced him; they took him into their arms like thin-fingered women, and soon he was buried in the mossy hump up to his neck. The girl knelt beside him and her face was calm and regretful. For some reason her nakedness didn't embarrass him any more. It was almost as if he knew her too well. But without saying anything more, she lowered the blanket of moss over his face and his world went completely dark.

He took a deep, damp-tasting breath, and then he began to insinuate his way under the ground. At first, he was crawling quite level, but he soon reached a place where the soil dropped sharply away into absolute blackness. He thought he could feel a faint draft blowing, and the dull sound of hammering and knocking. This must be it: the end of Underbed, where Under-Underbed began. This was where the darkest things lived. Not just the fear, but the reality.

For the first time since he had set out on his rescue mission he was tempted to turn back. If he crawled back out of the moss-blanket now, and went back through the forest, then the darkest things would never know that he had been here. But he knew that he had to continue. Once you plunged into bed, and Underbed, and Under-Underbed, you had committed yourself.

He swung his legs over the edge of the precipice, clinging with both hands on to the roots that sprouted out of the soil like hairs on a giant's head. Little by little, he lowered himself down the face of the precipice, his shoes sliding in the peat and bringing down noisy cascades of earth and pebbles. The most frightening part about his descent was that he couldn't see anything at all. He couldn't even see how far down he had to climb. For all he knew, the precipice went down and down for ever.

Every time he clutched at a root, he couldn't help himself from dragging off its fibrous outer covering, and his hands soon became impossibly slippery with sap.

Below him, however, the hammering had grown much louder, and he could hear echoes too, and double-echoes.

He grasped at a large taproot, and immediately his hand slipped. He tried to snatch a handful of smaller roots, but they all tore away, with a sound like rotten curtains tearing. He clawed at the soil itself, but there was nothing that he could do to stop himself from falling. He thought, for an instant: *I'm going to die.*

He fell heavily through a damp, lath-and-plaster ceiling. With an ungainly wallop he landed on a sodden mattress, and tumbled off it on to a wet-carpeted floor. He lay on his side for a moment, winded, but then he managed to twist himself around and climb up on to his knees. He was in a bedroom – a bedroom which he recognized, although the wallpaper was mildewed and peeling, and the closet door was tilting off its hinges to reveal a row of empty wire hangers.

He stood up, and went across to the window. At first he thought it was night-time, but then he realized that the window was completely filled in with peat. The bedroom was buried deep below the ground.

He began to feel the first tight little flutters of panic. What if he couldn't climb his way out of here? What if he had to spend the rest of his life buried deep beneath the surface, under layers and layers of soil and moss and suffocating blankets? He tried to think what he ought to do next, but the hammering was now so loud that it made the floor tremble and the hangers in the closet jingle together.

He had to take control of himself. He was an expert, after all: a fully trained potholer, with thirty years' experience. His first priority was to find Leonora, and see how difficult it was going to be to get her back up the precipice. Perhaps there was another way out of Under-Underbed that didn't involve twenty or thirty metres of dangerous climbing . . .

He opened the bedroom door and found himself confronted by a long corridor with a shiny linoleum floor. The walls were lined with doors and painted, with a tan dado, like a school or a hospital. A single naked light hung at the very far end of the corridor, and under this light stood a girl in a long white nightgown. Her blonde hair was flying in an unfelt wind, and her face was so white that it could have been sculpted out of chalk.

The hem of her nightgown was ripped into tatters and spattered with blood. Her calves and her feet were savagely clawed, with the skin hanging down in ribbons, and blood running all over the floor.

'Leonora?' said Martin, too softly for the girl to be able to hear. Then, 'Leonora!'

She took one shuffling step towards him, and another, but then she stopped and leaned against the side of the corridor. It was the same Leonora whose photograph he had seen in the fisherman's cottage, but three or four years older, maybe more.

Martin started to walk towards her. As he passed each door along the corridor, it seemed to fly open by itself. The hammering was deafening now, but the rooms on either side were empty, even though he could see armchairs and sofas and coffee tables and paintings on the walls. They were like tableaux from somebody's life, year by year, decade by decade.

'Leonora?' he said, and took her into his arms. She was very cold, and shivering. 'Come on, Leonora, I've come to take you home.'

'There's no way out,' she whispered, in a voice like blanched almonds. 'The darkest things are coming and there's no way out.'

'There's always a way out. Come on, I'll carry you.'

'There's no way out!' she screamed at him, right in his face. *'We're buried too deep and there's no way out!'*

'Don't panic!' he shouted back at her. 'If we go back to the bedroom we can find a way to climb back up to Underbed! Now, come on, let me carry you!'

He bent down a little, and then heaved her up on to his shoulder. She weighed hardly anything at all. Her feet were badly lacerated. Two of her left toes were dangling by nothing but skin, and blood dripped steadily on to Martin's jeans.

As they made their way back down the corridor, the doors slammed shut in the same way that they had flown open. But they were still ten or eleven metres away from the bedroom door when Leonora clutched him so tightly round the throat that she almost strangled him, and screamed. *'They're here! The darkest things! They're following us!'*

Martin turned around, just as the light bulb at the end of the corridor was shattered. In a single instant of light, however, he had seen something terrible. It looked like a tall, thin man in a grey monkish hood. Its face was as beatifically perfect as the effigy of a saint. Perfect, that is, except for its mouth, which was drawn back in a lustful grin, revealing a jungle of irregular, pointed teeth. And below that mouth, in another lustful grin, a second mouth, with a thin tongue tip that lashed from side to side as if it couldn't wait to start feeding.

Both its arms were raised, so that its sleeves had dropped back, exposing not hands but hooked black claws.

This was one of the darkest things. The darkest thing that Leonora had feared, and had to face.

In the sudden blackness, Martin was disoriented and thrown off balance. He half-dropped Leonora, but he managed to heft her up again and stumble in the direction of the bedroom. He found the door, groped it open and then slammed it shut behind them and turned the key.

'Hurry!' he said. 'You'll have to climb on to the bedhead, and up through the ceiling!'

They heard a thick, shuffling noise in the corridor outside, and an appalling screeching of claws against painted plaster walls. The bedroom door shook with a sudden collision and plaster showered down from the lintel. There was another blow, and then the claws scratched slowly down the door panels. Martin turned around. In spite of her injured feet, Leonora had managed to balance herself on the brass bed rail, and now she was painfully trying to pull herself through the hole in the damaged ceiling. He struggled up on to the mattress to help her, and as the door was shaken yet again, she managed to climb through. Martin followed, his hands torn by splintered laths. As he drew his legs up, the bedroom door racketed open and he glimpsed the hooded grey creature with its upraised claws. It raised its head and looked up at him and both its mouths opened in mockery and greed.

The climb up the precipice seemed to take months. Together, Martin and Leonora inched their way up through soft, collapsing peat, using even the frailest of roots for a handhold. Several times they slipped back. Again and again they were showered with soil and pebbles and leaf-mould. Martin had to spit it out of his mouth and rub it out of his eyes. And all the time they knew that the darkest thing was following them, hungry and triumphant, and that it would always follow them, wherever they went.

Unexpectedly, they reached the crest of the precipice. Leonora was weeping with pain and exhaustion, but Martin took hold of her arm and dragged her through the roots and the soft, giving soil until at last they came to the blanket of moss. He lifted it up with his arm, trembling with exhaustion, and Leonora climbed out from under it and into the clearing. Martin, gasping with effort, followed her.

There was no sign of the forest-girl anywhere, so Martin had to guess the way back. Both he and Leonora were too tired to speak, but they kept on pushing their way through the branches side by side, and there was no doubt of their companionship. They had escaped from Under-Underbed, and now they were making their way back through Underbed and up to the worlds of light and fresh air.

It took Martin far longer than he thought to find the underground cavity which would take them back to Leonora's world. But a strong sense of direction kept him going: a sense that they were making their way *upwards*. Just when he thought that they were lost for good, he felt his fingers grasping sheets instead of soil, and he and Leonora climbed out of her rumpled bed into her bedroom. Her father was sitting beside the bed, and when they emerged he embraced them both and skipped an odd little fisherman's dance.

'You're a brave boy, you're a brave boy, bringing my Leonora back to me.'

Martin smeared his face with his hands. 'She's going to need treatment on her feet. Is there a doctor close by?'

'No, but there's lady's smock and marigolds; and myrtle, for dismissing bad dreams.'

'Her toes are almost severed. She needs stitches. She needs a doctor.'

'An idea will do just as well as a doctor.'

'There's something else,' said Martin. 'The thing that hurt her . . . I think it's probably following us.'

The fisherman laid his hand on Martin's shoulder and nodded. 'We'll take care of that, my young fellow.'

So they stood by the shore in the mauvish light of an early summer's evening and they set fire to Leonora's bed, blankets and sheets and all, and they pushed it out to sea like an Arthurian funeral barge. The flames lapped into the sky like dragons' tongues, and fragments of burned blanket whirled into the air.

Leonora with her bandaged feet stood close to Martin and held his arm; and when it was time for him to go she kissed him and her eyes were filled with tears. The fisherman gratefully clasped his hand. 'Always remember,' he said, 'what might have been is just as important as what actually was.'

Martin nodded, and then he started walking back along the shore-line, to the tussocky grass that would lead him back to Legg's Elbow and the caves. He turned around only once, but by then it was too dark to see anything but the fire burning from Leonora's bed, 300 metres out to sea.

His mother frantically stripped back his sheets and blankets in the morning and found him at the bottom of the bed in his red-and-white striped pyjamas, his skin cold and his limbs stiff with rigor mortis. There was no saving him: the doctor said that he had probably suffocated some time after midnight, and by the time his mother found him he had been dead for seven and a half hours.

When he was cremated, his mother wept and said that it was just as if Martin's was a life that had never happened.

But who could say such a thing? Not the fisherman and his family, who went back to their imaginary cottage and said a prayer for the tunneller who rescued their daughter. Not a wild, half-naked girl who walked through a forest that never was, thinking of a man who dared to face the darkest things. And not the darkest thing, which heaved itself out from under the moss and emerged at last in the world of ideas from a smoking, half-sunken bed; a hooded grey shape in the darkness.

And, in the end, not Martin's mother, when she went back into his bedroom after the funeral to strip the bed.

She pulled back the blankets one by one; then she tugged off the sheets. But it was just when she was dragging out the sheets from the very end of the bed that she saw six curved black shapes over the end of the mattress. She frowned, and walked around the bed to see what they were.

It was only when she looked really close that she realized they were claws.

Cautiously, she dragged down the sheet a little further. The claws were attached to hands and the hands seemed to disappear into the crack between sheet and mattress.

This was a joke, she thought. Some really sick joke. Martin had been dead for less than a week and someone was playing some childish, hurtful prank. She wrenched back the sheet even further and seized hold of one of the claws, so that she could pull it free.

To her horror, it lashed out at her, and tore the flesh on the back of her hand. It lashed again and again, ripping the mattress and shredding the sheets. She screamed, and tried to scramble away, her blood spotting the sheets. But something rose out of the end of the bed in a tumult of torn foam and ripped-apart padding – something tall and grey with a face like a saint and two parallel mouths crammed with shark's teeth. It rose up and up, until it was towering above her and it was as cold as the Arctic. It was so cold that even *her* breath fumed.

'There are some places you should never go,' it whispered at her, with both mouths speaking in unison. 'There are some things you should never think about. There are some people whose curiosity will always bring calamity, especially to themselves, and to the people they love. You don't need to go looking for your fears. Your fears will always follow you, and find you out.'

With that, and without hesitation, the darkest thing brought down its right-hand claw like a cat swatting a thrush and ripped her face apart.

Before she could fall to the carpet, it ripped her again, and then again, until the whole bedroom was decorated with blood.

It bent down then, almost as if it were kneeling in reverence to its own cruelty and its own greed, and it firmly seized her flesh with both of its mouths. Gradually, it disappeared back into the crevice at the end of the bed, dragging her with it, inch by inch, one lolling leg, one flopping arm.

The last to go was her left hand, with her wedding-ring on it.

Then there was nothing but a torn, bloodstained bed in an empty room, and a faint sound that could have been water trickling down through underground caves, or the sea, whispering in the distance, or the rustling of branches in a deep, dark forest.

NIGHT OF THE WENDIGO
(co-written with Tony Campbell)

According to the sheriff's deputy, my brother Jack couldn't have known what had hit him. He had stepped out of the North Star Bar and walked across the parking lot in the thickest of snowstorms, the flakes whirling all around him like a thousand burst-open pillows, when something ripped across the side of his head, tearing off his right ear and half of his scalp. He fell face-first to the ground, breaking his nose, but he managed to roll over on to his back to protect himself, even though he must have been blinded by blood and snow.

A hostess called Alma Lindenmuth heard him screaming out, 'No!' She said she couldn't see anything very much, because of the furious blizzard, but she told the sheriff's deputy that Jack had twisted and wriggled with his arms wildly flailing and his legs kicking in the air. Then she had seen blood jumping everywhere, 'like them dancing fountains', and Jack had screamed, 'Get off me! Christ! Get off me!'

'He was shouting out, "Get off me!" but I never saw nobody else, only Jack. I swear it. He was fighting only with himself. He was hurting himself.'

'You're sure about that?' I asked her.

'I know what I saw, that's all.' She was fitfully smoking, as if she couldn't decide whether she really liked it or not. She had heaps of blonde curly hair with black roots showing. She wore a short denim skirt and a tight denim jacket with metal studs in it. In her cleavage there was a scattered pattern of moles like a star-map of Cassiopeia. She smelled of Tommy Girl cologne and cigarette smoke. I could smell something else, too, something sexual, like burying your nose in the bed sheets on the morning after.

'Next Thursday at nine-oh-five p.m. I would have known him for seven weeks exactly. He used to celebrate our anniversary at nine-oh-five p.m. every Thursday. Two tequila sunrises, there on the bar. He was such a doll.'

She paused, and sipped at her cigarette, and then said, 'He was the only guy I ever met who made wood interesting. Well,' she added, laughing 'when I say wood I mean, like, pine and fir and that kind of stuff. Timber-type wood. Not just, you know, wood. But he was very physical, you know. He really carried himself, if you understand what I mean.'

'Sure,' I told her, and I knew exactly what she meant. Jack had always been outdoorsy with an upper-case O. He had always loved climbing and hiking and snowboarding and most of all he had always loved forests. The smell of them, and the awesome silence. I can remember the two of us standing in the middle of the Northwest Angle State Forest one summer's afternoon with the sun shining down through the pines like a medieval cathedral and him closing his eyes and saying, 'Don't ever let anybody tell you that heaven's somewhere up there in the sky. It's right here, Bill. Right here among the trees. Can't you hear them whispering, Bill? They're alive, for God's sake. They're alive.' And all I could think of was swatting away all those pesky midges and how much I would have given for a long tall cool one.

The North Star Bar was smoky and noisy and a three-piece band was playing the kind of music that can make you cry even when you don't feel like crying. Ridiculous, sentimental Gopher-State music, like 'I Left The Only Woman I Ever Loved At Thief River Falls Regional Airport'. An intermittent neon sign flashed Past Blue Ribbon, as if it were a secret message. Past. Blue. Ribbon.

I was still talking to Alma when a tall, stooping man appeared at our table. He wore a long black coat that made him look like a mortician. His hair was white and thick and sat on top of his head as if it could have been a toupee, yet there was an over-combed absurdity about it which made me believe that it was probably real. He wore a striped shirt and a dark blue necktie with the letters NEWS embroidered on it, in yellow.

'You a reporter?' I asked him.

'Why?'

'Says NEWS on your necktie.'

'Oh, that. You're reading it wrong. North East Wood Society, that's what it means. We're here to protect forests. Like our fathers did, and our fathers did before us.'

I held out my hand. 'Pleased to meet you, in that case. My brother was into forestry.'

'Jack Ballard? Yes, I had more than one discussion with Jack Ballard. You brother was very interested in cutting down tress. In fact, your brother was almost obsessive about cutting down trees.'

'Of course. That's what forestry is all about. Growing, cutting, preserving. It's all part and parcel of the same process.'

'Not necessarily. Depends which trees you're cutting down, and why.'

'Should I know your name?' I asked him.

'For sure. John Shooks. You ever been to Shooks, on the Cormorant River, near the Blackduck State Forest? My great-great-grandfather founded that community, with the specific assistance of the Ojibwa.

'Can't say I've been there, no. I'm a liability lawyer. Fire insurance claims mainly. Some auto-wreck stuff. From Minneapolis. Here's my card.'

'Married?'

'That's right. Two kids, boy and a girl.'

'Very different from your brother, then?'

'In some ways, yes. What are you getting at?'

John Shooks turned his head towards the bar. I beckoned the bar girl in the electric-blue satin blouse with the ruffles at the front and she came over and said, 'Yah?'

'Give me another Jack Daniel's, would you? And a tequila sunset. And whatever the gentleman's having.'

'Seven-Up'll do me. You're drinking Jack Daniel's?'

'My younger brother was torn to bits three days ago. You don't drink warm milk to get over a thing like that.'

John Shooks stared at me for a while. His eyes were heavily lidded, like a lizard's, and his irises were pale grey. His nose was awkwardly broken and his chin was prickly with white stubble. He looked like a week-long forecast of seriously bad weather.

'Your brother was torn to bits because he forgot who these forests belonged to.'

'I don't get you. The medical examiner thinks that he was probably attacked by a bear.'

'In the middle of town? That never happened before.'

'There's always a first time,' I challenged him.

'I never saw no bear,' put in Alma. 'Well, there could have been a bear . . . but I never saw one.'

'There was a force-six blizzard blowing at the time,' I reminded her. 'Visibility down to fifteen yards.'

John Shooks picked up his 7-Up and sipped a little from the bottle, keeping one eye on me while he did so. 'You ever seen a bear? Bear's a hard thing to miss, even in a blizzard,' he remarked.

'What are you trying to tell me? You're not trying to suggest that my brother was killed deliberately?'

'Well . . . I wouldn't use the exact word "deliberately".'

'All right, then. What exact word would you use?'

He licked his lips with the blue-grey tip of his tongue. 'I would use the word "unavoidably".'

'You want to explain that?'

John Shooks shrugged. 'What happened to your brother was an unavoidable consequence of the fact that he was felling over two thousand acres of trees in the Lost River Forest without taking the trouble to ask who those trees belonged to.'

'Oh, come on,' I retorted. 'He was employed to do it, by the Minnesota Forestry Department. Those trees belong to the state. My brother was employed to clear away jack pine and pitch pine, and replant the area with some threatened strains like white pine and Austrian pine, really good timber trees. That's the way I understand it, anyway. So I don't see the beef.'

'Beef? Your brother was considering the commercial value of all of those two thousand acres of trees, and not what they represented in spiritual terms.'

'Spiritual terms? I'm sorry, Mr Shooks, I don't understand what you're talking about.'

'The forests belong to those who used to live in them, sir, ever since. Every tree has a human spirit in it, that's what the Ojibwa used to believe. Every tree is like somebody's shrine. And what was your brother going to do? Fell them, fell them in hundreds and thousands. What would you do, if somebody came to the cemetery where your grandparents were buried, and tore up their headstone, and dug up their graves?'

'Mr Shooks—'

He waved me away with a pale, long-fingered hand. 'Your brother got what was coming to him, don't try and tell me different.'

'Mr Shooks, you're talking about forestry here. Economic rejuvenation. My brother was doing everything he could to save a very profitable species of pine. It was almost wiped out by the white pine blister, as far as I understand it, but he was going to plant a highly resistant strain that was going to turn northern Minnesota into the timber centre of the western world.'

'Forest conservation isn't all about money, Mr Ballard,' said John Shooks. 'There was human life in Roseau County well before the Ice Age, and Native Americans were living in these forests more than seven thousand years ago.'

'So what are you trying to tell me?'

'I'm trying to tell you that the forests don't belong to the state of Minnesota. They belong to the spirits who live in the trees.'

I looked at him for a long time, and then I beckoned to the bar girl for yet another Jack Daniel's.

'Do you know what I think, Mr Shooks?' I told him. 'I think there's a place waiting for you at the Zipple Bay Home for the Seriously Weird.'

After John Shooks had left the North Star Bar, I drank about nine whiskeys too many and when the bar closed at two a.m. Alma had to help me into my sheepskin jacket and my flap-eared tartan cap while I was staggering on one leg and falling repeatedly into the forest of coats in the cloakroom. When the barkeep opened the door to let us out, the cold hit me in the face like somebody throwing a bucketful of crushed ice. Alma kept me steady while I stood on the crunchy rock-salted sidewalk, swaying backward and forward and trying to find my horizon. The town square was deserted. The snowplows had come churning through it in the dark, but since then the snow had been falling softly and steadily, and now everything was white, with only a few random footprints to show that Roseau was inhabited, and even these were quickly filling in.

On the roof of Wally's Supermarket an illuminated sign told me that it was 2.06 a.m. and that the temperature was minus eleven degrees centigrade.

'You need to drink about a gallon of water and get some sleep,' Alma advised me.

'I need cuddling,' I told her. 'I need a warm pillowy bosom.'

'Come on, one foot in front of the other. You can't stand here for the rest of the night.' I looked up. The sky was intensely black, as black as if there was nothing there at all.

'Did you ever see anything so fucking black?' I said. 'Tell me,

Alma, did you ever in your whole life ever see anything so—' I stopped, and frowned at her. 'What did you say?'

'I didn't say anything. Let's get you back to your hotel.'

'I heard you say something. I distinctly—'

'Listen, I didn't say anything. You're drunk. Let me get you back to your hotel and tuck you into bed and then you can—'

I turned around, almost keeling over as I did so. I had heard something. I could feel something. Somebody had whispered close behind my back, and when I say close they must have been close enough to touch me. Yet there was nobody there. Nobody at all.

'How do you do that?' I demanded.

'How do I do what?' Alma was growing impatient now.

'Is that some kind of – what do you call it – ventriloquism?'

'Come on, sugar,' she said, tugging my arm. 'I'm freezing my buns off out here. If you want a cuddle I'll give you a cuddle. But for Christ's sake let's just get you to bed.'

Another whisper, even closer. I didn't turn around this time because I knew it had to be Alma. I couldn't work out what she was whispering: it wasn't quite distinct enough. But for some reason it sounded deeply unpleasant and perverse.

'Are you trying to make a monkey out of me?' I demanded. You know what it's like when you're seriously drunk: you can get paranoid about almost anything.

'What are you talking about? Just move.'

'I just want to know what kind of stupid stunt you're trying pull here, you know? All this—'

Whisper – whisper – whisper.

'Alma, if you have anything you want to say to me . . .'

We weaved our way across the town square, leaving footprints that looked like one of those dance-instruction diagrams. I stumbled once or twice, but I was so drunk that I was beyond the normal laws of gravity, and I didn't fall over.

Whisper – whisper – whisper.

'What?'

'You said something. You whispered.'

'I fucking whispered?' she retorted. 'Why the hell should I whisper? In this town, everybody's asleep by seven o'clock. That's if they're not in the boneyard.'

We reached a snow-covered bench right in the middle of the

square, under a snow-mantled statue of Martin Braaten, the city's
founding father, and sat down. My brain was going around like a
carousel, dipping and rising, music playing, lights revolving. I
couldn't remember what I had eaten for supper that evening, but
whatever it was, it was going up and down in my stomach like a
spotted carousel horse.

Alma said, 'You're so different from Jack. It's hard to believe
you were brothers.'

I gave her a little shake of my head. 'I was always the city brother
and he was always the country brother, that's all. I loved concrete
sidewalks and traffic. He loved the woods, and nature. Birds, bugs,
mosquitoes and slugs. Even when he was a kid. He was like Daniel
Boone and James Audobon and *The Last of the Mohicans*, all put
together. I miss him, though, Alma. I feel like I've lost an arm.'

'I miss him, too. He always gave me such respect, you know.
Most men wouldn't know what respect was if it was tattooed on
their ass.'

The snow was falling on her hair. She looked almost beautiful,
her eyes shining, her shoulders glittering with snow, like a fairy.

'You deserve it,' I said solemnly. 'You deserve respect.'

She looked away and nodded. And as she nodded, I heard that
whisper again, although it was more than a whisper this time; it
built up from a whisper into a sudden rush, and something flashed
past my cheek, so close that I could feel the wind of it, and there
was a crackling sound like somebody wrenching the leg-joint off a
Thanksgiving turkey, and Alma's head flew off her shoulders and
bounced on to the snow-covered concrete, her face still amazed,
rolling past the fire hydrant and into the gutter and lying there,
steaming in the sub-zero cold, while her headless body sat next to
me on the bench, with blood jetting out of its severed neck, warm
still, can you believe it, all over my hands and my sleeves and even
spraying into my face.

I can't remember if I shouted, but I remember ducking off the
bench and rolling on to the snow and looking wildly around me to
see what had hit her. But there was nobody standing behind the
bench. There was nobody anywhere in the square at all.

'Jesus Christ,' I kept repeating, lying on my side in the snow,
my breath smoking in terror. 'Jesus Christ Almighty.'

I cautiously climbed to my feet, holding on to the bench to steady myself. I couldn't even begin to imagine what had happened. There was blood spattered everywhere, all over the bench, all over my face, loops and squiggles of blood all over the snow. Alma's body remained where she was sitting for almost half a minute, and then she suddenly collapsed like a puppet with its strings broken. I skipped and jumped away from her, and my heart was banging so hard that it hurt.

Again, I looked around, and it was then that I thought I saw something flickering out of the corner of my eye. I tried to focus on it, but it was gone, like those imaginary black cats you can see when you're really tired.

I ran back to the North Star Bar, or loped, rather, like Groucho Marx. I banged on the door and shouted, 'Help! For God's sake! Help me!' And while I waited for the lights to be switched on, and the alarms to be switched off, and the bolts drawn back, I turned around and there was Alma's head still lying in the snow, staring at me in bloodied bewilderment, as if she couldn't understand why I had left her there.

The sheriff's deputy had a bristling ginger moustache and a lazy left eye and he chewed gum incessantly. He also had the biggest ass that I had ever seen north of the thirty-fifth parallel. His name was Norman Sturgeon. We sat in the cocktail lounge of the Roseau Rose Motel, on textured brown vinyl seats, and he asked me the same questions over and over, not because he was trying to wear me down, but because he obviously couldn't think of anything else to ask.

'You were sitting on the bench under Martin Braaten and her head flew off?'

'That's right. It just – flew off. Just like that.'

'And you weren't having any kind of altercation with her, nothing like that?'

'Even if I had been, Deputy, how could I have knocked her head off?'

'I'm not saying you did, sir. I'm simply doing my best to find out what happened here.'

'I've told you. She was sitting on the bench right next to me and I heard this whispering noise and then this rushing noise and the next thing I knew, whack! Her head was rolling across the ground. And her body was still sitting next to me.'

Norman Sturgeon blew out his cheeks in bewilderment. 'We've checked the square, sir, and apart from me and you and a few dozen people who ran out to see what was going on, and the paramedic crew, well, there's no suspicious footprints.'

'There was nobody there, Deputy. Nobody. Apart from Alma and me, the square was absolutely empty.'

'So what do you think happened?' asked Norman Sturgeon.

'I don't know,' I admitted. 'Something came rushing up to us. Something hit her and killed her, but whatever it was I never saw it.'

John Shooks was waiting for me outside my hotel. It was a sharp sunny morning and I had to lift my hand to shield my eyes from the snow-dazzle. He was sitting in a 1969 Lincoln Continental Sedan, in highly polished black, wearing tiny little sunglasses and a large fur hat that looked even odder than his hair. As I came past he rolled the window down.

'I want you to know that I'm truly sorry about what happened,' he said.

'But what? It was unavoidable? What did Alma ever do to upset anybody?'

'She was your brother's lover, sir. You cut down one of those trees, and you've started a blood feud. They'll come after you and yours, all of your kith and kin, all of your friends, all of your lovers and business associates, until they've wiped out anybody who ever had a good memory of you.'

He paused, and then he said, 'That's why I've come here this morning. I've come to warn you to go away and stay away. Never come back.'

'I'm not going until I know what it was that killed my brother and Alma Lindenmuth.'

John Shooks had a long think about that, and then he climbed out of his car. 'You and me better have a talk, in that case.'

We went to the Happy Raccoon Donut Bar. We picked a corner table, next to the window, and John Shooks ordered black coffee and sugared donuts.

'You see this town?' he asked me. 'In 1885 it had only four settlers. By 1895 it had grown to six hundred, and four years later farmers raised forty thousand bushels of hard red spring wheat.

Telephone lines were strung in 1903, and in the same year the town had its own light plant. A four-hundred-pound sturgeon was taken from the Roseau River in 1907 and had to be hauled up the river-bank by a team of horses.

'Those early settlers worked hard and they suffered all kinds of hardships, but one thing they never did was to disrespect their environment.'

'My brother respected this environment more than anybody. He wanted to preserve it, not destroy it.'

'You know that and I know that. But one man's preservation is another man's destruction. In 1924 five college students went camping in the Lost River Forest north of Roseau. They were expected in the neighbouring town of Warroad by dusk on August twenty-first. They never appeared, but six years later their skeletons were found by a fur-trapper called Kevin Dubuqe, still scattered around the ashy remains of a six-year-old campfire. Kevin Dubuqe said it looked as if their bones had been blown apart by all the winds in hell.'

'So what had happened?'

'They had made the mistake of cutting down a tree for their campfire, one of the sacred trees belonging to the spirits of the Ojibwa. They didn't do it deliberately, but spirits don't usually make allowances for ignorance. They were attacked and killed by some-thing called a Windigo, or Wendigo.'

'I've heard of that, but it's only a story, isn't it?'

'A lot of people think that it was created by Algernon Blackwood, the horror writer. But the Ojibwa have their own tales about the Wendigo, going back so far that they can't remember when the story hadn't been told. The Ojibwa say that it's a tall figure wearing white robes, and that it has an appetite for human flesh that beats my appetite for donuts.

'Some say that it follows you through the woods and drives you mad because it's always up close behind you, but whenever you swing around, there's nothing there, because it's dodged behind you again.

'Others say that it swoops down from the sky and catches a-hold of you and makes you run so fast that your feet catch fire. There are newspaper stories about black-charred footprints running right across fields of winter stubble.

'But there's one thing that all the storytellers agree on. The Wendigo is so thin that you can only see it when it decides to confront you face-on. It can come right up to you edgewise, and you'll never see it until it's too late.'

I put down my coffee cup. There was sugar all around John Shook's mouth. 'And you believe this is true? I asked him. 'You believe this is what really killed my brother, and took off Alma's head?'

'It's sunny now,' he told me. 'But it'll be dark by four, and there's snow forecast. If I was you, I'd put your brother's passing down to misfortune, and see if you can't make Thief River Falls by twilight.'

One of the skills I'd honed during my years as a liability lawyer was an ability to read between the lines, to see the truth through the countless layers of lies. Liability cases were never cut and dried, clients usually proffering just enough information to sway a court ruling in their favour. When I got that telltale feeling, that fluttering down in the pit of my stomach, I knew it was time to dig a little deeper.

I looked directly into John Shook's eyes and waited for counsel from my spirit guide – this analogy seemed appropriate with all this talk of Ojibwa and the Wendigo. 'I think,' I said, cracking my mouth open in a wide grin, 'I'll stick around for another couple of days. Might see if I can get a hunting rifle; see if I can bag a Wendigo.'

John Shooks' expression remained impassive. 'You will die if you stay here, Mr Ballard. Just like you brother and Miss Lindenmuth. It's only a matter of time.' He stood up, wiped the sugar from his mouth then wiped his fingers on his coat. 'I don't expect I'll be seeing you again, Mr Ballard. I bid you farewell. Please try and make the right decision.'

As he ducked through the door of the Donut Bar I suddenly felt extremely alone, sitting sipping coffee in a dingy café in a strange town, no one around that knew my name except a crazy local man foretelling my death.

A chill tickled the back of my neck and my hands developed a film of glistening sweat. I needed to hear a friendly voice, the dulcet tones of Marie, Tabitha, Conrad.

She answered after the fourth ring.

I took a deep breath. 'Hey, how's it going?'

Her reply was terse. 'Fine. We're all fine. The real question is how are you?'

'Listen, Marie, I think I'm on to something. I've been threatened by a local guy called John Shooks. He says he knew Jack. He warned Jack to stop cutting down trees but Jack wouldn't listen. Marie, I think he killed Jack. He's trying to scare the forestry company into pulling their operation.'

'For Christ's sake, Bill, have you told the authorities?'

'Yes. Well, no, not quite. They told me to get out of town.'

'I hope you're doing what he asked,' said Marie. Her voice now reflected concern.

'What if it was this Shooks character? I can't just give up and let him get away with murder.'

There was a pause. 'Listen, Bill, I'm not going to yell. I don't want another fight. Come home and leave the investigation to the experts.'

I felt prickly. I'd called her for support. For a friendly voice. 'I don't think you're listening. Jack's girlfriend was decapitated last night right in front of me and I'm sure it was this freak, Shooks.'

'What?' Marie screamed. 'You're going to get killed, you idiot. Then where will we be? Stuck here without a husband. Tabby and Conrad without a dad. You're always so goddamned selfish.'

'Jesus, Marie, I called you for some support, not a goddamned lecture.'

'Right,' she snapped, 'if you won't come home, we'll come to you.'

'No, it's too—' My words trailed off as I heard the line drop and go dead.

Goddammit!

I hurried back into town, straight for the glitzy tackle shop on Roseau Avenue, right across the parking lot from the North Star Bar.

'It's got a lovely action on it,' said the clerk, handing me a .338 Winchester hunting rifle. 'You could take out Bigfoot's left eye at four hundred paces with that.'

He checked my ID and then, after making a couple of phone calls to verify I was who I claimed, he swiped my credit card and sent me on my way with the rifle, ten boxes of ammunition and a cheery, 'Happy huntin'.'

The next few hours I spent locked in my hotel room familiarizing myself with my new toy. The instruction book was more pamphlet than book, but it seemed a pretty simple device. The bullets went in the top, cock the lever underneath, point it at the target, and blow its head off. Simple. You didn't need a big manual or course to teach you simply to point and shoot.

By mid-afternoon I was an experienced hunter, a woodsman of legend, so I decided to ring home again. No answer.

Dammit!

I phoned the airline enquiries desk at Thief River Falls and asked when the next flight from Minneapolis was due in. Shirley, the cheery lady on the flight desk, confirmed that Marie, Tabitha and Conrad were scheduled on board the 18.15, and my heart sank. Why the hell had I married such an obstinate woman? I guessed if they arrived in TRF at 18.15, they'd be another hour or so getting their luggage then the long drive to Roseau would take at least until midnight. No doubt Marie would call me when they landed, so I decided it was time to get to work. The rifle broke down into three pieces and fitted neatly inside my rucksack with the ten boxes of ammunition. I dressed in my warmest outdoor clothes and headed out.

The North Star Bar wasn't as busy as it had been the previous evening, but it was still early. I ordered a large Jack and Coke and sat down in the corner behind the pool table, studying the local barflies, people who might know something more about the peculiar John Shooks.

I nodded at a swarthy bear of a man who wore a bushy brown beard and peered back at me with black, soulless eyes. He was dressed in the traditional garb of the North American logger, checked shirt and heavy cord trousers, feet the size of snowshoes inside well-worn boots.

'Hey,' I said, pulling my stool alongside his. 'Bill Ballard.' I extended my hand and smiled. 'You from around here?'

The big man stared vacantly at me, as if appraising this dweeb trying to latch on to his serenity, then his expression softened and he smiled. 'Name's Bobby Ray.' Bobby Ray gripped my hand and squeezed.

'Some grip you got there, Bobby,' I said, gasping as he squeezed even harder.

'What'cha doin' in Roseau?' Bobby Ray asked, still gripping my hand like a vice.

'Passin' through,' I replied nonchalantly. He must have seen the tears welling up in my eyes since he released his grip and returned to his drink.

'Wanna Bud, Bill Ballard?' asked Bobby Ray, beckoning to the hostess. I nodded.

The squat, middle-aged woman waddled to our end of the bar and slapped a notepad down on the worktop. 'What's it gonna be, boys?' She hovered her biro over the blank pad.

'Two Buds,' said Bobby. She turned to the fridge without scribbling on the pad, before Bobby shouted, 'Oh, Norma, get us a couple packets o' them cheesy chips from out back, will ya?'

Norma grunted something unintelligible then disappeared through the door to the kitchen. I was alone with Bobby Ray.

'Do you believe John Shooks is trying to kill you, Bill?'

The question knocked me sideways. I looked at the big man and felt the blood drain from my face. He obviously knew more than he'd let on, so I came clean. 'He killed my brother,' I said. 'And I'm damned sure he killed Alma Lindenmuth.'

'Not sure old John'd be too happy 'bout you spreadin' rumours like that,' said Bobby. 'Maybes you should pack up and get yourself outta Roseau before you go causin' any more trouble.'

'I need to know where Shooks is,' I said to Bobby. I belched a foul combination of Jack Daniel's and donuts. 'Can you help me find him?'

'I've lived around here all my life,' said Bobby, 'and the one piece of advice I've learned is to keep away from the natives. Shooks is not all that he seems. But one thing is for sure, he ain't no killer. If he says it's the Wendigo, then that's what it is.'

'I need to find him,' I repeated. 'I need to know who killed Jack.'

'Get out of town,' said Bobby. 'Go to your family and never return.'

I noticed the edge of Norma's frock through the doorway. Bobby Ray followed my gaze, and upon seeing the hostess's return he fell silent.

'Thanks,' I said, as the hostess handed over our order.

I'd taken my first mouthful of icy Bud when my cellphone vibrated in my trouser pocket. I glanced at the antiquated clock mounted beside the head of a stuffed moose and shivered, noting that it was already 18.30. My eyes widened. Written in big bold neon green letters on my cellphone's LCD was the name I'd been dreading.

Marie.

'Bill,' she spluttered, 'I'm not staying on. We've landed in Thief River Falls and I've managed to get a cab to take us all the way into Roseau tonight. Stay at the hotel. We'll be with you by midnight.'

I was dumbstruck, so I said the only think I could think of. 'OK . . . I love you.'

Bobby Ray looked at me with disdain as I slid the cellphone back into my pocket. 'I can't believe you've placed your family in danger by bringing them out here.'

'It wasn't my idea—'

'Listen,' said Bobby Ray, his voice urgent. He leaned closer and whispered, 'If you wanna get through tonight, you'll do exactly as I say. Follow me.'

Donning our coats, we hurried from the bar, taking our beers into the parking lot. Night was fast approaching. The cold light of day had been reduced to an animated grey streak on the horizon, just visible through the trees at the edge of town. High above us, the Great Bear, Ursa Major, resolutely pointed north towards Polaris at it had done for countless millennia. I turned to face Bobby Ray, feigning an air of confidence I certainly wasn't feeling inside. The alcohol, mixed with the shock of the cold north wind, made my voice quiver. 'What's the plan, Bobby?'

'Things, Mr Ballard, are not entirely as they might seem. To defeat the Wendigo, you need to believe in its power. You'll need to understand what drives it if you expect to survive.'

I listened intently. I had to; I had no option. This was my only lead. Nodding slowly to Bobby Ray, I said, 'Go on.'

'I'm only agreeing to help you because of your family, Mr Ballard. Children have no place in a feud with the spirits, but the spirits care not for the sanctity of the innocent. Souls are souls, Mr Ballard, and tonight, the Wendigo will feast.'

I gulped. He was sincere. Even if I didn't believe his words, I believed this burly logger was frightened. More scared than I'd ever seen anyone. Christ, he really did believe we were in mortal danger.

'What can I do?' I said, voice breaking in the growing darkness.

'It can be killed,' said Bobby Ray, 'but you'll need help.'

'Will you help me?' I implored.

'I can guide you, but I cannot kill it. Only you, whom it seeks, can kill the Wendigo. It was summoned against you, and only you can send it back to the spirit world.'

I must have looked scared out of my wits. 'What . . . what do I need to do?'

Bobby Ray pointed to the trees where the last frontier of dark-grey daylight blipped out and night took us, and the fear came rushing at me like a steam train running with a full head. 'We've got quite a trek ahead. It's a two-mile hike to Timber Wolf Crag. We must be there by one.'

'One?' I asked.

'We must begin preparations at least a half-hour before the ritual.'

'Ritual?'

'John Shooks will explain when we get to Timber Wolf Crag,' Bobby Ray said. 'Come.' He beckoned to me to follow. 'We must collect a package from my trailer.'

'We'll die of exposure if we're up there all night,' I said. I hadn't lost all threads of logic just yet.

'Unless we die at the hands of the Wendigo, we'll be fine,' Bobby Ray said. 'Hurry, we can afford no time for chatter.'

We climbed into my rented Ford Explorer and drove to the edge of town where we entered the forest. After a short walk we came to the river bounding the town from the wild borders of the hills. Bobby Ray trudged over the wooden bridge then turned sharp right down the riverbank into the darkness. 'Hurry,' he called.

The gap between us increased with every stride. I picked up the pace, then without thinking I began to run. As I rounded a corner, I stopped dead in my tracks. A massive shape loomed out of the darkness in front of me. The thing was thirty feet long, black and menacing with a silhouetted horn on top, and it smelled sweet, yet somehow fetid.

I let out an audible screech as its single illuminated eye lit up the night. Then as fast as I'd panicked, I felt stupid and ridiculous. This was no beast: it was Bobby Ray's trailer. The big man had ducked inside and switched on the kitchen light, illuminating the satellite dish on top of the roof, and casting a laser beam of light on to the split bin bag on the ground in front of me. I chuckled to myself, commanded myself to get a grip. Jesus, this whole affair really had me spooked.

Bobby Ray emerged from the caravan with a black carry case under one arm. It was flat, five feet long and looked heavy even for him.

'What's in the case?' I asked.

'To kill the beast, you must first see that which you intend to kill.'

I must have looked confused. Bobby Ray smiled. 'John Shooks told you the beast is only visible when viewed face-on.'

I was still baffled. What did he mean? 'I know what John Shooks said, but I don't see how . . .'

'Look,' said Bobby Ray. 'To see the Wendigo, you must see all of it at once.' He began to unzip the canvas shroud. When he'd exposed no more than three inches of the contents, everything snapped into place. The light from the caravan window glinted off the mirrored surface and I counted the number of flat polished panels.

'With these twelve mirrors,' said Bobby Ray, 'we encircle the site of the ritual. Shooks' magic will summon the creature to the site . . .'

'Then it's my job to kill it,' I said.

Bobby Ray smiled and refastened the zip. 'Where you will kill it,' he confirmed.

'You had these mirrors made specially? I asked him.

'Them's as don't make no inquiries don't have to listen to no evasions,' said Bobby Ray. 'Come on now, the night's running out and it's time we hauled ass.'

'Wait up a minute,' I told him. 'Why would anybody have twelve custom-made mirrors in a case, except for the specific purpose of trapping a Wendigo?'

Bobby Ray stopped, and looked around, as if he was sure that he had heard somebody asking a stupid question, but couldn't think who it was.

'Well?' I persisted. I was shaking with cold, and I was terrified of trapping the Wendigo, but this was one of those situations where you need to know who your friends are, and what their motivation is. From years and years of liability law, I can absolutely assure you that no two people ever have the same agenda.

Bobby Ray came back toward me, and loomed over me. He smelled of body odour, and tobacco, and something else which I couldn't identify but I didn't like.

'All you need to know, Mr Ballard, is that I am your enemy's worst enemy.'

'So what are you telling me?' I would have laughed if I hadn't been so cold. 'You're a professional Wendigo-hunter?'

'Something like that.'

'You're serious?'

'How serious do you want me to be? I was called in by the Lost River Logging Corporation, round about April-time. Ever since they started cutting down the trees in the forests north-east of here, they started to lose their loggers – six or seven men a day sometimes. Heads torn off, guts ripped out. Naturally they thought it was bear, to start with, but as soon as I saw those cadavers I knew what'd done for them.

'I advised the company to keep their men out of the forests after sundown, and to bivouac them twenty miles away, in Wannaska. They gripe about the commute but at least it keeps their heads on their shoulders. I patrol the logging operations during the day, but that's mainly for show. The Wendigo, that son of a bitch only comes at night.'

I listened. The forest was unnaturally silent. Even in the dead of winter, as this was, you could usually hear owls hooting, and small creatures scurrying through the underbush. Not tonight, though.

Bobby Ray said, 'You may as well ask why the company called me in. Well let me tell you this, Mr Ballard, I know more about the Wendigo than most, having lived here in Roseau all of my life, and I've made it my business to know. When I was away in the service, my father came out here to the forest to cut down some trees. Three nights later our family home was torn apart and my father was killed and my mother was killed and my three little sisters were reduced to rags.

'That's when I first got to know John Shooks, because John Shooks made a point of coming up to me after the funeral and explaining what had happened. First of all, I didn't believe him, any more than you did, I'll bet. I was only twenty-four, and I thought I knew everything about everything, in them days. But Roseau is a pretty small town and I saw him a few years later and asked him to tell me more.

'I talked to him again in April, after I was given the job of hunting down that Wendigo and coming home with its hide. He told me that you couldn't set a trap for the Wendigo, not like you can with a bear. The Wendigo only appears when it's getting its vengeance for the spirits that live in the trees, and that means you have to go out looking for it with somebody it's hell-bent on killing. You have to have bait.'

'Bait?' I hesitated for a moment, and then said, 'Bait? You mean that's what I am? Bait?'

Bobby Ray gave me a nonchalant shrug. 'I'm sorry, Mr Ballard. You were determined to stay here in Roseau and you probably would've gotten yourself killed anyhow, so I thought I'd kind of make the most of the situation.'

'And John Shooks? What about him?'

'I called him and he's supposed to meet us here round about one thirty a.m.

'For the ritual, right?'

'Well, it's kind of a ritual. John Shooks will whistle for the Wendigo and once that thing has caught the smell of you, it won't need any further encouragement, any more than it did with your brother, or Alma Lindenmuth.'

'So once the Wendigo has caught the smell of me, then what?'

'It'll come rushing in, determined to take your head off. But you don't have to sweat it none. John Shooks isn't Ojibwa himself, of course, but he knows all of their magical hocus pocus, and he can do that shaman whistling stuff. I'll have set up my mirrors, John Shooks can whistle north, and he can whistle east, and that should keep the Wendigo turning around and around in front of my mirrors so that he can never turn edgewise on to you, and vanish. That's when you do the necessary business with that .388 rifle you're carrying there.'

I hefted up the Winchester and dubiously tucked it into my shoulder. It must have weighed nearly ten pounds, and after a few seconds my hand started to tremble and I had to lower it.

'I just hope this does the job, that's all.'

Bobby Ray grinned. 'You don't want to worry about that particular piece of ordinance, Mr Ballard. That's what we call a North Forty, because south of the fortieth parallel there's no indigenous animals big enough to shoot at with a sucker like that. That sucker can drop a bull elk at four hundred yards.'

'OK, then,' I said. 'We'd better go do it. I just wish you'd told me all this stuff sooner.'

'You can't say that I didn't warn you to go, Mr Ballard.'

'I'm a lawyer, Bobby Ray. I can recognize when a warning is a veiled encouragement.'

'Last veiled encouragement I ever saw was my Betsy, the day that I married her.' We made our way down a steep, dark slope, with ferns almost up to our shoulders. The shadows from Bobby Ray's flashlight jumped and danced through the forest like attenuated devils. The forest was still holding its breath. The only sound was our boots sliding down the loose pebbles, and the crackling of twigs, and Bobby Ray occasionally saying, 'Shee-it!'

At last we reached the edge of a steep, craggy, eighty-foot precipice, overlooking the Lost River itself. As we emerged from under the pines, we could see that it had started snowing again, and occasional gusts of wind made the snowflakes twirl into ghostly shapes. Below us I could see the dim, silvery curve of the river, with three oxbows, and a thin tributary that meandered all the way to Foxville and Etheridge and Skeleton Head.

'Used to bring Betsy up here in the summer,' said Bobby Ray, kneeling down and tugging open the zipper of his carrying case. 'As a matter of record, I used to bring all my girlfriends up here in the summer. Should have renamed it Busted Cherry Crag.'

He arranged his mirrors in a circle about twenty yards across, keeping each of them upright with four metal spikes. They looked like a circle of reflected headstones. 'There . . . no matter which way the Wendigo spins itself around, you're going to be able to see where it is. Don't worry where you hit it so long as you hit it. That North Forty of yours has a two-fifty-grain bullet which travels at two thousand feet per second.'

I checked my watch. It was 1.20 a.m. My nose was running and my throat was sore from breathing through my mouth. I took out my cellphone and tried to call Marie at the AmericInn, but there was no signal out here in the forest. I couldn't tell her I loved her. I couldn't even tell her goodbye.

Bobby Ray knocked in the last of his spikes and then came over to me, his breath smoking. 'John Shooks should be here in five. You ready for this?'

'I don't think I have a whole lot of choice, do you?'

'You realize, don't you, that if you bring down this Wendigo here tonight, I'm going to be looking for a new job?'

We waited and waited. Eventually I sat down on a rock. Bobby Ray lit a cigarette and paced up and down, whistling between his teeth.

At 1.51, I said, 'Do you think he's going to show?'

'Let's give him ten more minutes, OK? He's coming through Foxville but it's still pretty slow going, especially in this weather.'

We waited ten more minutes, then another ten. At last, I said, 'He's not coming, is he?'

'No, sir. I guess he ain't. I reckon I'd better take down all of these mirrors and call it a night.'

'I don't think he had any intention of coming. The way he talks, anybody who cuts down one of these sacred trees deserves to be ripped to pieces by the Wendigo.'

Bobby Ray was struggling to pull out one of his metal spikes. 'He swore blind that he'd show. He said he had some family business to take care of, but after that he was going to be here for sure. He said he wanted to finish things off for good and all.'

He was furiously working the spike from side to side, trying to get it free. 'Damn ornery thing,' he said; but even as he said it, I heard an extraordinary crackling noise, followed by a loud groan.

I lifted up my Winchester and released the safety. There was a moment's silence, but then the crackling started again, and then a sharp splitting sound, and a rush like a hundred people running down a corridor. A huge jack pine came tilting out of the forest and fell down on top of Bobby Ray with a thunderous crash.

'Bobby Ray!' I scrambled through the branches and picked up his flashlight. He was lying face down in the undergrowth with the tree resting right on top of him. He was still alive, although his face was badly lacerated and his right eye was hanging out of his cheek.

'Bobby Ray! Can you hear me! I'm going to get you out of there!'

Bobby Ray coughed up a gout of bright-red blood. 'I'm crushed,' he said, in a thick, bubbly voice.

'Just hold on. I'll get you out of there!'

I took hold of two of the larger branches and tried to roll the tree sideways. But as it was over a hundred feet high, and where the trunk was resting on top of Bobby Ray it was over four feet in diameter, I couldn't budge it an inch.

'I'll have to get help!' I shouted. 'It's going to take a chainsaw to get you out of there!'

Bobby Ray coughed more blood. 'Don't worry about me. Go find Shooks.'

'What?'

'Go find John Shooks. If he ain't here, where is he, and what's he getting up to?' I stood up. The snow blew steadily against my back and the trees swayed against each other as if they were getting ready to shuffle toward me. I thought I could hear voices, and somebody close behind me talking in a fast, sibilant whisper, but it was probably nothing more than the wind beginning to rise.

Bobby Ray let out another cough. 'Go find Shooks,' he repeated.

It was then that I remembered what John Shooks was supposed to have said to him. 'He had some family business to take care of. He said he wanted to finish things off for good and all.'

Maybe the family that he had been talking about wasn't his family, but my family. *'You cut down one of those trees and you've started a blood feud. They'll come after you and yours, all of your kith and kin, all of your lovers and all of your friends, until they've wiped out anybody who ever had a good memory of you.'*

I looked back down at Bobby Ray. His left eye had closed, even though his right eye was staring at the ground. Even if he wasn't dead yet, there was no chance that he would still be alive by the time I got back here with help.

I said, 'Sorry, Bobby Ray.' Then I picked up my rifle and started to run back through the forest.

By the time I reached the wooden bridge, I was sweating and gasping. It was snowing even more thickly, and my SUV was covered three inches deep. I swept my arm across the windshield to clear it as much as I could, and then I climbed in and started the engine.

I swerved away from the bridge and headed back toward town. As I drove, I tried the AmericInn again.

'AmericInn Roseau, good evening.'

'Mrs Ballard, please.'

'Hold on, sir.'

I could hear the phone ringing and ringing. Marie, for Christ's sake, pick up. Marie, for Christ's sake, pick up.

The phone stopped ringing, and clicked.

'Hallo? Marie? Is that you? Marie – can you hear me, Marie?'

There was a long pause, and then a soft voice said, 'I did warn you, Jack Ballard's brother. I did warn you of the consequences.'

'Shooks? Shooks, you bastard, what are you doing there? I'm warning you now – you touch one hair of my family's heads . . .'

'Oh, they all say that, Jack Ballard's brother. But when the Wendigo sweeps in, there's nothing anybody can do to stop it.'

'Shooks!' I screamed at him, but he had put down the phone.

I slammed my foot down on the gas and the Ford swerved wildly from one side of the highway to the other. Luckily, there were no other vehicles in sight. I juggled with my cellphone, trying to dial 911, but then I dropped it on the floor, and no matter how much I groped around for it, I couldn't find it.

The AmericInn Roseau was on Highway 11 West, a low two-story building with a snowy collection of RVs and SUVs lined up outside. I slid the Ford into the parking lot, climbed out, and ran across to the front doors. Inside, it was almost intolerably warm, and a bored-looking young man was sitting at the front desk playing with a hand-held computer game.

'Ballard – which room?' I demanded.

He looked up and blinked at me. He was pale and spotty with a high, gelled-up pompadour. 'You'll have to check that hunting-rifle, sir.'

'Which fucking room?'

'Erm, Ballard. That'll be two-two-two. But you still have to—'

I couldn't wait for the elevator. I ran for the stairs and leaped up them three at a time. I ran along the overheated corridor, counting the rooms as I went. Here it was, 222. I hurled myself up against it and it burst wide open.

The sight that met me made my skin shrink. Marie was standing in the centre of the room, wearing her pink-and-blue Chinese bath-robe. She was very small, and somehow she looked even smaller than ever, and completely defenceless. Her face was drained of colour and her braided brunette hair had partly come loose. One arm was wrapped protectively around Tabitha, who was twelve, wearing her pink starry nightshirt; and the other arm was wrapped around Conrad, who was eight, in blue striped pyjamas.

In the far corner stood John Shooks, in his long black mortician's tailcoat, with his improbably white hair. In the gloomy light from the single bedside lamp, he looked even more cadaverous, and the shadow on the wall behind him looked like a hunchbacked monster.

'Daddy!' said Tabitha, as soon as she saw me.

'Oh God!' said Marie. 'Oh God what's happening? Who is this man? He just walked in here! I tried to stop him but I couldn't!'

John Shooks turned to me with a smile that opened like a knife wound.

'Well, well, Mr Ballard. I wasn't expecting you so soon.'

'Get the hell out of here, Shooks. Leave my family alone. Marie – pick up the phone and call the cops.'

'Oh, I'm afraid it's too late for that, Mr Ballard. Soon as I got your call, I whistled for the Wendigo, and it's on its way here.' He gave a loud, thumping sniff. 'Pity you ran into that fool Bobby Ray. We could've gotten this done and dusted by now.'

'Bobby Ray's dead. Jack pine fell on him.'

'That doesn't surprise me. The Wendigo protects the trees, but now and then the trees protect the Wendigo.'

'So you never had the slightest intention of helping us?'

'Of course not. I just wanted Bobby Ray out of the way. He could have been dangerous, with those mirrors of his, even though he was a fool.'

'But what the hell is the point of killing innocent people? Children?'

'You should have asked the U.S. Cavalry that question, before Wounded Knee. I told you before, Mr Ballard. We have to think of the spiritual value of these forests, before we consider their commercial value. My forebears owe the Ojibwa their lives, and that means I do, too.'

I lifted the Winchester and pointed it straight at his chest. 'I'm giving you a count of three to get the hell out of here.'

'Go ahead, shoot me. It won't do you any good. The Wendigo has been whistled for, and there's no way that you can stop it.'

I opened the door wider. 'Marie – Tabitha – Conrad – run for it. Go down to the desk and ask the clerk to call the police.'

'You can't escape!' John Shooks screamed at me, in such a shrill voice that I felt as if centipedes were pouring down my back. 'You can run wherever you like, but you can't escape!'

At that moment, the door slammed violently shut. I grabbed the handle with my left hand and tried to pull it open, but it felt as if it were locked and bolted.

'Can't escape,' John Shooks repeated, smiling and shaking his head.

I stepped away from the door. I could hear a noise in the corridor outside like a high wind rising. There was a pause, and then a hollow, breathy sound like a slide whistle.

Through the crack at the side of the door a figure appeared, white and transparent and entirely two-dimensional, like a figure on a movie screen. It was so tall that it reached the ceiling. It was wearing robes made out of tattered sheets, like torn shrouds, and hung all over with white animal pelts. Its head was covered by a long drooping hood, but in the darkness underneath the hood I could see eyes like two grey stones, and a mouth that bristled with jagged teeth.

As the figure entered the room, it was followed by a screaming wind, even though its robes didn't stir. Papers blew off the side table, one of the standard lamps fell over, and John Shooks' hair was blown into a fright wig.

'The Wendigo!' John Shooks yelled at me, with spit flying from his lips.

I took another step back, and then another, pushing Marie and the children behind me. I lifted the Winchester and aimed it. Instantly, the Wendigo turned edgewise and vanished.

I waved the rifle from side to side, frantically trying to see where the Wendigo had disappeared to. The wind was still blowing, and papers were still flying around the room. John Shooks was right in the far corner now, both arms held high above his head as if he were an evangelist preacher, his face grey with excitement.

Every now and then I caught a split-second glimpse of the Wendigo as it turned from one side to the other, but before I could take a shot at it, it was gone.

I thought: six shots at random . . . all spread out . . . one of them is bound to hit it. But as soon as I lifted the rifle I felt claws tear deep into my shoulder. I could actually hear my muscles crunch. I was lifted off my feet, and I dropped the rifle on to the floor. I was turned around, and then I was thrown through the air, right through the bathroom doorway, hitting my head against the basin. I tried to stand up, stunned and bleeding. Tabitha and Conrad were both screaming and Marie was waving one hand from side to side, trying to protect them from a creature that appeared only in tantalizing flickers, like a zoetrope.

With an explosive bang, the shower curtain suddenly billowed and the Wendigo tore into the bathroom, picking me up again and ripping at my clothes with its horny claws. I could feel my blood spraying everywhere and I was sure that I was going to die.

The Wendigo lifted me up. I felt as battered and helpless as a marionette with its strings cut. It looked down at me, and its eyes were totally unforgiving. *You have slaughtered my people. You have desecrated my holy places. You have cut down the trees that carry the souls of my ancestors. For that, you and your family will all be sacrificed.*

It held me in its claws. It pulled me close, almost like a lover. I could feel every spiny, bony excrescence that came out of its chest. When it turned sideways to look back at Marie, it disappeared, but when it turned back to look down at me, I could see its face, and its jagged teeth, and I could tell that it was relishing this moment.

And then – like a ludicrous comedy – the door crashed open and Deputy Norman Sturgeon was standing there, holding his .45 automatic in both hands, his hat askew, his legs wide apart.

'Freeze!' he shouted.

John Shooks lifted him arm to cover his face, as if he were trying to pretend he wasn't there.

'Where's the hunting rifle?' Norman Sturgeon demanded.

The Wendigo slowly dragged me out of the bathroom and into the bedroom. Marie and Tabitha and Conrad were staring at me in horror, and when I saw myself in the mirror, I could understand why.

I could see the Wendigo, because it was looking down at me face-on, but nobody else could. To everybody in the bedroom, it must have appeared that I was staggering out of the bathroom on my own. Blood was running in rivulets down my forehead, and my arms were held up because the Wendigo was carrying me.

'Mr Ballard,' said Norman Sturgeon. 'Where's the hunting rifle, Mr Ballard?'

I hesitated, and took a deep breath. This was going to be all or nothing. I opened my mouth wide and I screamed. I shoved myself forwards against the Wendigo's bony chest so that it lost its balance, and together we lurched toward Norman Sturgeon like a pair of deranged ballroom dancers. I dragged the Wendigo in between me and Norman Sturgeon, then the Wendigo dragged me back again. At the last moment I turned him around one more time.

'Hold it right there!' shouted Norman Sturgeon. But Norman Sturgeon couldn't see the Wendigo. He could only see me, with my mask of blood and my elbows cocked upward, and a grotesque look on my face like a Japanese horror mask.

Like the well-trained Roseau County deputy that he was, he shot at me three times, a tight group aimed at my heart. Except that I was shielded by the Wendigo.

With the first shot, the Wendigo gave a terrible flinch, and arched its spine backward. With the second, it tried to turn around. But then the third shot penetrated its internal organs. I felt its body ripple, if that's anything to go by. Gradually, painfully, it released me. Then it twisted sideways and collapsed to the floor.

I picked up the Winchester.

Norman Sturgeon shouted, 'Drop it! Drop it, Mr Ballard!'

But even if Norman Sturgeon couldn't see it, I could see the Wendigo, lying on the rug, its white face staring up at me; and it had killed my brother Jack, and Alma Lindenmuth, and who knows how many other people who had disturbed its sacred trees. And this wasn't the nineteenth century, this was today, and sacred trees didn't count for anything any more.

I fired the Winchester three times and bits of carpet and concrete flooring flew up into the air, and the Wendigo was blown apart. Tattered robes, animal pelts, beads and bones.

I laid the rifle down on the bed. Norman Sturgeon came up to me cautiously, pointing his gun at me. 'Keep your hands behind your head, Mr Ballard. No false moves or I swear to God I'll drop you.'

He looked down at all the remnants lying around the room. The wind had dropped now, but a few white feathers where still falling down to the floor.

'What the hell happened here?' he demanded. 'There wasn't nobody else in the room, was there? Who's this? And how come you didn't get shot, Mr Ballard? I shot you three times but you ain't even scratched.'

I couldn't have cared less. I put my arms around Marie and Tabitha and Conrad and we held each other close.

As for John Shooks, he gave two catarrhal coughs and headed toward the door. But I turned around before he could go and called out, 'John!'

He stopped. His lizard-like eyes wouldn't even look at me.

'It's finished, John. It's over. What we did, all those years ago, it might have been wrong, but it's over.'

John Shooks said, 'That's what you think.'

Norman Sturgeon turned around but John Shooks had disappeared, and outside the windows in the town of Roseau it was still snowing, and beyond Roseau lay the forests and the lakes and it was snowing there, too, and who knows what spirits still sleep beneath that snow.

Author's Note: *Night of the Wendigo* was originally titled *Edgewise* and appeared in *The Horror Express* magazine in September 2005. It was the result of a contest in which I supplied the beginning of a story and readers were invited to submit a middle for it, whereupon I would furnish the ending. The winner was Tony Campbell, a prolific writer of computer articles, as well as dark fiction. I used the title *Edgewise* for my full-length novel about the Wendigo, which was published in 2006.

SPIRITS OF THE AGE

Michael was sitting in Prince Albert's writing room when he thought that he could hear a woman sobbing. He sat up straight and listened. It was very faint, as if she had her face buried in a pillow, and after a few seconds it died away altogether, so that he couldn't be sure that he had heard it at all.

Outside, it was a blustery day, and for all its opulence Osborne House was notoriously drafty, especially when there were North Easterlies blowing across the Solent.

It could have been nothing but the wind, whining down one of the chimneys. It could have been water, quietly gurgling through the miles of elaborate nineteenth-century plumbing. But he stayed quite still, listening, and in the gilt-framed mirror over the fireplace his reflection listened, too – pale-faced, his glass tilted and his hair sticking up at the back.

After a long pause he went back to tapping at his laptop. It didn't take much to distract him. He was working as a research assistant for Buller & Haig, the art publishers, who were planning to bring out a lavish coffee-table book on all of Prince Albert's gardens. It wasn't the kind of job that Michael had ever wanted to do. He had left Middlesex University with a second-class English degree and ambitions of being a magazine journalist, the new Tom Wolfe, all coruscating adjectives and supercilious satire. But as one rejection followed another, it began to dawn on him that his entire university career had left him over-educated and out of touch. Magazines didn't want literary wasps any more. They wanted New Lads who told it like it was, with F in every other sentence.

The morning that his rejection letter from *Vanity Fair* arrived in the post, his girlfriend Sam called him to say that she was sorry, but she was leaving him for a Nigerian actor called Osibi with tribal scars on his face.

'He understands my *aura*,' she said, as if that explained every-thing, and put the phone down. He hadn't been to the Isle of Wight since he was eight. All he could remember was catching tiny green crabs in a bucket and peeing in the sea. But when his university friend Richard Buller had offered him this small research job at Osborne House, he had realized that it was just what he needed. Although the island was only a twenty-minute ferry journey away from Portsmouth, and was actually in sight of the mainland, it was strangely dislocated from the rest of England. It didn't just belong in the sixties, it belonged in some version of the sixties that had never happened anywhere else, except within the imaginations of retired folk who wore beige cardigans and lived in pebble-dashed bungalows called 'Meadhurst', as well as a few hippies with odd burring accents and mongrels on the end of a string. A community with a tenuous grip on reality.

But Michael badly needed to convalesce, and to concentrate on something other than his stalled ambitions and his lacerated emotions, and the Isle of Wight was the very best place to do it.

Queen Victoria had fallen in love with the island's detachment, too. She had had Osborne House built between 1845–51 as a country retreat where she and her family could be free from state ceremonial duties. It was a huge, sand-coloured building with two Italian-style *campanile*. It was surrounded by woods and gardens, most of them planted and laid out by Prince Albert himself, and to the east, it looked along a broad stretch of open land directly to the sea.

Usually, Osborne was filled with shuffling lines of white-haired sightseers, but it was off-season now, and Michael almost felt that the house belonged to him alone. There was a home for retired servicemen in the Household Wing, and occasionally one of them would wheel past him and raise a walking stick in salute, but sometimes he could go for days on end and see nobody at all except a distant gardener tending a fire.

Some days, bored with his work, he would wander from one room to another, each of them overwhelmingly decorated in high Victorian Gothic, with gilded and moulded ceilings and gilt-encrusted furniture and chandeliers made to look like giant convolvuluses climbing out of a basket. He found the Durbar Room especially overbearing. It was the state banqueting room, designed in the Indian style by Rudyard Kipling's father Lockwood and a craftsman from Lahore, Bal Ram Singh. It had a deeply coffered ceiling, like the inside of a temple, and for some reason Michael always felt uneasy there, as if he were intruding on a culture that was not his own; as if he should take off his shoes.

It echoed, because it was empty of furniture, but it had strange dead places where it didn't echo at all.

Michael liked Albert's writing rooms, though, where he was usually allowed to work. It was a modest size, with Adam green walls and early Renaissance paintings on the wall, as well as a portrait of Albert and his brother Ernest. Albert's presence was still remarkably strong. Everything around had been invented by him or designed by him, from Queen Victoria's shower to the fastidious engraving of Osborne House on his notepaper, of which there was still a great deal left.

Sometimes Michael found himself talking to Albert as if he knew him.

'God, you made a bloody fuss over that *magnolia grandiflora*, didn't you, Bertie? And those myrtles. And all that special Kentish mulch.'

It especially amused him when he found out that Albert's idea of hands-on garden 'planting' involved him standing on top of one of the *campanile*, directing his gardeners by semaphore.

It was mid-December, and by three o'clock in the afternoon it was starting to grow dark. Michael decided to call it a day and go into Cowes to do some shopping. He didn't need much: bread, milk and a newspaper. He packed up his laptop, but as he did so he was sure he heard that sobbing sound again, and this time it was very much clearer.

He listened for a while, and then he called out, 'Hallo? Is anybody there?'

There was no reply, but the sobbing persisted. He walked across the swirly patterned carpet to the door which led to the Queen's sitting room. This had a semicircular bay with tall windows that led to a balcony. There were no lights on, and the only illumination came from the pearly coloured fog outside.

'Hallo?' Michael repeated, but now the sobbing seemed to have stopped.

He walked cautiously into the room and looked around. In the centre were two desks where Victoria and Albert had sat side by side. Both desks were cluttered with framed portraits and memorabilia. On the side of the Queen's desk were three electric bell-pulls: one to summon Miss Skerret, her dresser; another to call for a page; and a third to bring in Prince Albert's personal attendant. Michael pulled each one of them in turn, but of course nobody came.

Except that he heard someone walking across the Queen's dressing room, next door. There was no mistaking it. A quick, furtive rustling sound.

He opened the door and he was just in time to see a black figure disappearing through the door into the Queen's bedroom. At least he thought it was a figure. It could have been nothing more than a shadow.

He hesitated for a moment, and then he went into the bedroom. There was nobody there. But as he walked around the high-canopied bed, he saw that one side of the pale, embroidered bedspread had been rumpled, as if somebody had been sitting on it. On the bedhead hung a pocket for the Prince Consort's watch, and a posthumous portrait of him, which Victoria had kept in every residence, so that she could touch his dear dead face before she slept.

Michael straightened the bedcover. He didn't know why. He looked into the corridor outside the bedroom just to make sure that there was nobody there. He even went out into the stairwell, where two flights of marble stairs led down to the floor below. A distorted, echoing voice reached up to him, and footsteps, but when he looked over the cast-iron railings he saw that it was only one of the cleaners.

He walked to the main entrance to catch the bus. The fog was much thicker now, and all the myrtle and laurel bushes hunched in the gloom. The only sound was the crunch of his footsteps on the gravel path, and the mournful cry of foghorns from the Solent.

He was passing the red-brick wall around the kitchen garden when he thought he heard somebody else's footsteps. He stopped, and listened, but there was nothing but silence. It must have been the echo of his own footsteps against the wall.

He walked a little further, and he thought he heard the footsteps again, off to the right, toward the little octagonal summer house where Victoria's children sometimes used to have their supper. He glimpsed a triangular black shape disappearing behind the summer house, so quickly that he couldn't be sure what it was. A dog? A badger? Or somebody trailing a black sack behind them?

'Hallo?' he called, uncertainly. There was no reply, only the lost and distant moan of the Portsmouth ferry. 'Hallo?' he called again.

He circled around to the front of the summer house. It was so dark that at first he couldn't see if there was anyone there. He approached it cautiously, and saw that the doors were five or six inches ajar. He had never seen them open before: the public wasn't allowed inside. Maybe it was a squatter, or a drunk, or somebody who needed some shelter for the night.

He climbed the first two steps and then he stopped, his skin prickling like nettle rash.

There *was* someone there. A small figure dressed in black, with a black hood over her head, and a face as pale as a lamp. Michael couldn't see her very well. She seemed to be blurry, like a figure seen through greasy glass. She didn't appear to be frightened of him, though. She stood still and silent, and he couldn't even tell if she was aware of his presence or not. But there was something about her that seriously unsettled him. Some coldness. But it was more than coldness. It was an aura of complete self-possession, as if she were unafraid of anything, or anybody.

'Are you – do you need some help?' he asked her. She didn't reply. It was hard for him to say how old she was. Pretty old, he guessed, by her small, stooped figure. But she could have been a dwarf, or a little child, or something else altogether.

'Are you lost? I can help you find your way out of here.'

'Not lost,' she said, in a small, dry voice. '*Lost.*'

'This is off-season. They don't have visitors here till Easter.'

'*Who* has no visitors?'

'They. The English Heritage people.'

There was a long pause – so long that Michael wondered if she were ever going to speak again.

'Lost,' she repeated. 'I expected to find him here.'

'I'm sorry. You expected to find *who* here?'

'This *is* the year 2000, isn't it?' she asked him.

'That's right. December sixteenth, 2000.'

'And the world has made many great advances, in the past hundred years? In science, in medicine, in saving human lives?'

'I'm sorry,' said Michael, 'I don't understand.'

He could hear the little figure breathing, but no vapour came out of her nostrils, not like his. 'We *have* found a cure for the typhoid fever?'

'Well, yes, as far as I know.'

'And has the way been found to galvanize the dead?'

'I'm sorry?'

'Has the way been discovered to restore the human heartbeat through electrical shock?'

'Well, yes.'

'Then where is he? I was assured that he would be here.'

Michael said, 'I think we'd better find somebody to help you.'

'I don't require help,' she said, in obvious distress. 'I just want *him*.'

'If I knew who you were talking about . . .' Michael began.

She stepped through the five-inch gap in the doors without opening them any wider. Even outside, her face was white and indistinct. 'I . . . was assured,' she said. 'I was *assured* that by the end of the twentieth century, all diseases would have been cured, and that the deceased could be cured of those diseases from which they had expired, and brought back to life.'

Michael tried to take hold of her elbow, but his hand seemed to pass through it like a velvet curtain. He was beginning to feel seriously alarmed now, and the fog didn't help, nor the utter silence. Even the foghorns seemed to have stopped.

'Listen, why don't you come back to the house? Perhaps we can call somebody for you? A daughter, maybe? Do you have any daughters?'

'I have to stay here. I can't go anywhere until I find him. He *must* be here. I was assured.'

'Who assured you?'

'Abdul Karim, my *Munshi*. He said that he could foretell everything that would happen in the future. He said that people would be able to send their spirits flying around the world while their bodies remained in bed. He said that we would all be able to cure our loved ones, and bring them back to life, just the way they were. Living, breathing, laughing. The way that Albert used to laugh!'

'*Albert?*' said Michael. 'You've come here, expecting to find *Albert*? Albert died one hundred and thirty-nine years ago.'

She looked up at him, and he could feel the cold electricity of disapproval. 'The Prince Consort built this house. His heart was here, and this is where Abdul Karim promised me that he and I would one day be reunited.'

'Reunited?' said Michael, shaking his head. 'You and Albert are going to be *reunited*?'

'Don't you understand who I am?' she demanded. 'Has a hundred years erased my memory so completely?'

'I know who you are,' said Michael reassuringly. 'You're Queen Victoria, that's who you are. Now, why don't you let me walk you back to the main gate and you and me can talk on the bus up to Cowes.'

The small woman said nothing. But then she lowered her head and uttered a single sob of anguish, and turned around. She passed back through the doors of the summer house, and into the darkness of the summer house itself.

Michael followed her, flinging the doors open wider. The summer house was empty. He went all the way around it, feeling the walls, looking for any way in which the woman could have escaped. In the end he stood in the middle of it, his hand clamped over his mouth, wondering if he were starting to go mad.

Abdul Karim had come to Osborne in 1887 – first as a servant, and then as Queen Victoria's personal Indian Secretary. There was a fine painting of him in the Durbar Corridor. He was suave, handsome, with hooded eyes and a neatly trimmed beard and moustache. Michael stared at his picture for a long time; but Abdul Karim had his eyes averted, and always would.

That evening, back in his room at the top of the Household Wing, Michael combed the Internet for all the information that he could find about Queen Victoria and her Indian servants. There was very little about Abdul Karim, even though he had been a minor celebrity in his time. But there was one book: *Queen Victoria's Mystic*, by Charles Lutterworth, brought out in a limited edition in 1987 by the Vectis Press – a small specialist publisher with an address in West Cowes.

Michael didn't sleep well that night. He kept seeing the summer house doors opening, and a pale lamp-like face watching from the darkness within. At 3.20 in the morning, his bedroom door opened, and he sat bolt upright in bed, his heart clamped with alarm. He went cautiously over to the door and opened it wider, and looked out, and he thought he saw a small dark shadow disappearing down the end of the corridor.

He closed his door and locked it. He lay back in his cold, sweat-tangled bed but he couldn't sleep any more. Dawn found him sitting by the window, looking out across the woods and the first grey haze of light across the Solent.

He took the floating bridge across the River Medina to West Cowes – him and a motley collection of cars and vans and cyclists and women with baby buggies. The morning was sharp as a needle but bitterly cold. His breath smoked and he regretted that he hadn't worn his woolly hat.

He found Vectis Press down a sharply sloping side-turning next to a fish-and-chip shop. It had the name Vectis Press Publishers & Stationers written in gold on the door, and a dusty front window display filled with curled-up sheets of headed notepaper, faded calendars and dead flies. He opened the door and a bell jangled.

Inside, there was a cramped office with stacks of books and files and boxes of envelopes. Through the back door he could see an old-fashioned printing press, as well as a new Canon copier. He shuffled his feet and coughed for a while, and after a while a red-faced, white-haired man appeared, wearing a ski sweater with reindeers running across it and a baggy pair of jeans.

The man cocked his head to one side and looked at Michael and didn't say a word.

'I'm – ah – looking for a book you published. I don't know whether you have any copies left. Or perhaps you can tell me where I can find the author.'

The man waited, still saying nothing.

'It's *Queen Victoria's Mystic*, by somebody called Charles Lutterworth. Published 1987.'

The man nodded, and kept on nodding. 'Yes,' he said. 'Yes. I think I can help you there. Yes.'

Michael waited for him to say something else, but he didn't.

'I – ah – do you have a copy here? Could I . . . buy one?'

The man nodded. 'I've got eighty-six copies left. You can have them all if you like. Didn't sell very well, see.'

'Oh, well, I'm sorry to hear that.'

'So am I, considering I wrote it.'

'*You're* Charles Lutterworth?'

'Roger Frost, actually. Charles Lutterworth's my *nom de plume*.'

He went over to an old oak-veneered cabinet and opened it up. It was crammed with books of all sizes. 'Let me see now,' he said, and at last managed to tug out a copy of a thin volume bound in blue.

'There you are. Six quid for cash. What's *your* interest in it?'

'I was doing some research. I came across some reference to Abdul Karim's belief in the resurrection of the dead. I sort of got the idea that Queen Victoria might have found it . . . well, you know, that Queen Victoria might have been very interested in it, considering the loss she felt for Albert.'

Roger Frost tapped the cover of his book with an ink-stained finger. 'It's all in here. All meticulously documented. Chapter and verse. The trouble was, most of the first-hand information came from other Indian servants, and nobody believed what they said. Unthinkable, you know, that our own dear Queen was dabbling in Hindu mysticism.'

'Did she really think that she could bring Albert back to life?'

'That's what Abdul Karim led her to believe. He was more than her *Munshi*, her teacher – he was a highly respected holy man and mystic. It seems he told the Queen that by the end of the second millennium, all disease would have been wiped out, and your dead loved ones could be dug up, cured of what had killed them, and brought back to life.'

'And she believed him.'

'Well, why shouldn't she?' said Roger Frost. He hadn't realized that it wasn't a question. 'You've got to remember that Victoria's reign saw unbelievable strides in science and technology, and enormous advances in medicine, so it must have seemed like quite a reasonable prediction. She knew the story of *Frankenstein*, too – that was republished in 1831 – and if it could happen in a story, why not for real? After all, a lot of people still believe that resurrection is just around the corner – otherwise they wouldn't have their bodies frozen, would they? Idiots.

'It was partly Albert's fault. He was so enthusiastic about science that he convinced Victoria that, with science, absolutely anything was possible. And if you combine that idea with the terrible grief she felt at losing him, it wasn't surprising that she accepted what Abdul Karim told her.'

'And what *did* he tell her?'

'Some of it's hearsay but some of it's documented, too, at Windsor, and in the library in Delhi. Personally, I think that Abdul Karim was doing nothing more than trying to console the Queen – spinning her a bit of mystic yarn, like, to help her recover from Albert's death. But he performed a Hindu ritual which would ensure that the Queen's spirit would reappear at the turn of the next century.

'He actually left a letter attached to his will which required his executors and their assigns to resurrect Albert's body from the Royal Mausoleum at Frogmore as soon as it was scientifically possible, and to inform him that the Queen's spirit would be waiting for him on the anniversary of his death, at Osborne House, which is where they were happiest.'

'Why didn't he leave instructions for *her* body to be resurrected, too?'

'She wanted Albert to supervise *her* revival personally. After all, she was the Queen, Empress of India, and Albert was the only man she trusted to ensure that all went well. She didn't know how she was going to die, you see, and she might have been taken by an illness that wasn't curable yet in the year 2000. In that case, she said, it would be enough to know that *he* had returned to life and vigour, and that she could remain as a shadow at Osborne House to watch him fulfil his destiny.'

Roger Frost handed the book over. 'Unfortunately, as we all know, we still can't bring dead people back to life, no matter what they've died of, and no matter how much we used to love them. And I'm not saying that I don't believe in ghosts, but nobody's ever seen the ghost of Queen Victoria, have they?'

'I have,' said Michael.

'I beg your pardon?'

'There *is* a ghost of Queen Victoria. I saw her last night. I *talked* to her, for God's sake. How do you think I knew about Abdul Karim?'

Roger Frost looked at Michael for a while with his lips pursed. Then he said, 'It's all right. You can have the book for a fiver if you want to.'

'I saw her. She was crying in her bedroom. Then I met her in the children's summer house.'

There was a very long pause, and then Roger Frost said, 'You're serious, aren't you?'

It was eight o'clock, and dark. They stood together in Albert's writing room, listening to the grief-stricken sobbing coming from the Queen's sitting room next door.

'Do you want to see her?' asked Michael.

'I don't know,' said Roger Frost. 'I don't really think I do.'

Michael went to the door and eased it open three or four inches. He could see the small black figure sitting at the writing desk, her head bowed. He beckoned Roger Frost, who, after some hesitation, came to join him.

'Jesus,' was all he said.

Later, Michael said, 'There's only one thing I can think of.'

'What's that?' said Roger Frost, wiping his mouth and putting down his pint. They were sitting in the Old Anchor in West Cowes, a noisy, smoky bar full of yachtsmen.

'Well, we can't just let her wander around Osborne forever, can we? I mean, Albert's never going to come back, which means that she's going to spend the rest of eternity grieving for him. We've got to find a way to put her to rest.'

'Loads of ghosts do that – what's different about her? Just because she's royalty.'

'I can't let her do it, that's all. I can't let her suffer like that.'

'So what do you propose? Get in a priest, and have an exorcism?'

Michael shook his head. 'I read your book last night. In the appendix, you've set out the Hindu ritual that Abdul Karim used to bring her spirit back.'

'That's right. That was in some of his papers. I had it translated. Thought it was cobblers, when I first read it.'

'Well . . . supposing we use the same ritual to bring *Albert's* spirit back? Supposing we reunite them – not physically, we can't do that. But at least we can bring their spirits back together.'

Roger Frost sniffed and helped himself to another handful of dry-roasted peanuts, which he churned around his mouth like a cement mixer. 'I thought you had a screw loose the moment you walked into the shop.'

In the Durbar Room, half an hour before midnight, Michael laid out a pattern of candles on the polished floor, and drew with chalk the *Shri-yantra*, a circular pattern filled with overlapping triangles. If you meditated on this *yantra* long enough, you could look back into the dizzying mouth of space and time, back and back, to the beginning of creation.

The room echoed, except for its dead spots, and the dripping candle-flames made it look as if shadowy spirits were dancing across the coffered ceiling.

Roger came quietly into the room and stood beside him. 'I can't guarantee this is going to work, you know, just because I printed it in my book. For all I know, Abdul Karim was nothing but a shyster.'

'Well, we can only try,' said Michael. He picked up the book and turned to the ritual, the *Paravritti*, the 'turning back up'.

He began to recite the words. 'We who are looking back into time and space, we call you to find the spirit of our lost son, Prince Francis Charles Augustus Albert Emmanuel of Saxe-Coburg, and carry him forward on the stream of creation. Let his spirit rise from where it lies asleep so that it can come to join us here.'

Roger Frost, with a very serious face, began to recite the '*Om* . . .' There was a time when Michael would have found it ludicrous, but here in the Durbar Room, with midnight approaching, and the figures of Indian gods and goddesses leaping in the candlelight, it sounded sonorous and strange, as if it were a summons that could wake up spirits from days and years and centuries long forgotten.

'We call on our lost son Prince Albert to open his eyes and return to the house of his greatest happiness. We call him to rejoin the ones he loved so dearly.'

It was then that Roger touched Michael's arm. From the far door, a small dark shadow had appeared, a small dark shadow with a pale, unfocused face. It made no sound at all, but glided toward them across the floor, until it was standing just outside the circle of candles.

Roger said, 'I'm seeing things.'

'No,' said Michael. 'She's there.'

'What are you doing?' she said, in that tissue-papery voice.

'The ritual,' said Michael. 'Abdul Karim's ritual. We can't bring back the Prince Consort's body. We don't have the power to do that. But perhaps we can bring back his spirit.'

'What? What are you talking about?'

'You can have his spirit back here, at Osborne. You can both be together again.'

'What?' She sounded aghast. 'Don't you understand? Once you've called up a spirit, it can never go back.'

'What do you mean?'

'I mean that, once you've summoned him, he'll have to stay with me, whether he wants to or not, forever.'

'But I thought that's what you—'

Michael was interrupted by a sound like nothing he had ever heard before – a low, agonized moan that made him feel as if centipedes were running up his back. He felt a sudden draft, too – a draft that was chilly and smelled of dust and long-enclosed spaces. The candle flames were blown sideways, and some of them were blown out altogether, so that the Durbar Room became suddenly much gloomier.

Out of the darkness, a dusty-grey figure appeared, so faint that it was almost invisible. It seemed to be moving toward them, but Michael couldn't be sure. The small shadow woman took two or three steps away from it, toward the door. Michael stood where he was, his fists clenched tight, his breath quickening, his heart pounding harder and harder.

The figure stood still for a moment. It was no more substantial than a grey net curtain hanging at a window. Michael thought that he could see a luminous white face, and the indistinct smudges of side whiskers, but that was all. Gradually, as it came nearer, its substance began to thicken and darken.

By the time it was standing by the pattern of candles, the shape was clearly Prince Albert, a small, portly man in young middle-age, deathly white, with a sharp nose and an oval face, and drooping moustaches. He was wearing a dark uniform decorated with medals and a large silver star.

His image wavered, in the same way that a television screen wavers when somebody moves the aerial. He turned this way and that, as if he couldn't understand where he was or what was happening.

'Albert,' Roger whispered. 'It's Albert, you've brought him back.'

The figure opened and closed its mouth but didn't seem able to speak. Michael kept squeezing his eyes tight shut and opening them again, because he simply could not believe that this was real.

It was then that the shadow-woman walked around the *Shri-yantra* and glided slowly toward Albert with both arms outstretched.

'My love,' was all she said. 'Oh, my love.'

Albert stared at her. At first it was obvious that he didn't recognize her. She came closer, and took hold of both of his hands, and said, 'It is *I*, my love. They've brought you back to me.'

'Back?' he whispered, his voice thick with horror. '*Back?*'

'This is Osborne,' she said. 'You never lived to see this room. But this is Osborne. We can be happy again, my darling. We can stay here forevermore.'

Albert slowly pushed her away from him, still staring at her. 'What's happened to you?' he asked her. 'Can this really be you? What's happened to you? Your hair! Your skin! You've withered away! What kind of devilish spell have they cast on you?'

Michael said, 'No spell, sir. Only time.'

Albert frowned at Michael like an actor peering into a darkened audience. '*Time?*'

'You died at the age of forty-two, sir,' put in Roger. 'Your Queen here was eighty-one when she went.'

Victoria looked up at him in anguish. 'I am still myself, my love. And I have kept my love for you intact, for so many years.'

Albert's mouth opened and closed, but he still couldn't speak. Something glistened on his cheeks, and Michael realized that he was witnessing an extraordinary spiritual phenomenon – the sight of a spirit, crying.

'I am still your darling,' begged the shadow-woman, reaching out again to touch him. 'I am still your wife and the mother of your children.'

'And they?' asked Albert, his mouth puckered with grief.

'Dead, sir,' said Roger. 'All long dead. I'm sorry.'

Albert gradually sank to his knees, and his head dropped as if he were waiting for an execution that would never come. The shadow-woman put her hands on his shoulders, but he was inconsolable. She had lost her young husband when he died, but now he had woken from the dead to discover that he had lost his sparkling young wife.

'Can you not find it in your heart to love me, now that I am old?' asked the shadow-woman.

Albert couldn't answer. All he could do was bury his face in his hands and remain where he was, too grief-stricken to move, while the candles in the Durbar Room guttered and died.

Michael saw them only once more, on the afternoon that he was due to leave. He was carrying his suitcase out to a waiting taxi when he happened to turn and look along the broad avenue that led to the shore of the Solent. It was difficult to see them, in the foggy half-light, but it looked as if they were walking very slowly toward the house. She was leaning on his arm for support. He had his face turned away from her.

Michael watched them for a while, then climbed into the taxi.

'Are you all right?' asked the taxi driver.

'Yes, why?' said Michael, and it was only then that he realized that his eyes were filled with tears.

WITCH-COMPASS

On his last night in Libreville, Paul went for a long, aimless walk through the market. A heavy rainstorm had just passed over and the air was almost intolerably humid. He felt as if he had a hot Turkish towel wrapped around his head, and his shirt clung to his back. There were many things that he would miss about Gabon, but the climate wasn't one of them, and neither was the musty smell of tropical mould.

All along the Marché Rouge there were stalls heaped with bananas and plantains and cassava; as well as food stands selling curried goat and thick maize porridge and spicy fish. The stalls were lit by an elaborate spiderweb of electric cables, with naked bulbs dangling from them. Each stall was like a small, brightly coloured theatre, with the sweaty black faces of its actors wreathed in theatrical steam and smoke.

Paul passed them by, a tall rangy white man with short-cropped hair and round Oliver Goldsmith glasses, and already he was beginning to feel like a spectator, like somebody who no longer belonged here.

A thin young girl with one milky eye tugged at Paul's shirt and offered him a selection of copper bracelets. He was about to shoo her away when he suddenly thought: what does it matter any more? I won't be here tomorrow; I'll be on my way back to the States, and what good will a wallet full of CFA francs be in New Milford, Connecticut?

He gave the girl five francs, which was more than she probably made in a week, and took one of the bracelets.

'*Merci beaucoup, monsieur, vous êtes très gentil*,' she said, with a strong Fang accent. She gave him a gappy grin and twirled off into the crowds.

Paul looked down at his wallet. He had hardly any money left now. Three hundred francs, an American Express card which he didn't dare to use, and a damp-rippled air ticket. He was almost as poor as the rest of the population of Gabon.

He had come here three and a half years ago to set up his own metals-trading business. Gradually he had built up a network of contacts amongst the foreign mining companies and established a reputation for achieving the highest prices for the least administration costs. After two years, he was able to rent a grand white house near the presidential palace and import a new silver Mercedes. But his increasing success brought him to the attention of governments officials, and before long he had been summoned to the offices of the department of trade. A highly amused official in a snowy short-sleeved shirt had informed him that, in future, all of his dealings would attract a 'brokerage tax' of eighty-five per cent.

'Eighty-five per cent! Do you want me to starve?'

'You exaggerate, Mr Dennison. The average Gabonese makes less in a year than you spend on one pair of shoes. Yet he eats, he has clothes on his back. What more do you need than that?'

Paul had refused to pay. But the next week, when he had tried to call LaSalle Zinc, he had been told with a great deal of apologetic French clucking that they could no longer do business with him, because of 'internal rationalization'. He had received a similar response from DuFreyne Lead and Pan-African Manganese. The following week his phones had been cut off altogether.

He had lived off his savings for a few months, trying to take legal action to have the 'brokerage tax' rescinded or at least reduced. But the Gabonese legal system owed more to Franz Kafka than it did to commercial justice. In the end his lawyer had withdrawn his services, too, and he knew there was no point in fighting his case any further.

He walked right down to the western end of the Marché Rouge. Beneath his feet, the lights from the market stalls were reflected like a drowned world. The air was filled with repetitive, plangent music, and the clamour of so many insects, that it sounded as if somebody were scraping a rake over a corrugated iron roof.

At the very end of the market, in the shadows, an old woman was sitting cross-legged on the wet tarmac with an upturned fruit box in front of her. She had a smooth, round face and her hair was twisted into hundreds of tiny silver beads. She wore a dark brown dress with black-printed patterns on it, zigzags and circles and twig-like figures. She kept nodding her head in Paul's direction, as if he were talking to her and she was agreeing with him, and as she nodded her huge silver earrings swung and caught the light from the fish stall next to her.

On the fruit box several odd items were arranged. At the back, a small ebony carving of a woman with enormous breasts and protruding buttocks, her lips fastened together with silver wire. Next to her feet lay something that looked like a rattle made out of a dried bone and a shrunken monkey's head, with matted ginger hair. There were six or seven Pond's Cold Cream jars, refilled with brown and yellowish paste. There was a selection of necklaces, decorated with teeth and beads and birds' bones. And there was an object which looked like a black gourd, only three or four inches long and completely plain.

Paul was about to turn back to his hotel when the woman said, '*Attendez, monsieur! Ne voulez-vous pas acheter mes jouets?*'

She said it in surprise, as if she couldn't understand why he hadn't come up to her and asked her how much they cost.

'I'm sorry, I'm just taking a walk.'

She passed her hands over the disparate collection on top of her fruit box. 'I think that is why you come here. To buy from me something.'

'No, I'm sorry.'

'Then what is bringing your feet this way?'

'I'm leaving Libreville tomorrow morning. I was taking a last look around the market, that's all.'

'You come this way for a reason. No man comes looking for Jonquil Mekambo by accident.'

'Listen,' said Paul. 'I really have to go. And to tell you the truth, I don't think you have anything here that I could possibly want.'

The woman lifted up the ebony figure. 'Silence those who do you bad, *peut-être*?'

'Oh, I get it. This is ju-ju stuff. Thanks but no thanks. Really.'

The woman picked up the bone with the monkey's head and tapped it on the side of the box. 'Call up demons to strangle your enemy? I teach you how to knock.'

'Listen, forget it. I got enough demons in my life right now without conjuring up any more.'

'Jonquil knows that. Jonquil knows why you have to go from Libreville. No money, no work.'

Paul stared at her. She stared back, her face like a black, expressionless moon. 'How did you know that?' he demanded.

'Jonquil knows all thing. Jonquil is waiting for you here *ce soir*.'

'Well, Jonquil, however you found out, there's nothing you can do to help me. It's going to take more than black magic to sort my life out. I'll have to start over again, right from scratch.'

'Then you need witch-compass.'

'Oh, yes? And what's a witch-compass going to do for me, whatever that is?'

Jonquil pointed with a red-painted fingernail to the gourd. 'Witch-compass, genuine from Makokou.'

'So what does a witch-compass do?'

'Brings your feet to what you want. Money, woman, house. Work all time.'

'I see. Never fails. So what are *you* doing, sitting in the street here, if you could use the witch-compass to guide you to whatever you want?'

'Jonquil has what she wants. All thing.'

Paul shook his head. 'It's a great idea, Jonquil. But I think I'll pass.'

'Pick it up,' Jonquil urged him.

Paul hesitated for a moment. For some reason, the pattering of drums sounded louder than usual, more insistent, and the insects scraped even more aggressively. He picked up the black gourd and weighed it in his hand. It was quite light, and obviously hollow, because he could hear something rattling around inside it. Beads, maybe; or seeds.

'See in your head the thing that you want,' said Jonquil. 'The witch-compass makes its song. Quiet when you want is far off distance. Louder – louder when close.'

'Kind of a Geiger counter, then,' smiled Paul. 'Except it looks for luck instead of radiation.'

'Money, woman, house. Work all time.'

Paul rolled the witch-compass over and over in his hand. There was something very smooth and attractive about it, like a giant worry-bead. 'I don't know,' he said. 'It depends how much it is.'

'*Il y a deux prix*,' said Jonquil.

'Two prices? What do you mean?'

'*En termes d'argent, le prix est quatorze francs. Mais il y a également un prix moral à payer, chaque fois la boussole pointe sur ce que vous désirez.*'

'I have to make a moral choice? Is that what you said?'

Jonquil nodded again. 'No thing that you truly desire come free.'

Paul gently shook the witch-compass and heard its soft, seductive shaking sound.

'All right,' he said. 'Fourteen francs. If it works, I'll come back and thank you in person. If it doesn't, I won't be able to afford to come back.'

'You will come back,' Jonquil assured him, as he counted out the money. 'Your feet will bring you back.'

It was dry and breezy when he arrived back in New Milford. The sky was startlingly blue and red and yellow leaves were whirling and dancing on the green. He drove his rental car slowly through the town, feeling just as much of a ghost as he had on his last night in Gabon. He saw people he knew. Old Mr Dawson, with a new Labrador puppy. Gremlin, his previous dog, must have died. Jim Salzberger, leaning against a red pick-up truck, talking to Annie Nilsen.

The same white-painted buildings, dazzling in the sunlight. The same town clock, with its bright blue dial. Paul drove slowly through but he didn't stop. He didn't want anybody to know that he was back, not just yet. He had been crackling with ambition when he left this town, and his parents had been so proud of him when he made his first hundred thousand dollars in Libreville. But here he was, back and bankrupt, more or less, without even the will to start over.

He drove out along the deserted highway to Allen's Corners, past Don Humphrey's general store. The sunlight flickered through the car windows, so that he felt that he was watching an old home movie of his previous life.

At last he took the steep turn up through the woods that led to his parents' house. It wasn't much of a place: a single-storey building on the side of a hill, with an awkwardly angled driveway and a small triangular yard. His father was out back, sawing logs with his old circular saw, and there was a tangy smell of woodsmoke in the air.

He parked behind his father's Oldsmobile and climbed out. His father immediately called out, 'Jeannie! Jeannie! Look who's here!' and came hurrying down the steps. He was a tall man, although he wasn't as tall as Paul, with cropped grey hair and the slight stoop of somebody who has worked hard in an office all his life, and never quite managed to fulfil himself. Paul's mother came out of the kitchen still carrying a saucepan. She was tall, for a woman, and although her hair was grey she looked ten years younger than she really was. She was wearing a pink chequered blouse with the sleeves rolled up, and jeans.

'Why didn't you say you were coming to see us?' asked his mother, with tears in her eyes. 'I don't have a thing in!'

His father slapped him on the back and ushered him up the steps into the house. 'I guess he wanted to surprise us, didn't you, son?'

'That's right,' said Paul. 'I didn't know that I was coming back until the day before yesterday.'

'It's great to see you.' His father smiled. 'You've lost some weight, haven't you? Hope you've been eating properly. All work and no lunch makes Jack a skinny-looking runt.'

'I should have gone to the market,' said his mother. 'I could have made your favourite pot roast.'

'Don't worry about that,' his father said. 'We can eat out tonight. Remember Randolph's Restaurant? That was taken over, about a year ago, and you should see it now! They do a lobster chowder to die for!'

'Oh, Dan, that's far too expensive,' said his mother.

'What do you mean? Our son here's used to the best, aren't you, son? How's that Mercedes-Benz of yours running? Or have you traded it in for something new?'

'Oh . . . I'm maybe thinking about a Porsche.'

'A Porsche! Isn't that something! A Dennison driving a Porsche! Listen, how about a beer and you can tell us how things are going.'

'Well, to tell you the truth, I'm kind of pooped.'

'Sure you are, I'm sorry. Why don't you go to your room and wash up? You can fill us in when you're good and ready.'

His mother said, 'How long are you staying for?'

He gave her a quick, tight smile. 'I don't know . . . it depends on a couple of business deals.'

She held his eye for a moment and there was something in the way she looked at him that told him she suspected he wasn't entirely telling the truth. His mother had always known when he was lying. Either that, or he always felt guilty when he lied to her, and it showed.

He hefted his bag out of the car and carried it through to the small room at the back. It was depressingly familiar, although it had a new green carpet and new curtains with green and white convolvulus flowers on them. His high-school football trophies were still arranged on top of the bureau, and there was a large photograph of him at the age of eleven, clutching a shaggy red dog. He sat down on the bed and covered his face with his hands. Eleven years of work. Eleven years of talking and travelling and staying up till two or three in the morning. All of it gone, all of it – and nothing to show for it but a single suitcase and twenty-three CFA francs – not convertible into dollars, and not worth anything even if they were.

His father came in with a can of Coors. 'Here – I'll bet you can't get this in Libreville.'

'No, we get French beer mainly. Or there's the local brew. OK for cleaning drains.'

He opened up the suitcase. Two pairs of pants, one crumpled linen coat, a pair of brown leather sandals, socks and shorts. His father said, 'You're travelling extra-light. The last time you came, you had so many cases I though that Madonna was visiting.'

'Well . . . I wasn't given too much notice.'

He took the witch-compass out of the side pocket in his suitcase and put it next to his football cups.

'What the two-toned tonkert is that?' asked his father.

'It's kind of a good-luck charm.'

'Oh, yeah?' His father picked it up and shook it. 'Looks like a giant sheep dropping to me.'

Paul hung his clothes up in the closet.

'You're quiet,' said his father. 'Everything's OK, isn't it?'

'Sure, sure. Everything's OK.'

His father laid a hand on his shoulder. 'I'll tell you who else is around. You remember that Katie Sayward you used to like so much? Her marriage broke up, so she's back here with her aunt, to get over it.'

Paul said, 'What? I didn't even know she was married.'

'Yeah. She married some actor she met in New York. Real good-looking guy. *Too* good-looking, if you know what I mean. I met him once when she came up to Sherman to see her aunt. So far as I know, he had an affair with some girl in the chorus-line and Katie was totally devastated. If you do see her, I wouldn't mention it if I were you. Not unless she brings it up first.'

Paul went to the window and pressed his forehead against the cold glass. Outside, the yard sloped steeply uphill towards a thicket of dry brown bracken. Katie Sayward. He had always adored Katie Sayward, even when he was in grade school. Katie Sayward, with her skinny ankles and her skinny wrists and her shining brown hair that swung whenever she turned her head. Even when she was younger, her lips always looked as if she had just finished kissing someone. She had grown into a beautiful young woman, with a head-turning figure. Paul had only plucked up the courage once to ask her for a date. He could remember it even today – walking into the home room in front of all the other girls, and saying, 'Katie, how about you and me going out for a burger tonight?' Katie had clamped her hand over mouth, and widened her eyes, and then she had burst out laughing. The memory of it still made him feel hot and uncomfortable.

So Katie Sayward had married. Well, of course she had married, a lovely girl like that. It was just that he hadn't wanted to hear about it. And worse than that, her husband had cheated on her. How could he have cheated on Katie Sayward, when she was the perfect, perfect girl?

His mother came into the room. 'You're sure you don't want anything to eat? I could make you a bologna sandwich. I don't suppose you get much bologna in Gabon.'

'I'm fine, Mom. Honestly. Let me grab a few zees, that's all.'

'OK,' said his father, giving him another affectionate clap on the shoulder. 'I'll wake you up in time for dinner.'

Randolph's Restaurant was decorated in the style of an old colonial inn, with wheelback chairs and softly shaded lamps on the tables and antique warming pans hanging on the walls. They sat right in the middle of the restaurant, and Paul's father kept turning around in his chair and calling out to people he knew.

'Dick! Janice! Paul's back from darkest Africa! Sure, doing real good, aren't you, Paul? Business is booming! Counting on buying himself a new Porsche, top-of-the-range!'

Paul glanced at his mother. She was still smiling, but he definitely had the feeling that she knew something wasn't quite right.

His father ordered two large martinis to start, and a mimosa for his mother. Then he opened up the oversized leatherbound menu and said, 'OK! Let's push the boat out!'

He ordered oysters and caviar with sour cream and blinis. He ordered steak and lobster and fresh chargrilled tuna. They drank Roederer champagne with the hors d'oeuvres and Pauillac with the entrées, $97.50 a bottle.

Paul's father did most of the talking. Paul sat with his head lowered, chewing his way unenthusiastically through his meal. He couldn't even taste the difference between the steak and the lobster, and he left his beans and broccoli untouched.

'You must be feeling jet-lagged,' said his mother, laying her hand on top of his.

'Yes . . . kind of. I'll be OK tomorrow.'

The pianist on the opposite side of the room was playing a slow bluesy version of 'Buddy, Can You Spare A Dime?' and he almost felt like standing up and walking out.

'You know something?' said his father, with his mouth full, and a shred of lobster dangling from his lip. 'I'm so proud of you, Paul, I could stand right up in this restaurant and shout it out loud. My only son, started from humble beginnings, but had the guts to go to Africa all on his own and make himself a hundred million.'

'Well, I'm not so sure about the hundred million,' said Paul.

'You mark my words – if you haven't made a hundred million yet, you sure will soon! That's what you're made of! That's why I'm so proud of you!'

They finished the meal with Irish coffees in the cocktail lounge. Paul's father grew more and more talkative and when he started to tell stories about his high-school days, losing his shorts in the swimming pool and falling into the rhododendron bushes, Paul asked for the check.

'That's real generous of you, Paul.' His father beamed. Then he turned to his mother and said, 'How many people have a wealthy young son who can take his folks out for a night like this?'

Paul opened the leather folder with the check inside. It was $378.69, gratuity at your discretion. Suddenly he couldn't hear the piano music any more.

'How is it?' asked his father. 'National debt of Gabon, I'll bet.'

'Something like that,' said Paul, numbly, and reached into his coat with fingers that felt as if they were frostbitten. He took out his wallet and opened it, while his mother watched him silently and his father chatted with the cocktail waitress.

'In Gabon, you understand, they respect Americans. They trust them. Wouldn't surprise me at all if Paul ends up running a big mining corporation over there.'

Paul said, 'Shit.'

'What? What is it?'

'All the money I changed . . . I left it back in my suitcase.'

'You can use your card, can't you?'

'No, no, I can't. It's only for use in Africa.'

'But that's an American Express card. That's good anywhere.'

'Not this one, no. I have a special deal. They bill me in CFA francs, so that I save myself twelve-and-a-half per cent handling charges.'

Paul's father pulled a face. 'Don't you have Visa, or MasterCard?'

'Left them back in my suitcase, too. Stupid of me. Mom's right. I must be jet-lagged.'

'Looks like we're going to have to wash the dishes,' said his father.

'I'll tell you what I can do,' Paul volunteered. 'I can come back early tomorrow, soon as you open, and pay you then. How's that? I can leave my watch if you like.'

'Oh, that's OK,' smiled the waitress. 'I think we can trust you, don't you? And what is it they say in those gangster movies? We know where you live.'

They all laughed and Paul tucked his wallet back in his coat and said, 'Thanks.' Shit. Where was he going to raise more than four hundred dollars by lunchtime tomorrow? He could pawn his watch, he supposed. It was a nine hundred dollar Baume & Mercier that had been given to him by the sales director of a French copper company. His ten thousand dollar Rolex had long gone, in legal fees. He just hoped that Robard's jewellers was still in business.

His mother took his arm as they left the restaurant and walked across the parking lot. It was a cold, dry night.

'Winter's coming early this year,' said his mother. His father was weaving ahead of them, singing erratic lines from 'Buddy Can You Spare A Dime?' 'Once I was a bigshot . . . now I'm broke.'

'Well, we don't get much of a winter in Libreville.'

'Is everything all right, Paul?'

'Sure. What do you mean? Everything's great.'

'I don't know. You look – I'm not quite sure what the word is. *Haunted*, I guess.'

'Haunted?' He laughed. 'You make me sound like Hill House.'

'But everything's OK? The business? You're not sick, are you?'

'I got over the dengue months ago.'

'You will tell me, though, if anything's wrong?'

He gave her a kiss and nodded, and then he hurried her along a little faster, so that they would catch up with his father. 'Dad! Dad! Come on, Dad, there's no way that I'm going to let you drive!'

That night he lay in bed listening to the leaves whispering in the yard outside. He felt infinitely tired, but he couldn't even close his eyes. The moonlight fell across the wall as white as a bone.

He ought to tell his parents that he was bankrupt. He ought to tell them that he was never going back to Gabon, couldn't go back. He knew his father would be crushed, but how much longer could he keep up this pretence? Yet he felt that if he told his parents, he would reduce himself to the level of a hopeless alcoholic, finally admitting that he couldn't summon up the willpower to quit on his own.

His parents' admiration was all he had left.

The digital clock beside the bed told him it was 3.57. It clicked on to 3.58 – and it was then that he heard a soft shaking noise, like dry rice in a colander.

He raised his head from the pillow. It must have been the leaves, skittering in the wind. But as he lowered his head he heard it again, much sharper this time. *Shikk – shikk – shikk!* And again, even louder. *Shikk – shikk – shikk!*

He swung his legs out of bed and walked across to the bureau. There, amongst his football trophies, lay the black smooth shape of the witch-compass. It was shivering, very slightly, and as it shivered, the beads or seeds inside it set up that *shikk – shikk – shikk!* sound.

Cautiously, he picked it up. It felt as pleasant to hold as it always did; yet tonight it seemed to have life in it. It vibrated, and shook again. He pointed it towards the window. It stopped vibrating, and the *shikk* sound stopped, too. He pointed it toward the closet. It vibrated again, but only softly. Next he pointed it towards the door. It gave a brisk shiver and almost jumped out of his hand.

It's guiding me, Paul thought. *It's guiding me to what I want.*

He tested it again, pointing it back at the window, back at the closet, back at the door. As soon as he pointed it towards the door, it became more and more excited.

Supposing it's showing me how to find some money. That's what I need more than anything.

Hurriedly, he pulled on his shirt and his pants and his shoes. Then, breathing hard, he eased open his bedroom door and stepped into the darkened hallway. He could hear his father snoring like a beached whale, and the clock ticking loudly on the wall. He pointed the witch-compass north, south, east and west. It shook most vigorously when he pointed it towards the front door. It was guiding him out of the house.

He walked as quietly as he could across the polished oak floor. He lifted a nylon windbreaker down from the pegs by the door. Then he eased open the chains, drew back the bolts and went out into the cold, windy night.

The witch-compass led him down the front steps and down the narrow, winding road that led to the main highway between New Milford and New Preston. Although it was only four in the morning, the sky was strangely light, as if a UFO had landed behind the trees. Paul's footsteps scrunched through the leaves at the side of the road and his father's windbreaker made a loud rustling noise. It smelled of his father's pipe-smoke, and there was a plastic lighter in the pocket.

And all the time, the witch-compass rattled in his hand with ever-increasing eagerness.

He had just reached the hairpin bend that would take him down to the highway, when he heard a car coming, from quite a long way off, but coming fast. He began to hurry around the bend and down the steeply sloping road, and as he did so he glimpsed headlights from the direction of New Milford. It looked as if it were travelling at more than seventy miles an hour.

He hadn't even reached the highway when he heard a sickening bang and a shrieking of tyres, and then a sound like an entire junkyard dropping out of the sky. Wheels, fenders, mufflers, windows, crunching and screeching and smashing. Then complete silence, which was worse.

Paul came running around the corner and saw the bloodied body of a dead deer lying in the scrub on the far side of the highway, its legs twisted at extraordinary angles, as if it were trying to ballet dance. Almost a hundred feet further up, a battered, dented Chevrolet was resting on its roof. Shattered glass glittered all over the blacktop.

'Jesus.' Paul started to run towards the wreck. As he came closer he saw that the driver was still in his seat, suspended upside-down in his seat belt. His deflated air bag hung in front of him, and it had obviously saved his life. He was groaning loudly and trying to wrestle himself free.

'Hold on!' Paul called out. He crunched though the glass and then he realized that he was splashing through a quickly widening pool of gasoline.

'Get me out of here,' the driver begged him. He was a heavily built, fiftyish man. His grey hair was matted with blood. 'I think my goddam legs are crushed.'

'OK, OK, just hold on,' Paul reassured him. He was about to put the witch-compass into his pocket when it gave a high-pitched *shikkashikkashikka!* that sounded like a snake hissing. Paul looked down and saw the driver's pigskin billfold lying on the road, right in front of him. Even without picking it up, he could see that it was stuffed with money.

'Oh God, please get me out of here,' moaned the driver. 'This is hurting so much.'

Paul reluctantly took his eyes away from the billfold. He took hold of the Chevrolet's door handle and tried to drag it open, but it was wedged solid. He went around to the other side of the car and tried the passenger door, but that wouldn't budge either.

He came back to the driver's side and reached into the broken window. He managed to locate the man's seat-belt buckle. But the crash had jammed it and the man's bulging stomach was straining against it. His shirt was soaked in warm, sticky blood.

'Please, I'm dying here. Please.'

Paul said, 'OK, but I can't get you out by myself. I'm going to have to call the fire department.'

'Hurry, please.'

Paul took hold of his hand and squeezed it. 'Just hold on. I'll be as quick as I can.'

But in his pocket the witch-compass went *shikkashikkashikka!*

Paul slowly stepped away from the wreck. He looked down and

there was the pigskin billfold. He could see fifties and twenties. More than enough to settle his restaurant bill. More than enough to buy him a new coat and a new pair of jeans and see him through the next few days. He hesitated for a second and turned back to the man hanging in the car, and the man was looking up at him, bleeding and broken and pleading with him: *Get me out of here, for Chrissakes.* But the worst possible idea came into his head – an idea so terrible that he could hardly believe that he had thought of it. And inside his pocket, the witch-compass rattled and shook as if it were a living thing.

He stooped down and picked up the billfold. The man in the car watched him, unable to comprehend what he was seeing. Paul took all of the cash out of the billfold except for $50. He didn't want to make it obvious that the man had been robbed. He held up the billfold for a moment and then he dropped it back on to the road.

Shikkashikkashikka.

'What are you going to do?' the driver asked him. 'Look, take the fucking money. I don't care. Just call the fire department, get me out of here.'

But Paul knew that it would be different once the man was released. *I was trapped, I was dying, and he stole my money, right in front of me.*

He walked a few paces back down the road. '*No!*' the driver screamed at him. '*Don't leave me here! Don't!*'

Paul stopped. He lowered his head. In his pocket he felt the witch-compass, warm and thrilling. The witch-compass was guiding him away from the wreck, back to his parents' house. Leave him, what does he mean to you? He was driving too fast anyhow. Everybody knows there are deer on these highways. Supposing you hadn't woken up? Supposing the witch-compass hadn't brought you here. The stupid bastard would have died anyhow, alone.

'*Don't leave me!*' the driver screamed at him. '*I'm dying here, for Chrissake! Don't leave me!*'

In one pocket, Paul felt the witch-compass. In the other, he felt his father's cigarette lighter. He turned around. There are two prices, Jonquil had told him. Fourteen francs; and a moral choice, every time the witch-compass finds you what you want.

The driver was suddenly silent. He had seen Paul flick the cigarette lighter, and stand in the road with the flame dipping in the early-morning breeze. The flame was reflected in the gasoline which was running across the road into the ditch.

Paul genuflected, and lit it.

The fire raced back towards the upturned car. The driver twisted and struggled in one last desperate effort to pull himself free.

'*You could have had the money!*' he screamed at Paul. '*I would have given you the fucking money!*'

Then the whole car exploded like a Viking fireship and furiously burned. Paul gradually backed away, feeling the heat on his face and the cold wind blowing on his back. He saw the driver's arm wagging from side to side, and then it kind of hooked up and bent as the heat of the fire shrivelled his tendons. As he walked up the winding road towards his parents' house he could still see it burning behind the trees.

Afterwards, he sat down on his bed and counted his money. Six hundred and fifty-five dollars, still reeking of gasoline. On top of the bureau, the witch-compass lay silent.

He drove into New Milford the next morning to pay off Randolph's Restaurant. 'Glad you didn't try to leave the county.' The owner smiled, counting his money. 'I'd have had to set my old dog out looking for you.'

The dog lay in the corner of the restaurant, an ancient basset hound, snoring as loudly as Paul's father.

On his way home, he took a different route, the road that led up to Gaylordsville and then meandered through the woods to South Kent. He didn't want to go past the scene of last night's auto wreck again. This morning, when he had driven by, the rusty and blackened Chevrolet was still lying on its roof in the road, surrounded by fire trucks and police cars with their lights flashing.

It was another pin-sharp day. All around him, the woods were ablaze with yellows and crimsons and dazzling scarlets. Every now and then he checked his eyes in the rear-view mirror to see if he could detect any guilt, or any emotion at all. But all he felt was reasonably satisfied. Not over-satisfied, but the edge had been taken off his anxiety.

He slowed as he reached the intersection where the road led back towards New Preston. About a quarter of a mile beyond it, screened by trees, stood the yellow-painted house where Katie Sayward's aunt lived, and where Katie was staying after the break-up of her marriage. The times he had driven past here when he was younger, hoping to see her. Maybe he should pay her a visit now. But what would he say? 'You thought I was an idiot when we were at school together, sorry about your marriage'?

He drove past slowly, no more than ten miles an hour, ducking his head so that he could peer beneath the branches of the trees. Nobody was in sight. But as he pressed the accelerator to move away, he heard a crisp *shikk! shikk! shikk!*

He slowed down again. The witch-compass was inside the glovebox. It started a series of quick, rhythmic rattles. As he drove further away from Katie's house, however, the rattles became less and less frequent. When he reached the next bend, they stopped altogether.

He pulled the car in by the side of the road. The witch-compass remained silent. *It's trying to tell me something about Katie. It's guiding me back.*

He turned the car around and drove slowly back towards the yellow-painted house. Inside the glovebox, the witch-compass started to rattle again *shikkaSHIKKAshikkaSHIKKA* like a Gabonese drumbeat.

Katie's marriage has broken up. Maybe the witch-compass is trying to tell me that she needs somebody. Maybe it's trying to tell me that Katie needs me.

Cautiously, he drove in through the gates and up the driveway to the house. Nobody came out to greet him and the place looked as if it were deserted. No vehicles around, and no smoke pouring from chimneys. Paul climbed out of the car and went up to the front porch and knocked. There was no answer, so he knocked again. He didn't like the knocker. It was bronze, cast into the face of a sly, blind old man. He waited, whistling between his teeth.

No, nobody in. The witch-compass must have made a mistake. He walked back to the car and opened the door. The rattling inside the glovebox was practically hysterical, and he could hear the witch-compass knocking from side to side, as if it were trying to break out.

'All right, already,' he said. He took the witch-compass out of the glovebox and held it in his hand. Then he walked back to the house, and knocked again – so loudly this time that he could hear the knocks echo in the hall. Still no reply.

'There, what did I tell you? There's nobody home.'

Shikkashikkashikka rattled the witch-compass.

Paul pointed it towards the front door of the house, and its rattling died away. He swept it slowly backwards and forwards, and the witch-compass rattled most excitedly when he pointed it to the side of the house.

'OK, let's check this out.'

He walked around the house, past a trailing wisteria, until he found the kitchen door at the back. He knocked with his knuckle on the window, just in case there was somebody inside, and then he turned the handle. It was unlocked, so he opened it and stepped inside.

'Hello!' he called. 'Anybody home?'

Shikkashikkashikka.

'Look, it's no good shaking like that. There's nobody home.'

Shikkashikkashikka.

The witch-compass guided him into the hall, towards the foot of the staircase. At the top of the staircase there was a landing with an amber stained-glass window, so that the inside of the house looked like a sepia photograph.

Shikkashikkashikka.

'Upstairs? All right then. I just hope you know what you're doing.'

Paul climbed the stairs and the witch-compass led him along the landing to the very last door. He knocked again, but there was no reply, and so he carefully opened it. The witch-compass was shaking wildly in his hand and he had to grip it tight so that he wouldn't drop it.

He found himself in a large bedroom, with an old-fashioned dark-oak bed, and a huge walnut armoire. The windows were covered in heavy lace curtains with peacock patterns on them, so the light inside the bedroom was very dim. The bed was covered with an antique patchwork quilt; on top of the quilt lay Katie Sayward, naked.

Now the witch-compass was silent. Paul took a breath and held it, and didn't know if he ought to leave immediately, or stay where he was, watching her. She was older, of course, and she had cut her long hair short, but she was still just as beautiful as he remembered. She was lying on her back with her eyes closed, her arms spread wide as if she were floating, like Ophelia. She was full-breasted, with a flat stomach and long legs. *My perfect woman*, thought Paul. *The kind of woman I've always wanted.*

He took two or three steps into the room. The floorboards creaked and he hesitated, but she didn't show any signs of waking. Now he could see between her legs, and he stood transfixed, breathing softly through his mouth.

He took another step closer. He wanted to touch her so much that it was a physical ache, but he knew what would happen if he tried. The same ridicule that he had suffered when he'd asked her for a date at high school. Shame and embarrassment, and trouble with the law.

It was then, however, that he saw the empty bottle of Temazepam tablets on her nightstand and the tipped-over bottle of vodka on the quilt and the letter she was holding in her right hand.

He took another step closer, then another. Then he sat on the bed beside her and said, 'Katie . . . Katie, can you hear me? It's Paul.'

Katie didn't stir. Paul gently patted her cheek. She was still breathing. She was still warm. But she was deathly pale. He peeled back one of her eyelids with his thumb. Her blue eye stared up at him sightlessly, its pupil widely dilated.

He lifted her right wrist so that he could read the note. 'Dearest Aunt Jessie. I know this is a selfish and horrible thing to do to you. But a life without James just isn't any kind of life at all.'

Paul felt her pulse. It was thready, but her heart was still beating. If he called the paramedics now, there was a strong possibility that they could save her. She would be grateful to him, wouldn't she, for the rest of her life? There might even be a chance that . . .

His arm brushed against her bare breast and it gave a heavy, complicated sway. There might be a chance in the future that he and Katie could get together. But if they got together *now*, then he could be sure of having her. Maybe just once. But even once was better than never.

He stood up and very deliberately took off his clothes, staring down at Katie all the time. He had never dared to dream that this could ever happen; and now it was, and he could do whatever he wanted to her, anything, and she wouldn't resist.

He climbed on to the quilt. His body was thin and wiry and his skin was very white, except for his face and his forearms and his knees, which had been tanned dark by the equatorial sun. He kissed

Katie on the lips, and then her eyelids, and then her cheeks, and he whispered in her ear that he loved her, and that she was the most desirable woman he had ever known. He squeezed her breasts and sucked at her nipples. Then he ran his tongue all the way down her stomach and buried his face between her thighs.

He stayed in her bedroom for over an hour, and he used her body in every way he had ever fantasized about. He couldn't believe it was real, and he wanted it never to end. He turned her over, face down in the pillow, and forced himself into her, but it was then that she gave a shudder that he could feel all the way through him, right to the soles of his feet.

He leaned forward, his cheek close to hers. 'Katie? Speak to me, Katie! Just let me hear you breathing, Katie, come on!'

She was silent and her body was completely lifeless. He took himself out of her and stood up, wiping the back of his hand across his forehead. *Shikk!* went the witch-compass.

Paul dressed, feeling numb; and then he rearranged Katie as he had found her. He cleaned between her thighs with tissues, wiped her face. He had bruised her a little: there were fingermarks over her buttocks and breasts, and a lovebite on her neck. But who would ever think that *he* had inflicted them? So far as anybody was aware, they hardly even knew each other.

He left the house by the kitchen door, taking care to wipe the door handle with the tail of his shirt. He drove back the way he had come, through Gaylordsville, crossing the Housatonic at Fort Hill so that he could deny having driven back towards his parents' house on the South Kent Road. He even made a point of tooting his horn and waving to Charlie Sheagus, the realtor.

And how do you feel? he asked his eyes, in the rear-view mirror.

Satisfied, his eyes replied. Not *fully* satisfied, but it's taken the edge off.

His father was waiting for him in the living room when he returned. He was wearing a chequered red shirt and oversized jeans and he looked crumple-faced and serious. His mother was sitting in the corner, in the shadows, her hands clasped on her lap.

'Where've you been?' his father wanted to know.

'Hey, why the long face? I went down to Randolph's to settle the check.'

'It's a pity you haven't been settling all of your checks the same way.'

Paul said, 'What? What are you talking about?'

'I'm talking about Budget Rental Cars, who just called up to say that your credit rating hadn't checked out. And Marriott Hotels, who said that you bounced a personal cheque for two hundred dollars. And then I called Dennison Minerals, your own company, in Gabon, and all I got was a message saying that your number was discontinued.'

Paul sat down in one of the old-fashioned wooden-backed armchairs. 'I've been having some cash-flow difficulty, OK?'

'So why didn't you say so?'

'Because you didn't want to hear it, did you? All you wanted to hear was success.'

His father jabbed his finger at him. 'What kind of person do you take me for? You're my son. If you're successful, I exult in it. If you fail, I commiserate. I'm your father, for Chrissakes.'

'Commiserate? Those Gabonese bastards took my business, my house, they took everything. I don't want commiseration. I want revenge.'

His father came up to him and laid both of his hands on his shoulder and looked him straight in the face. 'Forget about revenge. You can always start over.'

'Oh, like you started over when you lost your job at Linke Overmeyer? With a little house, and a millionth-of-an-acre of ground, and a row of beans? I had a mansion, in Libreville! Seven bedrooms, four bathrooms, a swimming pool, a circular hallway you could have ice skated on, if you'd had any ice, and if you'd had any skates.'

'So what?' his father asked him. 'That's what life is all about. Winning and losing. Why did you have to lie about it?'

'Because of you,' said Paul.

'Because of *me*? What the hell are you talking about?'

'Because you always expected me to do better than you. That was all I ever got from you, from the time I was old enough to understand anything. "You'll do better than me. One day, you'll be rich and you'll buy a house for your mother and me. With a lake, and swans." Jesus Christ! I was nine years old, and you wanted me to give you fucking *swans*!'

His father closed his eyes for a moment, trying to summon up enough patience not to shout back. His mother said nothing, but sat still in the shadows, a silhouette, only the curved reflection from her glasses gleaming. In the distance, Paul heard the dyspeptic rumbling of thunder. It had been a dry day, and the air had been charged with static electricity. Lightning was crossing Litchfield Hills, walking on stilts.

Paul's father opened his eyes. 'Are you going back to Africa?'

'There's nothing to go back to. I'm all washed up in Gabon. I still owe my lawyer seven thousand francs.'

'So what are you going to do?'

'I don't know. Right now, I don't want to do anything.'

'You're going to have to find yourself a job, Paul, even if it's waiting tables. Your mother and I can't support you.'

'I see. So much for my fucking four-hundred-dollar dinner then! "Who has a son who takes his parents out for a meal like this?" You didn't even offer to pay half.'

'I'm sorry. If I'd known that you were busted I wouldn't have suggested going to Randolph's at all. We could have eaten at home. And don't use language like that, not in this house.'

'Oh, I beg your pardon. First of all you won't support me, and now you take away my rights under the First Amendment.'

'The First Amendment doesn't give you the right to use profanity in front of your mother.'

Paul was about to say something else, but he took a deep breath and stopped himself. He felt angrier than he had ever felt in his life. But what was the point in shouting? He knew that he wouldn't be able to change his father's mind. His father had almost made a religion out of self-sufficiency. Even when Paul was young, he had never given him an allowance. Every cent of pocket money had been earned with dishwashing or raking leaves or painting fences. He would rather have burned his money than given anything to Paul for nothing.

'All right,' said Paul. 'If that's the way you feel.'

He walked around his father and went to his room. He slung his suitcase on the bed and started to bundle his clothes into it. His mother came to the door and said, Paul . . . don't be angry. You don't have to leave.'

'Oh, but I do. I might accidentally breathe some of Dad's air or flush some of his water down the toilet.'

'Sweetheart, he doesn't mean that you can't stay with us, just till you can get yourself back on your feet.'

'You don't get it, do you? I don't want to get back on my feet. I've spent eleven years working my rear end off, and look what I've ended up with. One tropical suit, two shirts, and a rental car I can't even pay for. I just want to lie down and do nothing. That's all.'

'Do you want to see Dr Williams?'

Paul pushed his way past her. 'I don't want to see anybody. I'm not sick. I'm not disturbed. I'm just exhausted, that's all. Is it a crime to be exhausted?'

'Paul . . .' his father began, but Paul opened the front door and went down the steps. 'Paul – we can talk about this. I'm sure we can work something out.'

'Sure,' Paul retorted. I can clean out your gutters and mend your roof and you'll pay me in hamburgers. Forget it, Dad. I'd rather go to the Y.'

With that, he climbed into his rental car and backed out of the drive with a scream of tyres. His father sadly watched him go.

By nine o'clock that night the rain was lashing all the way across Litchfield County and the hills were a battlefield of thunder and lightning.

Paul had driven into New Milford, where he spent his last $138 on a steak and fries and a bottle of wine at the Old Colonial Inn. Now he didn't even have enough money for a room. It looked like he was going to have to spend the night in the car, parked on a side road.

He left the inn, his coat collar turned up against the rain, but by the time he reached the car his shoulders were soaked. He wiped the rain from his face and looked at himself in the rear-view mirror. If only he had someplace to sleep. A warm bed, and enough money to last him for six or seven months, so that he wouldn't have to do anything but sit back and drink beer and think of nothing at all.

He started the engine, and the windshield wipers flapped furiously from side to side. It was then that he heard the softest of rattles. *Shikk – shikk – shikk.*

A prickling sensation went up the back of his neck. The witch-compass was telling him that he could have just what he wanted. A bed for the night, and money. But the question was, how was he going to get it, and what kind of moral decision would he have to make?

Shikka – shikka – shikka rattled the witch-compass, and Paul took it out of his pocket.

For one second, Paul was tempted to throw it out into the rain. But it felt so smooth and reassuring in his hand, and he knew that it would guide him to a place where he could sleep, and where he wouldn't have to worry for a while.

He nudged his car out of the green on to the main road to New Preston. He turned the wheel to the right, and the witch-compass was silent. He turned it to the left, and the witch-compass went *shikkashikkashikka*.

He was almost blinded for a second by a crackling burst of lightning. But then he was driving so slowly through the rain, hunched forward in his seat so that he could see more clearly, heading northwards.

After twenty minutes of silence, the witch-compass stirred again. *Shikk – shikk – shikk.* He had reached the intersection where the Chevrolet had collided with the deer – the intersection that would take him up the winding road towards his parents' house.

'Oh, no,' he said. But the witch-compass rattled even more loudly, guiding him up the hill. Another fork of lightning crackled to the ground, striking a large oak only a hundred feet away. Paul saw it burst apart and burn. Thunder exploded right above his head, as if the sky were splitting apart.

He drove around the hairpin bend towards his parents' house. Now the witch-compass was shaking wildly, and Paul knew without any doubt at all where it was taking him. He saw the roof of his parents' house silhouetted against the trees, and as he did so another charge of lightning hit the chimney, so that bricks flew in all directions and blazing wooden shingles were hurled into the night like Catherine wheels.

The noise was explosive, and it was followed only a second later by a deep, almost sensual sigh, as the air rushed in to fill the vacuum that the lightning had created. Then there was a deafening collision of thunder.

Paul stopped in front of the house, stunned. The rain drummed on the roof of his car like the juju drummers in Marché Rouge. He climbed out, shaking, and was immediately drenched. He walked up the steps with rain dripping from his nose and pouring from his chin. He pushed open the front door and the house was filled with the smell of burned electricity, and smoke.

'Oh, Jesus,' he said.

He walked into the kitchen and the walls were blackened with bizarre scorch-marks, like the silhouettes of hopping demons. Every metal saucepan and colander and cheese-grater had been flung into the opposite corner of the room and fused together in an extraordinary sculpture, a medieval knight who had fallen higgledy-piggledy off his charger.

And right in the centre of the floor lay his mother and father, all of their clothes blown off, their bodies raw and charred, their eyes as black as cinders, and smoke slowly leaking out of their mouths.

Shikk – shikk – shikk rattled the witch-compass.

So this was how he was going to find himself a warm bed for the night. However stern he had been, his father had always told him that he was going to inherit the house, and all of his savings, as well as being the sole beneficiary to their joint-insurance policies. No more problems. No more money worries. Now he could rest, and do nothing.

He slowly sank to his knees on the kitchen floor and took hold of his mother's hand, even though the skin on her fingers was crisp and her fingernails had all been blown off. He pressed her hand against his forehead and he sobbed and sobbed until he felt that he was going to suffocate.

'Dad, Mom, I didn't want *this*,' he wept. 'I didn't want this, I swear to God. I'd give my right arm for this never to have happened. I'd give anything.'

He cried until his ribs hurt. Outside, the electric storm grumbled and complained and eventually disappeared, *perdendosi*, into the distance.

Silence, except for the continuing rain. Then Paul heard the witch-compass go *shikk – shikk – shikk*.

He raised his head. The witch-compass was lying on the floor next to him, softly rattling and turning on its axis.

'What are you offering me now, you bastard?' said Paul.

Shikkashikkashikka.

'This doesn't have to have happened? Dad and Mom – they needn't have died?'

Shikk – shikk – shikk.

'What are you trying to tell me, you fuck? I can turn back the clock? Is that what you mean?'

Shikk – shikk – shikk.

He let his mother's hand drop to the floor. He picked up the witch-compass and pointed it all around the room, 360 degrees. 'Come on then, show me. Show me how I can turn the clock back.'

Shikkashikkashikka.

The witch-compass led him to the kitchen door. He opened it and the wind and the rain came gusting in, sending his mother's blackened fingernails scurrying across the vinyl like cockroaches. He stepped outside, shielding his face against the rain with his arm upraised, holding the witch-compass in his left hand, close to his heart. He wanted to feel where it was taking him. He wanted to know, this time, what it was going to ask him to do.

But of course it didn't. He stumbled on the wet stone step coming out of the kitchen and fell heavily forward, with his right arm still upraised. It struck the unprotected blade of his father's circular saw and the rusty teeth but right through the muscle, severing his tendon and his axillary artery. For a terrible moment he hung beside the saw-table, unable to lift himself up, while blood sprayed on to his face and all over his hair. The rain fell on him like whips, and his blood streamed across the patio in a scarlet fan-pattern and flooded into grass.

Jonquil was waiting for him at the very end of the Marché Rouge. On the upturned fruit-box in front of her stood the carved figure of a woman with her lips bound together with wire, and a rattle with a monkey's head on top of it, and several jars of poisonous-looking unguents.

He walked along the row of brightly lit stalls until he reached the shadowy corner where she sat. He stood in front of her for a while, saying nothing.

'Your feet brought you back,' she said.

'That's right,' he told her. 'My feet brought me back.'

'How is Papa and Mama?' she asked, with a broad, tobacco-bronzed smile.

'They're good, thanks.'

'Not dead, then? Bad thing, being dead.'

'You think so? Sometimes I'm not so sure.'

'You'll survive. Everybody has to survive. Didn't you learn that?'

'Oh, sure. Even if I didn't learn anything else.'

He reached into the pocket of his crumpled linen coat and produced a smooth black object that looked like a gourd. He laid it down on the fruit-box, next to the carving.

'I don't give refunds,' said Jonquil, and gave a little cackle.

'I don't want a refund, thanks.'

'How about a new arm?'

He looked down at his empty sleeve, pinned across his chest. He shook his head. 'I can't afford it. Not at your prices.'

She watched him walk away through the equatorial night. She picked up the witch-compass and put her ear to it and shook it.

Shikk – shikk – shikk it whispered. Jonquil smiled, and set it back down on the upturned fruit-box, ready for the next customer.

RESONANT EVIL

Martin drew into the curb and turned off the engine. 'There,' he said. 'Tell me that isn't perfect.'

Serena looked at the white two-story house with its patchy front lawn and its overgrown ninebark bushes and its peeling window frames. Six or seven of the uprights in the veranda rail were missing, which gave the house a gap-toothed appearance, and the shutters of one of the upstairs windows were hanging askew.

'You didn't say it was a fixer-upper,' she said. 'How much are they asking for it?'

'Five nine nine. It's a steal. It has five bedrooms, two and a half bathrooms, and a totally private yard with a view of Little Pond if you stand on a stepladder.'

'I don't know. It looks like a whole lot of work. And I won't be getting any more agile, will I?'

'Just take a look inside,' Martin coaxed her. 'I promise you, you're going to love it.'

'Well, OK,' said Serena, reluctantly. Martin climbed out of the car and walked around to open the door for her. Although she was six months' pregnant, she was still quite skinny, except for her bump. Her long blonde hair was tied back with a pale blue scarf, and she was wearing a pale blue smock and tight black leggings. Her blue denim sandals had five-inch wedges but Martin didn't mind because he was seven inches taller than she was, lean and dark-haired and gangling, more like a basketball player than a neuroscientist.

They walked up the path together and climbed the steps. Martin took out the key that the realtors had given him and unlocked the faded green front door. A corroded brass knocker was hanging on it, in the shape of a snarling wolf's head.

'Maybe I should knock first. You know – in case there are any ghosts still inside. I wouldn't want to startle them.'

'Don't you go scaring me,' said Serena. 'The house looks creepy enough as it is.'

'Don't worry,' Martin told her. 'Ghosts are all in the mind. Trust me. I'm a professional.'

He pushed open the door and its hinges made a thick grating sound, as if they hadn't been oiled for years. 'Do you know who used to live here before? Vincent Grayling. How about that for serendipity?'

Serena peered into the hall. It was dark and airless, because all of the shutters in the house were closed, and it was panelled in brown-varnished oak. She stepped inside, her sandals crunching on the gritty oak floor. On the left-hand side of the hallway there was a steep colonial staircase, which led up to a galleried landing. Some of the risers were rotten and needed replacing, and four or five of the banisters were missing, like the veranda outside. A huge crystal chandelier was suspended from the ceiling, trailing cobwebs like rags.

She sniffed. 'It smells like nobody's lived here for *years*.'

'They haven't. Vincent Grayling died in 1957. The realtors told me that the house remained in his family, but none of them wanted to live here so they rented it until it got too run down. They wanted to sell it but they couldn't agree on which member of the family was supposed to get the biggest share of the proceeds. It's only come on to the market now because the last but one of them has gone to meet his Maker.'

On their right, a wide doorway led into a living room. Although it was so gloomy in there, they could make out a worn-out brown leather couch, two mismatched armchairs with stretch nylon covers, a 'contemporary' coffee table shaped like an artist's palette and a standard lamp with a broken shade.

'You don't want to live here just because it was Vincent Grayling's house, do you?' asked Serena. 'I mean – sweetheart – have you worked out how much it's going to cost us to remodel? Not to mention all the new furniture.'

'All right,' said Martin, 'I confess. Vincent Grayling is one of my great heroes. But look what we'd be getting for the money. There's a much smaller house further down the street and it's nearly eight hundred.'

'I always thought that Vincent Grayling was some kind of a nutball,' said Serena, as she followed Martin along the hallway to the kitchen. 'Didn't he do some experiment when he spoiled the taste of people's food just by showing them horrible pictures while they ate?'

'That was one of his experiments, yes. And most of his research was pretty far out, I have to admit. But he did some incredible work on synaesthesia. That's when you stimulate one sense, like for instance *hearing*, and it affects another sense, like *taste*. He discovered that some people, whenever they hear a telephone ringing, taste salt on their tongues.'

'How about smell?' said Serena. 'I'm looking at this kitchen and I can definitely smell drains.'

The kitchen was still fitted in 1950s style, with green Formica worktops and a cream Westinghouse gas range, and wall cupboards with frosted-glass windows. The faucet was dripping monotonously into the sink, and all those years of dripping had stained the sink several shades of brown.

Serena pulled open the dome-topped Frigidaire. On the middle shelf there was a single Tupperware container with something black and speckled inside it. She looked at Martin, who could see that she was almost about to tell him that she wouldn't move into this house if the entire MIT tug-of-war team tried to drag her into it.

'First thing we'll do is we'll rip out this kitchen,' he promised her. 'We'll put in one of those fancy American Range ovens with a banquet burner broiler, or whatever it's called. And a fridge you could fit a family of Inuits into.'

'Hmm,' she said.

'Come on upstairs,' he said, taking hold of her hand. 'You ain't seen nothing yet.'

They gingerly climbed up the half-dilapidated staircase, until they reached the landing. 'Can't you imagine it?' he asked her. 'Your guests are waiting for you downstairs in the hallway, and *ta-da!* you appear right here, dressed up like Scarlett O'Hara. Slowly you descend the stairs, the chandelier shining on your diamond necklace . . .'

'What diamond necklace?'

'The diamond necklace I'm going to buy you when they make me head of my department.'

'Do I really have to wait that long? I won't be able to dress up like Scarlett O'Hara when I'm eighty-five years old.'

He gave her a playful slap on the bottom. 'Oh ye of little faith. Now, just take a look at this – the master bedroom!'

He opened the door. The master bedroom was enormous, dominated by a huge four-poster bed with carved oak pillars and dusty orange drapes. In the centre of the opposite wall there was a pair of French windows, covered by shutters, so that the afternoon sunlight shone on to the floor in narrow parallel bars. Martin crossed over to the windows, pulled back the bolts which secured them, and then forced open the shutters.

Outside, a balcony overlooked the yard, which was crowded with blossoming cherry trees. Beyond the cherry trees they could see Little Pond, blue and sparkling, with two rowboats tied together in the middle of it, and children swimming.

Serena came out on to the balcony and stood there for a while, with her eyes half-closed. The warm wind blew a few stray blonde hairs across her forehead.

'Well?' asked Martin.

'You've convinced me,' she smiled.

They looked into all four of the other bedrooms. Three of them were quite small, and empty, without even a bed in them, but the fourth was almost as large as the master bedroom, and it had obviously been used as a study. The walls were lined with bookshelves, although there were no books on them now, apart from a dog-eared telephone directory and a residents' association newsletter. In the worn beige carpet there were two rectangular indentations with a dark scuffed patch in between them, where a desk had once stood. A dusty black telephone with a rotary dial had been left on the window sill.

At the far end of the study there was a red-brick fireplace, and in the alcoves on either side of the chimney breast, oak-fronted closets had been built. Martin went over and tried to open them, but they were both locked, and neither of them had keys.

'This would make a fantastic den for you,' said Serena. She peered through the shutters to see what was outside. 'There's a girl next door, washing her car. She has thick glasses and a *very* large ass. I think I can trust you in here.'

'Does that mean you want us to buy it?'

Serena reached up and put her arms around his neck and gave

him a kiss. 'I think you've persuaded me, yes. Let's go talk to the realtors, shall we?'

It was seven more weeks before the paperwork was completed and they were able to move in. By now the air was feeling sharper every morning and the trees all around Little Pond were beginning to turn rusty-coloured.

Because their baby was expected in less than two weeks, Serena's sister Emma came to help them move, although Serena was blooming. Her hair was shiny and her skin glowed and Martin had never seen her so happy. They were going to have a girl, and they had chosen the name Sylvia Martina.

'Just because we're naming her after you, Martin, that doesn't mean I want her to be a neuroscientist,' Serena had told him. 'I want her to be a singing star.'

'What *we* want her to be is irrelevant,' Martin had replied. 'My mom wanted me to go into the grocery business, like my dad. Can you imagine me in an apron, slicing salami?'

'Actually, I just want little Sylvia to be healthy,' Serena had said, resting her head against his shoulder. 'I don't care what she does, so long as nobody ever hurts her.'

On the third day, the sky was dark grey and it was raining hard, which made the trees rattle. Serena and Emma were cleaning the kitchen together, and Martin was waiting for a house-clearance company to take away the living-room furniture, which was out on the front veranda now, looking old and worn-out and sorry for itself.

He stood on the veranda watching the rain for a while. The truckers were over an hour late now and he wondered if they were coming at all. He went back inside. Serena and Emma were singing some Rihanna song in the kitchen, out of key, and laughing together, so he decided to leave them to it. He climbed the stairs to the study. All his books were up there now, in eleven cardboard boxes, and he could make a start on unpacking them.

His desk was there, too, although it looked distinctly out of place in a colonial room like this because it was made of chrome and smoked glass. He would have to see if he could find an antique one, with brass handles and an embossed leather top.

He went across to the closets beside the fireplace. He had asked the realtors if anybody in the Grayling family had keys for them, but there had been no response. The Graylings had never taken an interest in the house, except as an investment, and they probably didn't even know that these closets existed, let alone where their keys might be.

He took out his Swiss army knife, opened out the longest blade, and slid it down the crack at the side of the left-hand door. He could feel the metal tongue of the lock, and he wiggled his knife from side to side to see if he could dislodge it from its keeper. It held firm, and so he gave up. He didn't want to damage the colonial oak beading.

In a last attempt to open the door, he opened out the corkscrew and inserted it into the keyhole. He jiggled it, and twisted it, but the door still remained firmly locked. He took out the corkscrew and gave the door a frustrated thump with his fist. As he turned away, the lock softly clicked and the door opened up, almost as if somebody had very gently pushed it from the inside.

He stood and stared at it. *No*, he told himself, *you're a neurobiologist; you're an associate professor in Brain and Cognitive Sciences at MIT. You do not believe in ghosts, or any kind of paranormal activity. Ghosts aren't supernatural; they're synaptic. Like you told Serena, they're all in the mind.*

Cautiously, he swung the door open wider. Inside, there were three shelves. The top shelf held half-a-dozen black hard-backed notebooks. On the centre shelf stood a portable record player from the late 1950s, cream and brown, an RCA Victor High-Fidelity autochange. On the bottom shelf there was a large cardboard box, with a lid, marked '*S-Disks #5 – #31*'.

Martin tried to lift the box out of the closet but it was so heavy that he had to drag it. When he opened the lid he found that it was full of long-playing vinyl records, all in brown paper sleeves. He picked out the first one and slid it out of its sleeve. On the white paper label in the middle there was scrawly purple handwriting: '*Lavender, recorded D Lab, 77 Massachusetts Avenue, 08/13/54.*'

Lavender? thought Martin. What the hell did that mean, *lavender*? How do you record lavender?

He lifted out the next record. '*Smoke, recorded D Lab, 77 Massachusetts Avenue, 08/21/54*'. Then, '*Lightning flash, 0.03 sec, recorded 76 Oliver Road, Belmont, 08/23/54.*'

Each successive record had a similar notation on its label. There were 'Moving Shadows', 'Apples', 'Faces', 'Snow', 'Cold Fingers' and 'Child'.

He stood up and took down the notebooks. On the front of each of them was a white label with the same scrawly handwriting. The first one read '*Experiments in Synaesthesia, 1954–55. Vincent D. Grayling, PhD.*' When he opened it, and read Vincent Grayling's handwritten introduction, he began to understand what he had found.

'I am working toward the stimulation of one sense through the stimulation of another. My first experiments are with hearing. I have successfully used sound recordings to evoke smells, visions and various physical sensations, such as the feeling of being stroked, touched, prickled, and even burned.

'I am firmly convinced that there is almost no limit to what the human mind can be persuaded to perceive through the manipulation of the various senses. We are already aware that music can dramatically sway our emotions. Sad songs can make us cry. Martial music can make us feel aggressive. But this is only scratching the surface. I believe that we can create an alternative "reality" through sensory stimulation – a "reality" so convincing that a subject will not be able to distinguish between "real" and actuality.

'In the same way that a pilot can feel in a flight simulator that he is actually flying, we can allow people to experience "real" events, such as walking through a scenic garden and smelling the flowers, or swimming in the ocean, or making love, or even meeting relatives or loved ones who have died.'

Vincent Grayling's explanation of how he had managed to conjure up 'real' sensations by the use of sound recordings went on for page after page. Martin sat at his desk, fascinated. It was hard to believe that nobody at MIT had made any effort to find out what had happened to Vincent Grayling's notebooks and records after he had died. Martin had read that he had been a difficult man to get on with, and that his arrogance and overwhelming self-belief had antagonized many of his associate professors. Even today, though, his work on synaesthesia was cutting-edge, and had limitless potential for psychiatric therapy and who knew what other possibilities. Maybe troops could be trained by thinking that they were fighting in Afghanistan, when they were simply sitting in a laboratory with earphones on. Maybe surgeons could separate conjoined twins before they actually made an incision. Maybe widows could meet their dead husbands again, and talk to them as if they were still alive.

He turned the next page and found a black-and-white photograph had been tucked into the margin. It showed a stocky man in a wide-shouldered grey suit, standing in the back yard, with the cherry trees behind him, although it must have been winter or early spring, because their branches were bare. He had black, slicked-back hair and a large, pale face, with near-together eyes and a heavy chin. Martin recognized him immediately as Vincent Grayling.

When he looked at the photograph more closely, he saw that there was a blurry white figure between the trees. It looked as if a child had been running past, just as the shutter was opened. It was impossible to tell if it was a boy or a girl, but Vincent Grayling didn't appear to be aware of it. He was staring straight at the camera as if he resented having his photograph taken at all.

Martin turned the photograph over. On the back was written, '*Vera, 01/16/55.*' Not '*Vincent*' or '*Me*' as he would have expected, but '*Vera*'. Maybe that blurry figure between the trees was Vera, whoever Vera might have been.

Martin took the record player out of the closet and placed it on his desk. He plugged it in and turned the knob and it immediately came to life. Its auto-change arm dropped a non-existent record on to the turntable with a complicated clicking noise.

'Martin!' called Emma, from downstairs. 'Your lunch is ready! Hot dogs!'

'Thanks, Emma!' he called back. 'Just give me a couple of minutes, OK?'

'Don't be long! You don't want cold dogs!'

Martin took out the first record, '*Lavender*', and laid it on the turntable. He carefully lowered the stylus on to it, and then turned up the volume. There were a few moments of hissing, and then he heard a very soft whispering sound, almost inaudible. The whispering went on and on, like somebody trying to say something confidentially in his ear, yet too close and too breathy for him to be able to make out what it was.

After about twenty seconds, the whispering was punctuated by an intermittent buzzing, which reminded him of the noise that a faulty fluorescent light makes just before it flickers off for good. These two noises went on and on, with the whispering rising and falling from time to time, and the intervals between the buzzing noises varying in duration, but that was all.

'Martin? Are you coming or not?' called Emma.

'OK, sure!' said Martin, and reached across his desk to switch off the record player. As he did so, however, he was suddenly aware of a strong smell of lavender, as aromatic as if he had found himself standing right in the middle of a lavender field.

He breathed out, and then breathed in again, deeply, just to make sure that he wasn't mistaken, or that he was deluding himself. But there was no question about it – he could smell lavender. Not only that, everything in the study seemed to have a lavender-coloured tinge to it, as if he were wearing sunglasses with purple lenses.

'*Vincent*,' he said, under his breath. '*I don't know how you found out how to do this, but you were a genius.*'

He lifted the '*Lavender*' record off the turntable and took out the next record, '*Moving Shadows.*'

'Martin!' shouted Serena. 'If you don't come down now I'm going to give your wieners to the cat!'

He placed the record carefully on his desk and went downstairs, swinging himself on the banisters to avoid the rotten risers.

'We don't *have* a cat,' he said, as he came into the kitchen. Serena and Emma were already sitting at the table, eating their hot dogs with coleslaw and curly fries.

'I know. But we will one day, and I was going to freeze your wieners until we do.'

'You women,' he complained. 'You're such sadists.' But before he sat down, he leaned over Serena and waved his hand under her nose. 'Here,' he said. 'Can you smell anything?'

She breathed in deeply. 'I smell *something*, yes . . . but I'm not sure what.' She breathed in again, and then she said, 'It's not your aftershave, is it? At least I hope not. Why? What have you been doing?'

'I'll tell you later,' he told her. 'I managed to open one of the closets in the study, and there was a whole lot of Vincent Grayling's notebooks and records in it. I should take them all in to the department, I guess. Well, I probably will, but I want to go through them first.'

Serena breathed in yet again, closing her eyes for a moment. Then she said, 'That smell . . . I think I know what it is.'

'Go on, then,' said Martin. 'Have a guess.'

'It's like when you first open a pack of ground beef from the supermarket.'

'What do you mean?'

'It's like blood.'

That night, after Emma had gone home to Watertown and Serena had retired to bed early, Martin went back to the study. He propped up the photograph of Vincent Grayling against the side of the record player, so that he could look at it while he opened his laptop and checked him out on Wikipedia.

Vincent Grayling, born October 17, 1908; died December 12, 1957. Assistant professor at the Department of Brain and Cognitive Science at Massachusetts Institute of Technology, 1934–1957.

Grayling was a neuroscientist specializing in various forms of synaesthesia, a condition in which senses are linked together, so that the stimulation of one sensory or cognitive pathway automatically stimulates a second or even a third pathway.

He married Joan Bannerman, the youngest daughter of Professor Humphrey Bannerman, in 1928. They had one daughter, Vera Joan, born 1931, who was fatally injured in a traffic accident at the age of six, while Vincent Grayling was driving.

Martin looked across at the photograph. Vincent Grayling had written '*Vera, 01/16/55*' on the back of it, and yet the blurred image between the trees couldn't be Vera – at least not the same Vera. If she had died when she was six, his daughter had been killed in 1937, which was eighteen years earlier.

Martin read on: *Joan Grayling died in 1952 of ovarian cancer. After her death, Professor Grayling became extremely reclusive, although he published several papers on synaesthesia, notably* Cognitive and Perceptual Processes in Congenital And Adventitious Synaesthetes. *None of these papers was very well received, because research into synaesthesia had been more or less abandoned by the scientific community, and after 1955 he submitted no more.*

He was found in his study, having bled to death from a fatal wound to his carotid artery. There was some bruising to his body, and one of his shirt sleeves was torn, but because the study was locked from the inside, with the key still in the door, the Middlesex county medical examiner decided that he had taken his own life.

Martin closed his laptop and sat back. He wondered if he ought to try listening to the '*Lavender*' record again. He couldn't understand why Serena had said that he had smelled of blood after he had come downstairs, when he was quite sure that he had still been carrying the lingering scent of lavender. Maybe – with Sylvia's birth so imminent – her sense of smell had been thrown out of whack by her raging hormones. He was much more keen to put on the second record, '*Moving Shadows*', and find out what happened when he listened to that.

He was just about to put the record on when he heard Serena calling him. He went along the landing to the master bedroom and opened the door.

'Are you going to be long?' she asked him.

He crossed the bedroom and bent over to give her a kiss on the forehead. 'Only a half-hour or so. I'd like to listen to one more record, that's all.'

'It's just that I feel strange in this house.'

'Strange – like how?'

'I feel like we're not alone. That there's other people here.'

'Of course there's other people here. There's Sylvia.'

Serena slapped the pillow. 'I don't mean Sylvia, stupid. I feel like there's other people walking around the house.'

'Really? Have you seen them? Have you heard them? Have any of them left their dirty coffee mugs in the sink?'

'No, of course not. It's a feeling, that's all. I'm probably letting my imagination run away with me. I've never lived in an old house like this before. I'll get used to it.'

'OK, darling,' he told her, and kissed her again. 'Why don't you try to get some sleep? You've done a lot today, cleaning up the kitchen and everything. I don't want you going into labour before you're due.'

'I don't think there's any chance of that, Martin. I feel like I'm going to be pregnant for ever.'

Martin left the bedroom door ajar in case she wanted to call out to him again, and he left the study door open, too. He sat down at his desk, lowered the '*Moving Shadows*' record on to the turntable, and started to play it.

After the initial hiss of the stylus, he heard a rustling sound, like a breeze, blowing through trees. It went on and on for almost a minute before it was joined by some awkward, sporadic tinkling. It could have been a wind chime, or somebody stirring a glass of Russian tea. Then both rustling and tinkling were punctuated by deep, distant, reverberating groans. The groans didn't necessarily sound human. They could have been caused by anything, like pit-props under tremendous strain, or dying animals calling out to each other across a swamp.

After the fourth or fifth groan, Martin glimpsed something out of the corner of his eye – a dark shadow that flickered across the open doorway, so quickly that he couldn't be sure that he had seen it at all. He stared at the doorway intently, waiting for it to reappear, but even though the rustling and the tinkling and the groaning continued, it seemed as if one fleeting shadow was the only illusion that this record was going to evoke.

He thought of playing the record over again, and he was just about to lift up the tone arm when he saw another shadow, halfway along the landing this time, as if it had just come up the stairs. It was very dim and indistinct, and it rippled like the shadow of somebody walking past a picket fence. But it was definitely the shadow of a person, and it was making its way toward the half-open bedroom door.

'Hey!' shouted Martin. 'Hey, you! *Stop!*'

He pushed back his chair and hurried along the landing. All the same, the shadow reached the bedroom door a split-second before he did, and stepped into it, without any hesitation at all. It was only a shadow, though. The door was still only half-ajar, and no human being could have walked through it without pushing it open wider.

Martin burst into the bedroom. Serena had already switched on her bedside lamp and was sitting up, wide-eyed.

'What?' she said. 'Who were you shouting at?'

Martin looked around. There was nobody else in the room.

'*Martin,*' Serena repeated. 'Who were you shouting at?'

Martin circled around the room and even looked behind the drapes. All he could see was the sparkling lights of the neighbouring streets of Belmont and, less then a half-mile away, the red and white river of traffic on the Concord Turnpike.

He opened the doors of the built-in closets but all he found in there were their clothes, hanging up, and their neatly folded sweaters and socks.

'Martin, you're scaring me now! What are you looking for?'

'Nothing,' he said. 'It's OK. It was just like an optical illusion, that's all.'

'What kind of optical illusion? Jesus, you haven't been smoking any of that skunk again, have you?'

'Of course not. I only tried that under laboratory conditions, for that neuropsychology program.'

'Well, it made you all jumpy, like you are now.'

'I haven't been smoking skunk, Serena, OK? Even if I wanted to, I don't have any. It was a visual aberration, that's all. Like a mirage.'

'A *mirage*? This isn't the Sahara, Martin, in the middle of the day. This is nine o'clock at night. Indoors. In Massachusetts.'

'I'm fine. I'm OK. I promise you.'

'Well, come to bed. You're freaking me out. Next thing I know, I'm going to start having contractions.'

Martin set aside the '*Moving Shadows*' record for now, but over the next few days he tried out several of the others, such as '*Apples*', '*Snow*', '*Cold Fingers*', '*Lightning*' and '*Faces*'.

Some sounds stimulated his other senses much more than others. '*Apples*', for instance, gave him a strong taste of Tremlett's Bitter apples in his mouth, and he could even smell apples, too. With '*Snow*', however, he could feel only the faintest of chills, as if he were standing in front of an open fridge, and he could see nothing more than a pale reflected light in the window of his study. When he looked outside, there was no snow in the yard, although the grass appeared whitish, as if an early frost had settled on it.

'*Lightning*' was more spectacular, especially when he played it in the evening. The record was a mixture of creaking and crackling, and after about thirty seconds Martin began to see static electricity crawling across his desk and around the window-frame like sparkling centipedes. Outside, over Little Pond, he could see branches of lightning flickering behind the trees, although he could hear no thunder, and the evening was completely calm.

'*Cold Fingers*' was the first record that actually made him jump.

It started with a light scampering sound, like a small rodent running, and then the scampering was accompanied by the shrill, sharp ringing of a bell. Immediately, Martin felt somebody drawing their chilly fingertips lightly across his cheek, even though there was nobody there. As the record continued, he felt it again and again. He stood up, knocking his chair over, and stumbled back across the room, holding up both hands to shield his face, but the chilly fingertips kept stroking him, faster and faster – not only his cheeks but his forehead and his ears and the back of his neck, even his lips. It was like being fondled by a dead but urgent lover.

He crossed over to his desk, still with one hand held up in front of his face, and pushed the record player so that the stylus scratched sideways across the record and stopped it.

'Martin?' called Serena, from the hallway. 'What's all that banging?'

'Sorry!' he called back. 'I'm rearranging my study, that's all!'

He slid the '*Cold Fingers*' record back into its sleeve. He felt guilty that he hadn't told Serena what he was really doing. After all, he had first met her when she was a student in the department of cognitive neuroscience, and she was quite capable of under-standing Vincent Grayling's research into synaesthesia. For several reasons, though, he wanted to find out more about the true psycho-logical effects of these records before he shared them with anybody, especially Serena. They were exciting, but he was concerned by the way in which they manipulated his senses so easily, making him see shadows where there were no shadows, and lightning where there was no lightning, and feel as if he were being intimately touched by somebody when he was alone. Serena was just about to give birth, and the last thing he wanted to do was mess with her mind.

He put on '*Faces*'. The sound of this record was quite different from the others. It was a jumble of hundreds of human voices, talking so quickly and indistinctly that it was impossible to make out what they were saying. He sat hunched at his desk, listening to them intently, but for over two minutes he didn't see anything, or smell anything, or feel that there was anybody else in the room. Maybe this was one record that wouldn't stimulate any of his other senses, and it would be interesting to know why.

He stood up and walked around the room, still listening. The voices made him feel as if he were surrounded by a huge crowd, still babbling away to each other, but a crowd which was completely ignoring him. Maybe that was the point of the record: to make him feel isolated, as if nobody cared about him.

It was only when he turned back toward his desk that he realized how wrong he was. '*Faces*' meant exactly that – faces. On the left-hand closet door, where he had found the records, he saw two faces, both of them in bas-relief, as if they had been carved out of the wooden door itself.

Martin stopped where he was and stared at them. One face was on about the same level as his own, a man's face, and even though it was fashioned out of wide-grained oak, he recognized it immediately as Vincent Grayling. Those near-together eyes, that heavy jaw, that suspicious, pugnacious pout.

Below Vincent Grayling's face, and slightly to his right, as if she were standing next to him, was the face of a young girl. She was quite plain, with a long nose and thin lips, but then she looked as if she were still too young for her features to have developed.

Martin thought: *Vincent Grayling and Vera. That's who these faces belong to. I can see them. I can actually see them, the way they must have appeared when they were alive. Not ghosts, not supernatural apparitions, but images created by stimulating my sense of hearing, and through my sense of hearing, my sight.*

He raised his hand toward Vincent Grayling's face, wondering if he ought to touch it – or, if he did, if he would actually feel anything. As he did so, however, a voice blurted out from all of the other voices. It was distorted, and some words were muffled and incomprehensible, but he could understand most of what it was saying.

'*Can you hear me? I said, can you hear me? I have to bring her back. It was my fault. I was –*' [incoherent] – '*and I should have known better. I can bring her back. I can. It's only a question of –*' [incoherent] – '*if I should fail, what future do I have? I will have lost everything. Joan, Vera. Everything.*'

Martin stared at Vincent Grayling's face on the closet door. Although he assumed that it was Vincent Grayling's voice that he could hear above the hubbub of other voices, the lips on the wooden face stayed motionless, and the eyes showed no sign of movement. Martin reached out again to touch him, but as he did so the record came to an end, and the tone arm lifted, and the face immediately melted away, leaving nothing but the flat closet door. The little girl's face disappeared, too.

'*I should have known better.*' What had Vincent Grayling meant by that? Martin would have to listen to the record again, more carefully, to find out exactly what he had said. Maybe he had blamed himself for his daughter's death. Maybe he had been driving under the influence of drink or drugs or even the mind-distorting influence of his own research.

It sounded to Martin as if he had been attempting to use synaesthesia to bring Vera back to life. Not physically, that was impossible, but by stimulating his own senses so that he could see her and feel her and talk to her. Maybe the photograph of '*Vera, 01/16/55*' showed that synaesthesia could evoke an image that could not only be perceived by people's neural pathways but by light-sensitive film. After all, if invisible voices could be recorded, why not invisible people?

He went downstairs. Serena was sitting in the living room, watching a repeat of *Party Line with The Hearty Boys*. He sat down next to her, put his arm around her and kissed her.

'Thinking of opening your own restaurant?' he asked her, nodding toward the TV.

'I think I'll have enough on my plate once Sylvia's born. I just want some ideas for when your parents come round.'

They sat in silence for a while, watching Dan and Steve make a three-cheese spaghetti. Then Serena said, 'There's something on your mind, Martin. I can tell.'

'It's nothing. Well, it's not *nothing*, but it's nothing for you to worry about. It's only that I've been listening to Vincent Grayling's records, and he really was on to something. It *works*, sweetheart. Synaesthesia actually works. Before I hand over any of his research to MIT, I want to find out how far he actually went with it. I may even be able to take it further, who knows?'

'If it worked, why didn't he win a Nobel Prize for Neuroscience? Or a Hartmann Prize, or whatever they had in those days? Not even his own department took him seriously. Come on, Martin, he was the archetypal mad professor, and you know it.'

Martin was about to come back at her, and tell her about the taste of apples, and the flashes of lightning, and the wooden faces on the closet door. Maybe if she hadn't been so close to giving birth he would have done, but he didn't want to argue with her, and he didn't want to upset her. Right now she needed him to be very normal and very dependable. The most important thing in their lives was Sylvia Martina, whose feet were churning under Serena's smock as relentlessly as the paddles of an old-fashioned washing-machine.

Martin reached across and stroked Serena's hair, which was shining in the afternoon sunlight. He wished he could think of words that meant *I love you, but a thousand times more than anybody else ever could.*

Sylvia Martina was born a day late at the Bain Birthing Centre at Mount Auburn Hospital. She weighed seven pounds two ounces and she was blue-eyed and fair-haired and when she was born showers of red and yellow leaves flew upward past the fifth-floor window of the maternity unit and rattled against the glass as if to welcome her.

On the third day they took her home to Oliver Road, and placed her in the crib in their bedroom. She would soon have a room of her own, but at the moment it was brown-wallpapered and bare and it would have to be decorated first.

Sylvia was a good baby, docile as well as pretty, and she hardly ever cried. A week after she was born, Martin came quietly into the bedroom at seven o'clock in the evening to find both Sylvia and Serena asleep. For the first time in his life, he knew what it was to feel blessed.

He went across and kissed Serena's cheek, and then he switched off her bedside lamp and left the bedroom, although he left the door a few inches open so that it wouldn't be totally dark.

He went into his study and poured himself a glass of Jack Daniel's. He hadn't listened to any of Vincent Grayling's records since Sylvia had been born, except for '*Lavender*', which he had played again while Sylvia was asleep and Serena was taking a bath, just to make sure that he couldn't detect any hint of blood. He had inhaled deeply while it was playing, and all he had smelled was lavender, *lavandula angustifolia.*

This time he put on '*Child*', and at the same time he leafed through Vincent Grayling's notebooks until he found a heading for '*Child*', handwritten in capital letters followed by several pages of Grayling's scrawling purple script. The handwriting on these pages was even more untidy than he had used for previous notes, with wild loops and fierce downstrokes, as if he had been angry or upset when he wrote it.

Martin lowered the tone arm on to '*Child*' and the first thing he heard was breathing. It was quick, and panicky, like the breathing of a small child fighting for air. It went on and on for more than three minutes before it was eventually joined by a very low grumbling sound, so deep that it was almost below the range of Martin's hearing – more like an earth tremor than a noise. His whiskey glass started to rattle against the side of the Jack Daniel's bottle, and all the pencils and ballpens that he kept in a white china mug on his desk began to jump up and down as if they were trying to escape.

The grumbling continued, drowning out the breathing altogether, although Martin couldn't be sure that the breathing hadn't stopped. Then, suddenly, there was a scalp-prickling howl. It was a man, no question about it, but a man howling in such agony that he could have been mistaken for a dog crushed under a truck.

On the opposite side of the study, next to the bookshelves, a shadowy figure materialized – the figure of a man, dressed in grey. His features were indistinct, but Martin could see that his mouth was stretched open wide, as if it were he who was howling. He was making his way toward the door, in a flickering motion, one image of him after another, a succession of grey shadowy men like a very early motion picture.

He reached the door. Although it was open already, Martin felt that it wouldn't have mattered if it had been closed; he still would have gone through it. He went out on to the landing, and as he did so the howling twisted itself into a cry of '*Vera! Vera! My dear little Vera!*'

Martin got up from his chair and went after him. He was just in time to see him enter the master bedroom, without opening the door any wider than it was already.

'*Vera! Oh, God, Vera! You've come back to me! My little Vera!*'

Martin pushed open the bedroom door and switched on the overhead light. Serena was already sitting up in bed, looking bewildered.

'Martin, what's . . . *Martin!* Who's that? Martin, what *is* that! Martin, *get it away from Sylvia!*'

This time, the figure hadn't vanished when it had entered the bedroom, but was standing by the side of Sylvia's crib, looking down at her. He was half-transparent. His face and hands were dark grey and his eyes were white, like a photographic negative, but at the same time Martin could clearly see that it was Vincent Grayling.

'Vera,' he said. *'My wonderful little Vera.'*

Martin could hear his voice quite distinctly, even though it wasn't coming out of his mouth, but playing on the record in his study.

'We thought you were gone, my darling one, but here you are again, alive and well.'

'Martin, get him away!' screamed Serena, pushing back the covers and climbing out of bed. 'Don't let him touch her!'

Martin seized Vincent Grayling by the shoulders and tried to twist him away from the crib, but he was jolted by an electrical shock that threw him back against the wall, jarring his spine. He lurched forward, snatching at Vincent Grayling's sleeve, but another electrical shock froze all of the feeling in his leg muscles, and he dropped on to his knees on the floor.

Vincent Grayling reached out for Sylvia. *'Come to daddy, my darling. I never thought to see you again.'*

But he wasn't quick enough. Serena bounded across the bedroom floor and snatched Sylvia out of the crib before he even had the chance to pull back her blankets. Then she ran for the door, gasping, 'Martin! Help me! Stop him!'

As Vincent Grayling flickered past him, one still image after another, Martin pitched himself sideways and tried to trip him up by grasping his ankle, but again he was stunned by a thrilling electrical shock.

Serena ran out on to the landing with Sylvia clutched tightly in her arms. The animated images of Vincent Grayling pursued her, only three or four feet behind, and as he did so the record in the study produced an eerie whining noise, as if Vincent Grayling were deliberately trying to panic her.

Martin reached the bedroom door just as Serena was starting to hurry down the staircase. Vincent Grayling was almost close enough to catch at her nightdress.

'Serena!' Martin shouted. *'Watch out for the stairs!'*

He didn't know if she had heard him or not, but she continued to run down the stairs as fast as she could. A third of the way down, they collapsed under her feet, cracking and groaning and then noisily crashing as the risers broke and the treads were ripped in sequence away from the wall.

Serena dropped into the space below the stairs, still holding Sylvia close. She didn't scream. She didn't utter a sound. In her nightdress she looked like an angel falling, until she was impaled by a capped-off gas pipe that ran vertically up through the floor from the basement. She was stopped with a jolt, her arms and legs flapping upward, and blood spurted out of her lips. She dropped Sylvia somewhere into the darkness and Sylvia didn't make a sound, either, not that Martin could hear.

The figure of Vincent Grayling turned around and stared at him with his white negative eyes. Martin had the feeling that he was about to say something. He thought he heard something like a croak of anguish. But then the record in his study abruptly came to an end, and Vincent Grayling vanished, and all Martin could hear was *hissss-clikkk! hissss-clikkk! hissss-clikkk!*

Shivering with shock, he climbed down the staircase, clinging to the balustrade. He looked down at Serena and it was clear that she was dead. Her bare feet were ten inches clear of the floor below her. She was wearing a bib of blood on the front of her nightdress and her pale blue eyes were staring at nothing at all.

He found Sylvia lying in a cardboard box full of spare electrical plugs and adaptors. Her eyes were open too, and she, too, was staring at nothing at all.

It was not until three weeks after the funerals that Martin found the strength to go back into his study and take the '*Child*' record off the turntable. He sat at his desk, holding it in both hands, and his overwhelming urge was to bend it backward and forward until it snapped in half.

But he needed to understand why an apparition of Vincent Grayling had appeared that evening, and why he had seemed to believe that Sylvia was Vera. Surely Vera had lived until she was six years old. She hadn't been a baby.

He took out Vincent Grayling's notebook again and started to read. Gradually, as he deciphered the scrawly purple handwriting, he began to realize what had happened, and why Vincent Grayling was a greater neuroscientist than any of his colleagues had been prepared to believe. Greater even than Marks or Cytowic or Patterson or Heidel.

Vincent Grayling had found out how to stimulate his own senses through sound – so that different noises could lead him to see, hear, touch and taste things that didn't actually exist. When somebody said 'blue', he could not only *taste* ink in his mouth, he could *see* and *touch* a bottle of ink, and even *spill* it, even though to any other observer it would make no mark. He had not only been able to see Vera when he played sounds that stimulated his senses into thinking of Vera, he had been able to hold her and kiss her and talk to her. To him, but to him only, she became real.

Because in fact Vera had not survived until she was six years old. Vera had died in her crib when she was only three weeks old.

'I cannot begin to describe the grief of losing her so soon, my little darling. I thought of her constantly, of what she could have done, of what she could have been, of what a happy life she could have led. I saw her dancing through fields full of daisies. I saw her sitting at her desk, her tongue protruding, carefully copying the letters of the alphabet, her blonde her shining in the light through the classroom window.

'That was when I decided that I would use synaesthesia to bring her back to me, and at least allow me to witness the life that was taken away for her, if nobody else.'

Martin sat back. The following pages were filled with Vincent Grayling's acoustic formulae, and how he had tuned various instruments and artefacts to produce the evocative sounds that would stimulate his senses into bringing his Vera back to him.

He succeeded. The notebooks that followed were full of descriptions of how he had been able to produce a virtual Vera who could grow, and learn to dress herself, and dance, and even have conversations with him.

The blow had come in January 1937, when Vincent Grayling had been driving into Cambridge one icy morning and crashed his Dodge Business Coupe into the rear of a garbage truck. He had suffered no serious physical injuries but he had struck his head on the steering wheel and been concussed, and when he had recovered from his concussion he had found that his synaesthetic sensitivity had been severely impaired.

He could no longer stimulate his senses to recreate Vera – or at least not as fully as he had been able to before the accident. He could glimpse her running through the trees, and he could hear her laughing, but that was all.

He tried for twenty years to bring her back the way she was. '*I need to hold her in my arms, if only once, if only for a moment,*' But his sensory perception was damaged for ever, and on December 12, 1957, in despair, he locked his study door and prepared to take his own life.

What he had failed to realize was that he had left himself on his records, his own longing, his own grief, all immortalized in vinyl. Just as Vincent Grayling had been able to bring Vera back to life, Martin's senses had been stimulated into bringing Vincent Grayling back to life.

Martin stayed in the house on Oliver Road for the next five years. He wrote numerous papers on various forms of synaesthesia, such as grapheme synaesthesia, in which letters and numbers appear to some people to have colours; and chromesthesia, in which music and other noises can produce the effect of waves, spots or even fireworks; and lexical-gustatory synaesthesia, in which words have distinctive tastes, like honey, or rust, or green.

However, he kept his most advanced research to himself – his continuation of the work that had been started by Vincent Grayling. He hated Vincent Grayling with a dark, bitter rage that would never diminish as long as he lived, but his records and notebooks were the only way in which he could back up something of what had been taken away from him.

He was writing up the results of his latest acoustic experiment when there was a tapping at his study door.

'What is it?' he asked.

A blonde-haired girl of five years old came into the room, wearing a pink knitted sweater and red OshKosh dungarees. Her hair was tied up with two red ribbons.

'*Dadd-ee,*' she said coyly, 'can we go out to the park, and have a slide on my sledge?'

Martin pushed his chair back and the little girl climbed on to his knee. 'Not today, sweetheart,' he told her. 'The roads are real icy, and we don't want history repeating itself.'

'What does that mean?'

Martin shook his head. 'You really don't want to know, believe me.'

At that moment, a voice called from downstairs, 'Sylvia? Are you bothering Daddy again?'

'No, Mommy!' the little girl called back. Then she turned to Martin and said, 'I'm not bothering you, am I, Daddy?'

'No, of course you're not. Not at all.'

She frowned at him seriously and touched his left cheek with her fingertip.

'If I'm not bothering you, then why are you crying?'

BEHOLDER

'Once upon a time in a faraway land, a princess was born who was so beautiful that nobody was allowed to look at her for fear they would be so jealous that they would try to harm her.

'She was so beautiful, in fact, that nobody could paint her portrait because the paints would burst into flames as soon as they were applied to the canvas, and no mirrors could be hung in the palace because they would shatter into a thousand pieces if she were to look into them.

'The beautiful princess had many servants, but they were all blinded before they were allowed into her presence by having their eyes spooned out of their sockets.'

Mummy had read Fiona that story so many times that Fiona knew every word of it by heart, and her lips used to move in silent accompaniment whenever Mummy read it. She loved it, because it made sense of her life. She would sit cross-legged on the end of her bed with the windows open, her eyes closed, feeling the sun on her face and listening to the chirruping of sparrows in the garden below. The garden into which she was never allowed to go further than the patio, in case one of the neighbours saw her, and were so envious of her beauty that they climbed over the fence and tried to disfigure her, or even kill her.

Mummy closed the book. It wasn't a proper printed book, but an exercise book with a purple marbled cover and the story of the beautiful princess had been written by hand. Fiona thought that Mummy was beautiful, although she knew that she herself was even more beautiful. At least Mummy could go out and meet other people, without them shouting at her or chasing her down the street or throwing acid in her face, which Fiona knew would happen to her, if *she* ventured beyond the front door.

It was a warm morning in the middle of May, and Mummy came into Fiona's room and said, 'Why don't you take Rapunzel into the garden, Fee-fee? I have to go to the shops and it's such a nice day.'

Rapunzel was Fiona's doll, which Mummy had made for her. Rapunzel had a completely blank face, with no eyes or nose or mouth, but she had very long fair hair, like Rapunzel in the fairy story, who had been locked up in a tower by an evil enchantress. When she had first given Rapunzel to her, Fiona had asked why she didn't have a face, and Mummy had said, 'You don't need a beautiful face to be beautiful. Beauty is in the eye of the beholder.'

'Who's The Beholder?' Fiona asked her.

'Anyone who looks at you. Anyone at all. They're all beholders.'

Mummy called out, 'Bye, darling, won't be long!' and Fiona heard her close the front door behind her.

Fiona picked up Rapunzel from her pillow, where she had been lying between Paddington Bear and Barbie. She went downstairs and out through the kitchen door, on to the York stone patio. The sun had moved around behind the horse-chestnut trees at the end of the garden, so the patio was in shadow now, but the stone was still warm. There was a low wall around it, with steps in the middle that led down to the lawn, and on either side of the steps stood two square pillars, with geraniums growing in them. Fiona thought that they looked like the towers of a fairy-tale castle, so she always knelt down and perched Rapunzel on top of one of them, amongst the geranium stems.

A breeze was rustling through the trees, as if they were whispering to each other, and she could hear the children next door laughing as they ran around their garden. Fiona sometimes wondered what it would be like if she hadn't been born so beautiful, and could play with them. She knew that the boy was called Robin and the girl was called Caroline, because she had heard them calling out to each other, but that was all. She had never seen them, even from her bedroom window, but she imagined that they were probably quite plain. Ugly, even.

'Rapunzel! Rapunzel! Let down your hair!' she repeated, in a creaky voice that was supposed to sound like the evil enchantress. In the story, there had been no door in the tower where Rapunzel was imprisoned, and no steps that led up to her room, so the only way in which the evil enchantress had been able to visit her was by climbing up Rapunzel's twenty-foot tresses.

Fiona took the hairgrips out of Rapunzel's silky blonde braid and hung it down the side of the pillar. Then she started to make her fingers crawl up it, spider-like, to represent the evil enchantress. But her fingers were less than halfway up to the top when a yellow tennis-ball came flying over the fence from the next-door garden, and bounced in the middle of the lawn.

She heard Caroline saying, '*Now* look what you've done, stupid! You'll have to go round and get it back!'

But then Robin said, 'There's somebody there . . . that girl we never see. I heard her.'

Fiona stopped her fingers from climbing Rapunzel's hair. She knelt up very straight, listening. She could hear Robin approaching the fence, and then he called out, 'Hey! Can you throw our ball back, please?'

Fiona stayed where she was, hardly daring to breathe. She knew that she couldn't go down the steps and on to the lawn to pick up the tennis ball because then Robin and Caroline would be able to see her, and realize how beautiful she was. Before she knew it they would be clambering over the fence with kitchen knives or broken bottles or bleach or who could guess what, to ruin her face.

Very, very carefully she stood up, lifting Rapunzel out of her flowery tower. Then she tiptoed backward toward the open kitchen door.

'Hey! Can you hear me?' Robin shouted. 'Can we have our *ball* back, please?'

'There's nobody *there*,' said Caroline, impatiently.

'Yes, there is, I heard her. All she has to do is throw it back.'

'She's probably gone inside. You'll have to go round and knock on the door.'

Just as Fiona was stepping back into the kitchen and closing the door behind her, she heard Robin shouting out one more time, 'Ex-*cuse* me! Deaf ears! Can you throw our ball back?'

Fiona locked the kitchen door and went through to the hallway. Over the front door there was a semicircular stained-glass window, so that the hallway was lit up with green and red and yellow light, like a small chapel.

'Mummy!' she cried out. 'Mummy, are you back yet?'

Silence. Fiona held Rapunzel tighter. 'Mummy?'

At that moment, the doorbell rang, one of those jangly rings that left a salty taste in Fiona's mouth. It must be the boy from next door,

Robin, wanting his tennis ball back. What if she opened the door and he saw how beautiful she was and attacked her? She stood in the hallway for a moment, clutching Rapunzel, not knowing what she should do, but then he rang the doorbell again and she ran quickly and quietly upstairs.

'Mummy!'

She stood on the landing outside Mummy's bedroom. The doorbell rang again and she was so frightened that she wet herself, a little bit.

'*Mummy!*'

'I can *hear* you!' said Robin. 'I know you're in there! We only want our ball back!'

Mummy always locked her bedroom door when she went out, but all the same Fiona pulled down the handle, and to her relief, it opened. Mummy must have come home and perhaps she had gone to the toilet and hadn't heard her.

'Mummy?' she said, stepping cautiously into her bedroom. There was still no reply. Mummy wasn't here, in the bedroom, and the door of her en-suite bathroom was open. She wasn't in there, either.

Fiona made her way around the bed, with its pink satin quilt and its array of lacy cushions. On the left-hand nightstand stood a gilt-framed photograph of Daddy, with his hair receding, but smiling all the same. Daddy had died when Fiona was only nine months old, although Mummy never said why he had passed away so young. There was a smell of talcum powder in the room, mingled with that distinctive dustiness of people who live on their own.

The doorbell rang yet again, but in Mummy's bedroom Fiona didn't feel afraid any more. She touched the quilt, which felt so cool and silky, and she went to the window and looked out, and saw the street outside, with its neat front gardens and cars parked in everybody's driveway. She felt like Rapunzel in her tower – not imprisoned by an evil enchantress, but by the beauty with which she had been blessed as an accident of birth. She was sure that one day a handsome prince would come to rescue her, just like the prince in Rapunzel.

In the story, the prince had tumbled from the top of the tower into the thicket of thorn bushes that surrounded it, and both of his eyeballs had been pierced, so that he had been blinded. Perhaps Rapunzel had been too beautiful for anybody to look at, too.

She went over to Mummy's built-in closet. Even with the doors closed, it smelled of Mummy's perfume and Mummy's clothes. Mummy had never let her look in her closet before, at all of her lovely clothes. She was sure, however, that Mummy wouldn't be cross if she had a quick peek. She needn't even tell her.

She turned the little key and opened the right-hand closet door. Hanging neatly inside were Mummy's dresses, in order of colour, and Mummy's skirts, and on the shelves were all of Mummy's jumpers and cardigans, neatly folded. On the floor of the closet were Mummy's shoes, her sandals and her court shoes and the high heels she never seemed to wear these days.

Then Fiona opened the left-hand door. Immediately she gasped in shock, and jumped back, almost stumbling over. Standing in front of her was a girl, wearing exactly the same pink gingham dress as Fiona, and with her blonde hair tied up with two pink ribbons, exactly the same as Fiona's hair.

This girl, however, had a hideously distorted face, with a bulging forehead and eyes as wide apart as a flatfish. Her nose was not much more than a small knot of flesh with two holes in it, and her mouth was dragged down as if she were moaning.

Fiona was about to demand what this monstrous girl was doing, hiding in Mummy's closet. But when the girl raised her hand in exactly the same way that Fiona was raising her hand, Fiona began to realize, with a growing sense of horror, who she actually was. On the back of the left-hand door there was a mirror, and the girl with the hideously distorted face was *her*.

She touched the surface of the mirror, and the girl with the hideously distorted face did the same, so that their fingertips met.

'But I'm beautiful,' she whispered, and the girl with the hideously distorted face whispered it, too. 'I'm so beautiful that nobody can look at me, because they'll be too jealous.

'I'm *beautiful*.'

It was then, however, that everything started to make sense. The reason why she could never go out, and meet other people. The things Mummy said to her. *Beauty is in the eye of the beholder.* She hadn't really understood what that meant, but now she did. She *was* beautiful. She was very, very beautiful. But too many beholders had looked at her, and every one of them had stolen a little bit of her beauty away.

Her beauty was still there, but now it was inside their eyes. Somehow she had to find a way of getting it back.

She took one more long look at herself and then she closed the closet doors and locked them. Her heart was beating very fast and she was breathing quickly, too, as if she had waded chest-high into an icy-cold swimming pool.

What could she do to get her beauty back? Mummy always kept her protected, inside the house, in case any more beholders saw her, and made her look even more hideously distorted than she was already. But had Mummy ever tried to confront those beholders, and demand that they return her daughter's looks? Perhaps she didn't know who the beholders were, or if she did, perhaps she was afraid to ask them. Anybody who would deliberately steal a young girl's beauty would probably be very selfish and vicious.

Fiona went downstairs, and as she did so the front door opened and Mummy came in, carrying a bag of shopping.

'Why aren't you out in the garden?' Mummy asked her. 'It's so lovely out there.'

'The boy from next door threw his ball over the fence and he came to the door to ask for it back.'

Mummy put down her shopping bag. 'You didn't open it, did you?'

Fiona shook her head, and now she was conscious of how loose and wobbly her lips were. 'I went upstairs to see if you were there, but you weren't.'

'Well, I'm here now. I'll throw his ball back over for him. Would you like some lunch? I can make you some sandwiches, and you can eat them outside, like a picnic.'

'Mummy . . .' Fiona began. She wanted to ask her about the beholders, and how Mummy had allowed them to take her beauty away, but then she thought better of it. Mummy always took such good care of her. She had probably done everything she could to keep the beholders away, and Fiona didn't want to upset her or make her feel guilty about something that she had been powerless to prevent.

There were many times when Fiona had heard Mummy sobbing in the middle of the night, or she had come downstairs late in the evening for a glass of water and Mummy had quickly torn off a sheet of kitchen towel to wipe her eyes.

They went outside. Mummy picked up the tennis ball in the middle of the lawn and threw it back over the fence. There was no reply from next door. Robin and Caroline must be inside, having their lunch, too. Fiona knelt down on the patio and put Rapunzel back on top of her tower.

'Rapunzel! Rapunzel! Let down your hair!'

As she said that, she saw a large brown snail creeping across the patio, leaving a silvery trail behind it. It had only one pair of tentacles sticking out from the top of its head, and she knew from her children's encyclopedia that the shorter tentacle was for feeling its way around, while only the longer tentacle had an eye on the end of it. All the same, that single eye was definitely looking at *her*.

She hesitated for a moment, and then she stood up and went back into the kitchen.

'Won't be long, darling,' said Mummy, spreading butter on four slices of bread. 'Would you like tomato in your cheese sandwich, or brown pickle?'

'Brown pickle, please.'

Mummy was standing with her back to her, so Fiona was able to slide open the drawer next to the cooker and quietly lift out the black-handled scissors which Mummy used to cut the tips off chicken wings. She dropped them into the pocket in the front of her dress and went back outside.

The snail was still only a third of the way across the patio. Fiona knelt down close to it, and peered at it intently. Its eye was unquestionably swivelling in her direction, so in its tiny way it, too, must be a beholder. Even if it had taken only the minutest part of her beauty – a pretty little dimple from her chin, perhaps – she wanted it back.

'What do you want to drink?' called Mummy. 'Orange squash or lemon barley water?'

She would be coming outside in a minute, so Fiona couldn't hesitate. She took the scissors from her pocket and snipped the snail's eye from the end of its tentacle. Instantly, the snail rolled both of its tentacles back into its head, but it was too late. Fiona had its eye now, and everything that its eye contained.

As Mummy stepped out of the kitchen, carrying a small tray, Fiona popped the snail's eye into her mouth and kept it on her tongue. It felt very small and bobbly, and it tasted *beige*, if there was such a taste.

'Here you are, Fee-fee,' said Mummy, and set the tray down on the top of the steps that led down to the lawn. 'Cheese-and-pickle sandwiches, and a strawberry yogurt.'

Fiona nodded and tried to smile. Mummy affectionately scribbled her fingers in Fiona's hair. 'You are a funny girl, aren't you?' she said, and then she went back inside.

With the tip of her tongue, Fiona pressed the snail's eye as hard as she could against her palate, but it refused to pop. In the end, she manoeuvred it between her front teeth, and bit it in half, and swallowed it. It was far too minuscule for her to taste any optical fluid, but she knew that she had taken back at least a tiny part of her beauty, and that was a good start.

The snail stayed where it was, not moving, as if it had been paralysed by the shock of losing its eye. Fiona watched it for a while, as she ate her first sandwich. After five minutes, when it still hadn't moved, she stood up and stamped on it, with a crunch. *Serves you right*, she thought. She touched her chin to see if she had regained a pretty dimple, and she was sure that she could feel some indentation. This seemed to work, taking the eyes from her beholders. She wondered how many more snails were carrying images of her beauty around in their eyes; or how many birds, for that matter.

As if in answer to her question, she heard a tinkle, and a grey tortoiseshell cat jumped up on to the fence, with a little silver bell around his neck. He belonged to old Mrs Pickens, who lived on the other side of Fiona and her Mummy. Fiona knew that the cat's name was Zebedee, because she had heard Mrs Pickens calling him in at night. Zebedee was always sitting on top of the fence, staring at her unblinking with his yellow eyes, so he must be a beholder, too.

'Here, puss!' Fiona called him. 'Come on, Zebedee! Come here, puss!'

Zebedee remained aloof on top of the fence. Fiona stood up and walked across the patio until she was standing directly beneath him.

'Come on, puss! Come down and play!'

Zebedee stared at her for a long time but still stayed where he was. Fiona took the top slice of bread off her half-eaten sandwich and threw it out into the garden, so that it landed on the lawn. Zebedee yawned and looked the other way.

Less than minute later, however, two fat pigeons landed on the lawn, and strutted toward Fiona's sandwich as if they had ordered it specially. They started to peck at it, and that was when Zebedee crouched himself down and arched his back and scratched at the fence with his claws as he repositioned himself, ready to strike.

'Go on, puss!' Fiona urged him. He ignored her at first, as he tried to balance himself in the best position for leaping off on to the lawn. But then – as the pigeons started to squabble with each other over the last remaining fragment of crust – he sprang off the fence and landed less than two feet away from them, making a southpaw lunge for the nearer pigeon and catching some of its tail feathers.

The two pigeons immediately flapped up into the air, and were gone. Zebedee circled around the lawn, looking up at the sky as if he had intended only to chase the pigeons away, and was just making sure that they didn't have the temerity to try to come back.

Fiona was sitting on the top step now, watching him. He came toward her, climbed the steps and started to sniff at her sandwiches.

'Cats don't like cheese and pickle,' said Fiona. Zebedee stared at her and licked his lips, as if he expected her to offer him something else, like sardines. Or maybe he only wanted to show her how much he relished the beauty that he had taken from her.

'You're a beholder, too, aren't you, Zebedee?' Fiona asked him. 'I can tell, because you're so beautiful. "What a beautiful pussy you are, you are."'

Zebedee came up closer to her and sniffed at her. She reached out and stroked his head, so that he half-closed his eyes and flattened his ears back.

It was then that Fiona suddenly snatched his green leather collar and twisted it around tight, so that it was almost strangling him. He yowled and struggled and scratched, jerking his body wildly from side to side, but Fiona held on to him, and pressed her thumb into his furry throat until he was whining for breath.

Gradually, his convulsive kicking became weaker and more spasmodic, and at last he stopped struggling altogether. Fiona laid him on his back across her knees, and tried to feel if he still had a pulse, but she couldn't find one. His eyes were closed and his upper lip was raised in a silent snarl.

'*Now* let's see who's beautiful,' she said. She picked up the small stainless-steel spoon that Mummy had given her for eating her strawberry yogurt. Then, with her thumb, she raised Zebedee's sticky left eyelid, so that his eye was exposed, with its sunflower-yellow iris. He didn't try to blink, so she assumed that he must be dead. She felt that it was a pity, in a way, that he was dead, because she would have liked him to be aware that she was taking back her beauty. He had stared at her. A cat may look at a queen, she thought, but that doesn't mean that the queen won't be angry for being looked at.

Very carefully, with the tip of her tongue clenched between her teeth, Fiona dug the tip of the yogurt spoon underneath Zebedee's eyeball. The eyeball made a slight sucking sound as she lifted it free from its socket, but it wasn't difficult to lever it out. Soon it was hanging on Zebedee's cheek, staring sightlessly at his whiskers. Fiona picked up the scissors and cut the optic nerve, and then she carefully placed the eyeball on the tray next to her plate of sandwiches.

She took out the other eye the same way, and then she had both eyeballs side by side. She couldn't help smiling because they were squinting, like cartoon eyes.

'Fee-fee!' called Mummy, from the kitchen. 'Have you finished your lunch yet?'

'Nearly!' Fiona called back. She lifted Zebedee off her lap and stood up. Then she carried his lifeless body over to the side of the house, where the dustbins stood. He was surprisingly heavy, and his legs swung from side to side like a pendulum. She opened the lid of the dustbin and dropped Zebedee into it, on top of a black plastic bag.

She had half-closed the lid when there was a frantic rustling of plastic, and a scrabbling sound, and then, with a screech, Zebedee came jumping up the inside of the dustbin, blindly scratching at the sides in an attempt to climb out. He managed to get his front legs and his head over the rim of the dustbin, but the plastic was too slippery for him to get any purchase with his back legs.

Fiona slammed the dustbin lid down on his neck, and pressed down as hard as she could. Zebedee spat and hissed at her, his eyeless face contorted with fury and pain. She pressed down harder still, and at last she heard a snap as the vertebrae in his neck were dislocated. He stopped hissing, and when she lifted the lid up a little he dropped back heavily on to the plastic bag full of rubbish.

Serves you right, too, thought Fiona.

She returned to the steps and sat down. She picked up one of Zebedee's eyes and held it up, so that she could stare into it. It stared back at her, sightlessly, with a shred of optic nerve hanging from the back of it. In there, that's where my beautiful face has been hiding. She hesitated for a moment, not because the eye disgusted her, but because she was so pleased that she had discovered how to get her beauty back, and it was a moment to savour.

She placed the eye on her tongue, and then she slowly closed her mouth. The eye felt like a grape, although it had a strange taste to it, oily and slightly musky. She waited a few seconds longer, and then she bit into it, so that it popped, and this time she could actually feel the small blob of optic fluid sliding down her throat.

She picked up the other eye, and bit into that, too. This eye had a longer string of connective tissue still attached to it, which stuck to the back of her throat and made her gag. For a few seconds she thought she was going to be sick, and lose all of the beauty which she had retrieved from Zebedee's eyes, but then she took a mouthful of lemon barley water and managed to swallow it.

She finished the second half of her cheese-and-pickle sandwich, and then she ate her strawberry yogurt. The sun flickered through the leaves of the horse-chestnut trees at the end of the garden and made Fiona feel as if she were an actress in a film. She kept touching her face and she was sure that she could actually feel her beauty coming back to her, little by little.

She sang, in a high, reedy voice, 'I feel pretty . . . oh so pretty! I feel pretty and witty and bright!'

From next door, she heard old Mrs Pickens calling out, 'Zebedee! Zebedee! Where are you, you naughty cat?'

Later that afternoon, when Mummy was busy in the kitchen, Fiona crept upstairs again and went into Mummy's bedroom. As quietly as she could, she turned the little key in the lock and opened the closet doors.

There she stood, in the mirror, the girl with the hideously distorted face. Fiona peered closely at her, so that their lumpy little noses almost touched, and she was sure that she wasn't quite as ugly as she had looked before. So it *did* work, finding beholders and swallowing their eyeballs. But it wasn't working as dramatically as she had hoped. She needed more – many more – and the bigger the eyeballs, the better.

A *person*, that's what she needed. A person who had seen her.

But who had seen her? Daddy was dead and presumably buried, or cremated, and Mummy had never taken her out of the house. She had never been to school, because Mummy taught her everything. She had never been to a shop, although she knew what they were because Mummy had shown her pictures of them.

She thought she could remember a man and a woman looking at her. They had both been wearing white coats and said things which she hadn't been able to understand. But that had been a very long time ago, and she had no idea who they were or where she could find them.

She carefully closed the closet doors and went back downstairs. Mummy was vacuuming in the sitting room so she was able to go through the kitchen and out on to the patio without Mummy seeing her.

She sat on the steps with Rapunzel and started to braid Rapunzel's hair, in the same way that Mummy braided *her* hair. The sunlight was still flickering through the trees, but it was much lower now, and the shadows across the lawn were much longer. After she had pinned up Rapunzel's braids, Fiona turned her around and looked at her blank, featureless face.

Beauty is in the eye of the beholder. That's what Mummy had said. And it was then that it occurred to her. *Mummy.* Apart from those two people in the white coats, Mummy was the only person who had seen her, all these years. There had been no other beholders, apart from the insects and the animals and the birds in the garden. Mummy was the only one.

Mummy came outside and sat beside her on the steps.

'Phew!' she said, with a smile, wiping her forehead with the back of her hand. 'That's all *that* done!'

Fiona stared at Mummy's eyes. Her irises were pale blue, like hers, but in the late-afternoon sunlight her pupils were only pinpricks. But now Fiona knew. Inside the blackness of Mummy's eyes, that was where her beauty was hidden. It must be. Nothing else made sense.

'What shall we do this evening?' asked Mummy. 'What about a film? We could watch *The Cat in the Hat* again, if you like.'

Fiona thought of that stringy shred of tissue sticking to her throat and shook her head. 'I've gone off cats.'

Once she was in bed, she was allowed to read for half an hour, but this evening her storybook remained unopened, because she was too busy thinking.

Mummy had always done everything she could to protect her and take care of her, ever since she was little, so she was sure that Mummy would understand why she needed to take out her eyes. Mummy would be blinded, yes, but blind people could still go shopping, couldn't they? And Fiona could help her around the house, cleaning and cooking. Fiona could roll out pastry and she knew how to make baked potatoes with grated cheese in them.

Perhaps they could get a guide dog, so long as the guide dog didn't look at her, and become another beholder. A guide dog with no eyes wouldn't be much good. The blind leading the blind!

The main problem would be keeping Mummy still, while she did it. And quiet, too. Zebedee had fought like a demon, even though he must have known that what was in his eyes belonged to her, and not to him.

At eight-thirty, Mummy came into her bedroom to tuck her in and give her a goodnight kiss.

'Sleep well, darling. Pleasant dreams.'

'Mummy?' said Fiona, as Mummy switched off the light.

'What is it, Fee-fee?' she asked, standing in silhouette in the doorway.

'If I did something terrible, but I did it because it made me happy, would you forgive me?'

'What do you mean by "something terrible"?'

'If I hurt somebody, really badly.'

'I don't know what you mean, darling. You don't *know* anybody, do you, apart from me?'

Fiona was tempted to tell Mummy what she wanted to do. Perhaps Mummy would agree to gouge out her eyes voluntarily, so that Fiona could be beautiful again. She had already given up her whole life for her, what difference would it make if she gave up her sight?

But then Fiona thought: what if she says no? What if she finds the idea really horrifying, and refuses to do it? After that, she will always be on her guard, and I won't be able to sneak into her bedroom in the middle of the night and take out her eyes, even though she doesn't want me to.'

'I know, Mummy. I was just being silly.'

Mummy blew her a kiss. 'You are a funny girl sometimes. You know that I'd forgive you anything, don't you? Since Daddy left, you're all I have.'

'Daddy *left*? I thought Daddy died.'

'That's what I meant, darling. Since Daddy left us, and went to Heaven.'

'Oh.'

Mummy closed the door, leaving Fiona lying in darkness, except for the illuminated green numbers on the digital clock beside her bed. For some reason, she thought that Mummy had sounded strangely unconvincing when she had said that Daddy had gone to Heaven. Perhaps he hadn't gone to Heaven at all. Perhaps he had gone to Hell.

She waited for over an hour, trying hard to keep her eyes open. She could hear the television in the sitting room below her, as Mummy watched the news and then some comedy program with occasional bursts of studio laughter.

This is the last time she'll ever be able to watch TV, thought Fiona. But she can listen to it, can't she? And she'll still have the radio in the kitchen.

At last she heard Mummy switch off the television and come upstairs. Mummy closed her bedroom door behind her and a few minutes later Fiona heard the bathwater running. The water tank in the attic always made a rumbling sound like distant thunder, followed by a high-pitched whistle.

Fiona waited for another half-hour, and then she sat up. She went across to her door and opened it. Mummy had switched off her bedside lamp, and the landing was in darkness. She knew that Mummy almost always took a Nytol tablet before she went to bed, so it was likely that she was asleep already. Mummy said she took Nytol because she found it difficult to get to sleep, and even when she did she had nightmares about monsters.

Fiona closed her door and turned on her light. She went over to the window and unhooked the pink braided cords that held her curtains back during the day. Then she took a small blue plastic-bound dictionary off her bookshelf, and a brightly coloured cotton scarf from the top drawer of her chest of drawers.

Last of all, she picked up a dessertspoon which she had taken from the cutlery drawer in the kitchen, as well as the poultry scissors.

She switched off her light and opened her door again. She stood there for a few seconds so that her eyes could become accustomed to the darkness. She didn't want to trip over something and wake Mummy up too soon.

In her head, over and over, she could hear Marni Nixon singing '*I feel pretty . . . oh so pretty! I feel pretty and witty and bright! And I pity any girl who isn't me tonight!*' She softly panted the words under her breath.

Very gently, she pulled down the handle of Mummy's bedroom door, and then opened it. When it was only a few inches ajar, she stopped, and listened.

At first she couldn't hear anything at all. But then Mummy turned over in bed, with a slippery rustle of her satin quilt, and muttered something that sounded like '*never*'. After that, Fiona could hear her breathing quite steadily, with a slight sticking noise in one of her nostrils.

Fiona crept across to Mummy's bedside. By the light of her luminous clock, she could see that Mummy was lying on her back, with one arm raised on the pillow beside her, and that she was deeply asleep.

With great care, she lifted Mummy's upraised arm a little further up the pillow, until Mummy's hand was poking through the brass rails of her headboard. She took one of the curtain cords and tied Mummy's wrist to the nearest rail, using the double knots that Mummy had taught her when she was showing her how to sew.

Next she walked around the bed and climbed up on to it so that she could gently tug Mummy's other arm out from under the bedcovers, and tie that to the headboard, too.

Now she lifted Mummy's head up from the pillow and slid the cotton scarf underneath it. Mummy stirred and said '*what?*' and then '*never!*' but still she didn't open her eyes. However, Fiona knew that what she did next was certain to wake her up. She took three deep breaths to steady herself and made sure that she had the little dictionary ready in her left hand and the spoon and scissors waiting on the bedside table.

I feel pretty, she breathed. *Oh so pretty.*

She parted Mummy's lips and then she pried her teeth apart. Mummy almost immediately opened her eyes and jerked at the cords that were keeping her wrists tied to the headboard. Without hesitation, Fiona jammed the dictionary between her teeth, as far as it would go, and then she took hold of the two ends of the scarf and tied them quickly in a tight knot over Mummy's mouth, so that she couldn't push the dictionary out with her tongue.

Mummy's eyes rolled in panic and bewilderment. She pulled at the cords around her wrists until the headboard rattled, and when she couldn't free herself she began to twist and kick and bounce up and down on the bed – all the while grunting and mewling at Fiona to untie her.

Fiona leaned over her, almost as if she were about to kiss her. Mummy stared up at her and stopped thrashing and kicking for a moment.

'Mmmm-mmmmfff-mmmmff,' she said, through the dictionary. Saliva was beginning to run down either side of her mouth.

'It's all right, Mummy,' said Fiona. 'I'll try not to hurt you, I promise.'

'*Mmmmmfff!*' Mummy retorted, and this time she sounded angry.

Fiona pinched Mummy's left eyelid between finger and thumb, and pulled it upward as far as she could stretch it. Mummy started kicking again, and trying to shake her head from side to side, but Fiona was holding her eyelid too tightly. She reached across to the bedside table for the spoon, turned it upside-down, and pushed the tip of it into the top of Mummy's eye socket. Mummy let out a harsh grating scream, and bounced up and down on the bed as if she were suffering an epileptic fit. But Fiona dug the spoon in deeper, until it curved around the back of the eyeball, and she could easily gouge it out on to Mummy's cheek. Blood welled out of her hollow eye socket and slid down on to the pillow.

Mummy started shaking uncontrollably. The mattress made a furious jostling noise and the bedhead banged repeatedly against the wall behind it.

'Mummy! Mummy! It's all right, Mummy!' Fiona pleaded with her. 'I promise I'll be quick!'

She hadn't realized how violent Mummy's reaction would be, and she started to sob. But it was too late now. She couldn't push Mummy's left eye back in and pretend that nothing had happened, and she so badly needed her beauty back. She reached across for the scissors but Mummy jolted her and she dropped them on to the floor.

Weeping, she climbed off the bed, but she couldn't see the scissors anywhere. She felt underneath the bedside table, but they weren't there. She felt underneath the bed, too, but there was a gap of only about an inch off the carpet and she couldn't feel them there, either.

Mummy was quaking and snorting now, with her gouged-out eye staring at Fiona accusingly from her cheek. There was only one thing that Fiona could do. She climbed back up on to the bed, and grasped Mummy's hair with her right hand to keep her head still. Then she took the eye between the thumb and middle finger of her left hand, leaned forward and bit it in half. She sucked the clear optic fluid out of it, and swallowed. Her eyes were still filled with tears, but she could almost feel her lost beauty slipping down her throat.

Mummy was still trembling, and she felt very cold, but she had stopped kicking and struggling. Fiona lifted her right eyelid, picked up the spoon, and gouged out her right eye, too. Again, she bit it in half and swallowed the fluid inside.

She knelt on the bed for a while, feeling slightly sick. Then she climbed off it again, untied the scarf that covered Mummy's mouth and gently wiggled the dictionary until it came out from between her teeth. Mummy had bitten almost halfway through it.

Next she untied her wrists and dragged up the bedcovers to try and get Mummy warm again. She didn't know what to do with the empty shreds of half-bitten eyes that were hanging out of each socket, so she carefully poked them back in again, and closed Mummy's eyelids, and then she tied the scarf around Mummy's head like a blindfold.

It didn't occur to her to call for an ambulance. She had seen ambulances on television, but they were only in stories. She had never seen a real one, and she didn't know that you could call one yourself, and it would actually come to your door.

Besides, the most important thing was that she had regained her beauty, and in spite of being so beautiful, she would risk going out

into the world, no matter how jealous other people might be. Mummy
might be blind now, but she was so beautiful that she would be able
to become a famous actress, and become rich, and support them
both.

It was only now that Fiona realized what a sacrifice Mummy had
made for her – keeping her beauty in her own eyes for all of this
time, in order to keep her safe. She must have known that one day
the time would come when she would have to give it back to her.

She crossed over to Mummy's closet and unlocked the doors.
There she was, in her pink pyjamas, which were spattered with a
fine spray of blood. But something was badly wrong. She wasn't
beautiful at all. She looked the same as she had before, with that
bulging forehead and those wide-apart flatfish eyes and that dragged-
down mouth.

Perhaps it took time for the beauty to make its way into your
body, she thought. After all, if you ate a bar of chocolate, you had
to digest it first, in your stomach, before the sugar went into your
bloodstream.

She sat down cross-legged on the bedroom carpet in front of the
mirror, and waited for Mummy's optic fluid to work on her face. It
had to work. Mummy had said that beauty is in the eye of the
beholder, and she had swallowed the beholders' eyes. What more
could she have done?

She woke up and the bedroom was filled with sunlight. She glanced
over at Mummy's bedside clock and saw that it was 7.17 a.m. It
looked as if Mummy was still asleep, with her blindfold over her
eyes. It was the blindfold that reminded her what had happened last
night, and what she was doing here in Mummy's bedroom.

She looked in the mirror. She hadn't changed at all. She was still
just as hideously distorted as she had been before. She couldn't
understand it. She had swallowed those eyes for nothing.

She slowly stood up.

'Mummy?' she said. 'Mummy, are you awake?'

She went over to Mummy's bedside. Mummy was very pale and
she didn't appear to be breathing. Fiona shook her shoulder but all
she did was joggle unresponsively from side to side.

'Mummy?'

She realized then that she must have misunderstood what Mummy had said to her. The snail hadn't been a beholder, and neither had Zebedee, or Mummy. *She* – Fiona – *she* was the beholder. It was *she* who had seen her own face in the mirror and thought that it was ugly. That was why Mummy had kept her away from mirrors, and stopped her from going out to meet other people. So long as she didn't know what she really looked like, she had remained incandescently beautiful.

She went back and stood in front of the mirror. Her hideously distorted face stared back at her. It always would, for the rest of her life, every time she saw her own reflection.

There was only one remedy. She went over to Mummy's chest of drawers. In the second drawer down, there was a purple biscuit tin with a picture of Prince Charles and Lady Diana on it, to celebrate their wedding. Mummy kept her sewing things in it – her spare buttons and her button thread and her needles.

Fiona picked out a large shiny darning needle and went back to face the mirror. With her fingers, she held her left eye open wide.

I feel pretty, she whispered, and stuck the needle into her pupil.

She felt nothing more than a sharp prick, but her eye instantly went blind. She held her right eye open in the same way, and stuck the needle into that eye, too.

She stood there, in total darkness. She couldn't see herself now. She couldn't see anything at all. But she could imagine how beautiful she was – so beautiful that if anyone tried to paint her portrait, their paints would burst into flames, and mirrors would shatter into a thousand pieces if she ever looked in them.

She started to circle around and around, and as she circled she sang 'I Feel Pretty', over and over, until she was so giddy that she dropped to her knees. Outside, in the street, she could hear traffic, and people talking, and her blind eyes filled with tears again, although she no longer knew why she was crying.